SIENNA MCKNIGHT

NEW PRAETORIANS 1

RK SYRUS

Editing:
Crystal "Godzilla" Watanabe
Taryn "Lois Lane" Lawson
Vanessa "Mother of Dragons" Ricci-Thode

Proofing:
Pikko's House

Cover:
James "Tiberius" Egan of Bookfly Design

Book Interior Design:
Crystal Watanabe

Paper book
ISBN10 1-910890-06-5 (ISBN13: 978-1-910890-06-6)

E-book
eISBN10 1-910890-00-6 (eISBN13: 978-1-910890-00-4)

"We don't see things as they are,

we see them as we are."

— Anaïs Nin
Seduction of the Minotaur

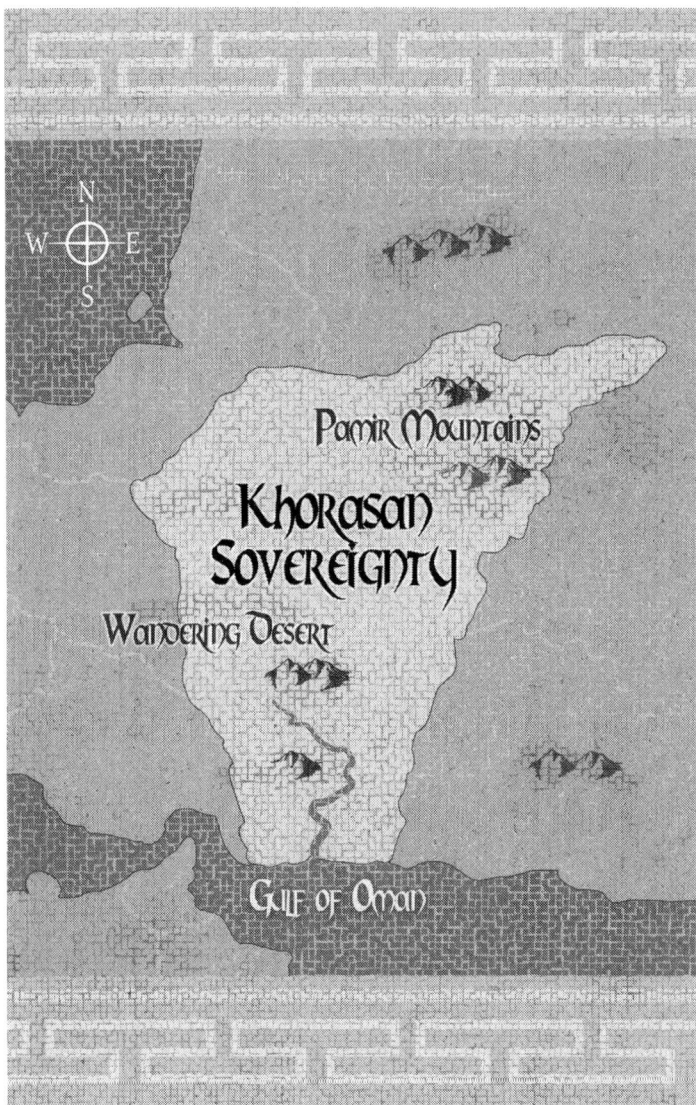

Pamir Mountains

Khorasan
Sovereignty

Wandering Desert

Gulf of Oman

1

ELEVEN YEARS AGO
WOODS NEAR THE BASE
NORTH CAROLINA

SIENNA

That sunny morning near her hometown she battled a ravenous beast with the help of a monster, the one that abides in her still.

Sienna McKnight looked up into the face of Uncle Bryan. Sarge Bryan. She squinted as rays of the mid-morning sun flared behind his head, blurring his bone-white features. Back then, he had his old eyes. As well, he sported fresh bruises swelling on his cheek and jaw. Over the years, her memory would graze over this small mystery tucked away amongst larger ones held by that day.

"Now git goin'." Exasperation dragged on his deep voice.

"Like heck." Sienna's empty hand, the one not holding a knife, slapped her leg. Long baggy shorts released a small puff of summer dust.

"Glantzer was tryin' to be nice. Tryin' to apologize."

That was impossible. A girl's 12th birthday was sacred and that no-account hillbilly had ruined it. All to pieces.

But Sarge, who did more ordering than persuading in his job, kept on at her. "Look, he lives off roadkill in a lean-to in the woods. That's probably the nicest thing he owned."

Sienna looked at Glantzer's let's-be-friends-again gift: nearly ten inches of high-carbon steel, polished to a mirror finish. That was rad. But the handle was gross, chipped and worn, and felt light, hollow. Felt like it wouldn't throw well.

"Old coot probably stole it."

"Watch your language, please." Bryan leaned back, like he was working some sore muscle obstinacy out of his back.

Good luck getting obstinacy out of me. A single yellow rose ain't gonna cut it.

Sienna never wanted to see that one-eyed loon again. Bryan went on, "And he probably didn't. His family had money. Owned a lot of land around Raleigh. He went to college and everything. Before. That there Bowie knife might be the last thing he had from his past."

"Oh yeah." Sienna recalled a fact useful to her argument. "You two are related, ain't you?"

"A little. You may find this comes in handy. It's one of the benefits of being adopted. Your family chose you, so you can choose your family. He's my dad's cousin eight times removed, or some such."

Sienna looked at the knife. She respected Bryan more than any of her teachers. Like her mother, he actually went out and fought bad people. But that damn old…

"You even had to burn my sweater."

"Along with my gloves," Bryan agreed. "And my pants."

"You knew he was gonna jump me? Then and there?"

That put Bryan on the defensive. Sienna had grown up an Army brat and knew soldiers hated losing the initiative.

"Well… sort of. If he's planning a surprise lesson, he has to tell me. But really, girl, I had no idea he'd drop out of a tree after he covered himself in some muck."

"Axle grease and dog crap."

Bryan's attempt to stifle a laugh came out as a snort. "That was a new one on me. Hey, come to think of it, Glantzer doesn't have a dog. You don't think…"

Sienna let out some real cuss words and tossed the knife. Contrary to her skepticism, it flew pretty good and stuck in some roots at the edge of the woods.

Man! People thought they were weird enough already. Sienna didn't care about that. But that sweater.

"In the man's defense, the lessons of the day were: never let your guard down, and never get distracted during a fight." Bryan had too much of a smile pulling at one side of his pale face.

"It wouldn't be funny if it was you he was trying to choke out jiu jitsu style."

"You got him back. Nearly knocked him out, and he's got to have thirty, thirty-five pounds on you."

"I weigh eighty-nine and fillin' out fast," she shot back.

Her anger was settling. But damn, that sweater was store-bought new. From Bonworthy's. In spite of herself, as she walked toward the trees to get her knife, she figured the fastest way through the woods to Glantzer's hootch. He probably had no other human friends. Maybe these knife-fighting lessons were the one thing keeping the few marbles he still had from rolling off for good. If Uncle Bryan chose to keep the crazy old sasser as a relative, even a distant one, that meant they were related. By choice.

Bryan was already walking to his Jeep. "There's a sale on at Cross Creek Mall, I'll pick you up at the end of Mac Ridge. Commandant needs me to check on something by the west gate," he called after her. "On the way over, could you check by Ellie's place? She's on medical, restin' up."

Sienna watched Bryan. Most people who saw him or his kind were shocked or disgusted, or fixed him with a stare marking the skin, hair, and eyes that made him different. She imagined the gawkers were stuck between hate, pity, or fear. If she had to pick something for those people to feel, fear was it.

She'd researched it online. Where US Army Sergeant Shetani Zeru Bryan came from, they cut up anyone who looked like him. They cut them up and made magic charms from parts of their bodies. She thought the other kids in social studies should know this. But Mr. Butterfield said they should not and disallowed her presentation idea. Some truths of the world were too gruesome for North Carolina middle school students.

Maybe Uncle Bryan was afraid for her. Maybe it was because he had seen enough, been through enough, and that was why he taught her as many Special Forces fighting moves as he thought she could handle. And when she asked to learn more, asked what a real fight was like, he stopped, thought a moment, and just said: "It's everything you don't expect."

Afterward, he asked—probably threatened or bribed— the most low-down, bat-pee crazy 'billy in the Carolinas to show her some highly irregular fighting secrets. These secrets included ambushing victims while they were walking to a bake sale.

She wished there was something she could do to keep Bryan safe. And her widowed mom Annalies, too. But it was Uncle Bryan, on account of being attached to Delta Unit, who got sent on worse deployments, ones which were never over until they were over. You never knew if he was all right until he showed up home or called from Ramstein in Germany.

That sucked, because it was Annalies and Uncle Bryan out of the whole world who she was certain she loved. Annalies and Theodora had adopted her, but really, Bryan did, too. He was in all of the mostly embarrassing pictures taken twelve years ago, when they brought her home as a baby.

Stopping at the tree line, she flipped the Bowie backward. Intending to catch it by the blunt, beveled spine, she was not familiar with its weight and had to use both hands to keep it from falling. Fingerprints smeared polish. Fingertips grazed the carefully, even fastidiously, honed edge. She felt dumb and clumsy. Had she caught it wrong, it was heavy enough and sharp enough to slice four fingers right off.

In her bare arm, some kind of blood vessel beat, pulsing under the scar across her arm. It was part of a matching set on her back and the sides of her legs. There was even a chunky scar divot at her ankle. They seemed all random, until she curled herself up in a ball. Then they aligned pretty straight into five slash marks. Keepsakes of a tragedy? A warning? Hogwash that had no meaning at all except to make you crazy thinking about it?

She could not read their true tale by sight or touch, not back then. Sienna looked at Glantzer's offering. Had a blade like this cut those scars into her body twelve years ago? No, she decided. There was no way a blade this beautiful could make marks that ugly.

***

Being jumped and befouled by that backwoods critter wasn't all that riled and bedeviled her. For some reason, her mom and Uncle Bryan chose *now* to tell her that her birth mother hadn't died in a car accident. She had been murdered. The fib didn't chafe, not really. Now she knew as much as they did, and understood as little. That knot in her gut was one she'd never untangle. Never ever. Even grown-ups were constantly getting flummoxed.

Past the tree line, the wooded areas in the hills around the Base got gnarly fast. There was always the chance of tripping over some rusted crap left by generations of Army since World War I. More than 50,000 active-duty soldiers and their families lived on government property at the outskirts of Fayetteville.

Sienna kicked a root. She did not imagine Glantzer's shin. She'd gotten more dirty and scuffed up by herself on the Green Beret's obstacle course. And maybe he hadn't mixed poop in with the grease. It all happened pretty fast. That had probably been her first- or second-best sweater, but they were going to the mall to get a replacement. As she stepped into the tree line, she figured she was mad for other reasons. She was mad at the whole military.

They were making her widowed mom ship out again. Sure, Bryan would stay over. But then he'd ship out, too. Dr. Theodora McKnight would never come back. An IED took her from them. Coffins came back to the Base airstrip at dawn. Probably so people wouldn't see them. Would they up and quit if they saw coffins coming home every day? There had been one for Dr. McKnight. Annalies told her it was empty. She was really buried in a faraway place inside the blown-up wreck of an ambulance. The military seemed to take and take and never give.

She wished she could change it all. But she was young and just a girl. It didn't matter what backwoods ninja skills she learned from Glantzer. Didn't matter a hoot she could shoot as well as the ROTC boys. She'd never be as strong as they were or as fast over the obstacle course. There was no guarantee she'd even be as smart as Dr. McKnight. Smarts were in the blood, and she didn't know whose blood she had. How could she be as brave as Annalies, then? She was just chicken-shit fraidy. Fraidy of everything.

Sienna could tell her mom was afraid sometimes. When she shipped out. She tried not to show it. When she had to leave. Nights before, night of, and nights after she deployed were worst. Bryan stayed at their house. Just like he had, they told her, when Theodora McKnight, Annalies's wife, was alive and they both had duty assignments. Until one day Dr. McKnight, the Army's best trauma surgeon, didn't come back. Still, Annalies went. She went when she was called on. Sienna was pretty sure it wasn't just for money.

Sienna, then, in those woods, found herself unable to name the power that could take Annalies away from safety, away from friends, away from her, whenever it chose. She could not name it, but she could hate it all the same. And she let out her preteen rage at something she could name. She hated the Army.

What seemed like a long time ago, back somewhere in her twelve years, she had felt differently. Once she felt pride and excitement at the sight of a long gray line of new recruits double-timing through the gates of the Base under the fluttering stars and stripes. She felt community when Uncle Bryan took her to eat at the mess hall. They'd give her double applesauce without her even asking. But between then and now were many people who had gone out. Out There. Only to come back wounded, or not at all. Sienna was tired of trying so hard to be brave, and that just made her ashamed, which was the worst feeling of all.

She scrambled up a small ridge and stopped. Dead still, it was. Dead quiet as woods ever get. Breeze, and leaves, and water unseen, all part of a silence she invited into herself. Delicately, she probed underneath for an unquiet. When she got mad it would sometimes get pipey. That thing, inside, underneath.

Nothing.

Down deep, quiet. That was good.

She scuttled sideways down the other side of the ridge. With practiced ease, Sienna rode a controlled hillside of loose rocks, moss, and logs eaten through by termites. A thorn vine blocked the trail. Sienna hacked it. The fat, green, hooky-spine crusted length of it hung unsupported for a second, not knowing it was severed, then fell. She stepped on it for good measure.

She imagined herself chopping her way through the deepest, darkest Amazonian jungle. Bloodthirsty natives were always hiding gold idols all over the place. Maybe the headhunters who worshipped animal gods were unaware of their cash value. If she found a golden idol, she'd sure as heck sell it and buy a new house. One for her and her widowed mom. As a single parent, she could retire from the service, but they needed the money.

If there was enough from the idol, and the loot that idols were normally found on top of, she'd definitely buy a place for Uncle Bryan. He lived in a house that smelled like wet socks. Heck, if it was one of those idols with jewels in the eyes, she might even get something for Glantzer. Nothing expensive, mind you. Maybe a tent without duct tape patches and a secondhand propane stove...

"Meerrrw."

Sienna stopped hacking.

"Meerr."

A cat. More like a kitten, in the low crook of a tree. The only house nearby was Ellie McNabb's. She had a kid, which was probably why Uncle Bryan asked her to stop by there on her way back to the road. If this was their kitten, returning it was a good excuse to take the longer way round to Glantzer's hootch.

Sienna tried to pick the warm fluffball off the branch. Ornery or scared, he hung on with scrabbling nails. Now, whether to stroke-pet the little fellow into line with her program or just yank the scruff of his neck. She was deciding when a sound behind her made her ears tick back. She looked.

From behind a log another pair of ears pointed at them, ones topped with reddish fur. She couldn't see it clearly. It stayed behind some bushes. Definitely not a dog. Must be one dumb coyote to come this close to houses. Sienna picked up a rock and whizzed it in the general direction of the ear tufts.

After the

thock

she expected to see a mangy, twenty-five pounder do a vigorous coyote skedaddle back up the ridge she'd just slid down. What she got was an energetic growl of aggression, the sort only truly wild things can produce. This was followed by a confronting leap forward by a ninety-pound critter. One starved lean, ribs showing, yellow eyes flaring, and a long mouth coated with fresh blood.

A red wolf.

Contact!

In science, they taught that increased precipitation from climate change had caused more vegetation growth in the Carolinas. This had spurred an increase in the populations of deer and rabbits, which had in turn resulted in a comeback for the endangered local predator. While she normally rooted for underdogs, she was instantly not a fan of this one.

Along with the half-dried blood and saliva on pulled-back lips, she noticed the wolf was missing a chunk of fur and most of his tail. The stump twitched and oozed. Angry, hungry, he took turns staring first at the appetizer in the tree, then at her knobby knees, like they were the main course. Drumsticks McKnight.

If she had a .22, this fight would already have been over. But she didn't. She forced herself to be aware of what was around her, without ever losing contact with two unblinking eyes that were threatening to block out everything else.

Tunnel vision: bad. *Be aware of your surroundings.*

No rifle. What she did have was a phone and a big tree angled up all nice for climbing, assuming you had thumbs.

Evade, regroup to the strong point, and call in ground support was the best option.

Hooah!

It was the smart option. The doable one. The only option that made sense. Until it was no option at all.

"Triskiiit."

Aw, man! A beautiful plan went in the crapper as some darn kid, a boy, about six years old, came crashing through the underbrush. Wolf ears, wolf eyes, and bared teeth flicked back and forth between her and the noisy newcomer, who was totally unaware of the deadly danger ahead.

"Tris-kit!"

The puff-ball kitten in the tree; that must be his name. Kind of appropriate for a side dish. The red wolf, sensing the kid was not a threat, turned back to her and her more meaty calves. Plan A was still viable. She could hurl her knife, larger rocks, even Triskit, at the threat, grab the kid, and pull or push him up into the tree with her. This would take longer. Chances of her drumsticks being gnawed to the bone increased if she took the kid up the tree with her. But she had to. You never left a man, or a noisy kid, behind. You just didn't.

New skirmish plan: covering fire. Grab the non-com. Up this tree. Reinforcements. Then a scraggy pelt with no tail hanging on a wall.

The wolf circled away. Silently and with intent. It was the bad kind of circling. This she knew from having watched every kind of stalking animal at play. This move came right before a serious dash forward at her flank. It would happen so fast and so violently her hamstrings and the tendons in the back of her knees would be crippled before she even got a good stab in.

This wasn't like the movies, where wild animals just stood there and let you kill them. Glantzer had taken her along on a varmint hunt for razorbacks. An aggressive sounder of ferals had destroyed a cornfield. All ten acres were rooted-up mud and pig dirt. They were legal to hunt year-round, so the 'billies went out for payback. Catch was, all of the men, for various reasons, were banned from having guns. They used spears.

Eventually, they cornered a feisty one in a gully. In the midst of a headlong charge, this wild hog got stuck. It took a 160-pound man for a ride on the end of the sticker. It was another five minutes of four guys avoiding being gored by a pair of eight-inch tusks before they finally killed it enough that it stopped moving. Forty pounds of bacon on hooves did that.

In front of Sienna was a meat eater more than twice as big. As she thought tactics, the wolf executed his. He zig-zagged forward. No more need for radio silence. The kid could not see the wolf. The wolf knew exactly where everyone was. Instinct told him who to attack first. If the kid ran, he'd be it.

"Yo! Kid! Your cat is safe. It's with me. Just stay still."

"Who are you? I'm not supposed to talk to—"

"Look, I'm not a stranger." *Damn.* It had to be Safety Kid wandering alone in the woods. "Your pa and ma work on the Base, right? You know a tall fellow, white skin, red eyes? Sarge Bryan, he's my uncle. So do what I say." As she made introductions, Sienna took off her jacket and wrapped it around her left arm.

Silence.

"Don't move. When you hear screaming, then you move. You run home, straight back home, and lock the door." And just in case he can remember it, she adds, "And get your folks to call an ambulance. Hooah?"

"W-who's gonna be screaming?"

"That would be me," Sienna said and hurled a nice jagged rock at the wolf. "Haw! C'mon and git sum!" she yelled, trying to sound like Sarge on the parade ground. The words came out really brave.

Then she noticed she wasn't. Her right hand shook so bad she almost dropped the Bowie. Her chances of cutting the wolf's eyes out of its head as it munched on her arm were entirely crappy. She had little expectation of future use of said left arm. She'd seen attack dogs rip apart K9 training dummies. Except all that came out of them was cotton and straw. Sienna expected the stuff that would come out of her arm to be more colorful.

The red wolf rolled with the missile strike to his rump. No telling if the rock drew blood. It did draw his attention. He came straight for her outstretched arm. Eyes narrowed to yellow-orange slits, black lips drew back, neck scruff puffed out to seem bigger. There appeared lines on his cheeks, brow, and snout she never knew existed, ones specifically carved into his attack face to freeze prey in its tracks for the instant necessary to clamp down. His only mission was to rip and tear, to search for jugular and windpipe, to suffocate and exsanguinate. In seconds, the wolf's jaws would do just that.

Tunnel vision now. Situational awareness, gone. Frame-step slo-mo, the attack played out in her head. The four-footed killer loped in. He drew up tailless hindquarters for a leap. That leap. The one that would be followed by the screaming she predicted.

The pain, it would come.

The knife, big before, now small. Shiny steel would tremble and fall and be lost among roots and leaves.

The kid. He was only trying to get his kitten back. What would happen to him was just so *wrong*. But there was nothing, totally nothing, she could do. That feeling hurt the most.

In mid-leap, the wolf's jaws clamped shut.

On air?

This desperate hurt released something. Like the first deep breath of sub-zero air, when it felt like the roof of your mouth would freeze solid. Except this went outward. A part of her, a part without feeling, separated. A cold shadow of herself, like an icy breath of fog, hovered out and clung. In those shady woods, it had to be seventy degrees. Still, chill it was. It was fear.

Not hers. The wolf's. Everything and anything he had feared in his life, all the things that had terrorized the lives of all his kind as long as there have been wolves, passed from girl into animal. This shadow settled into a form they both recognized: a bear. A pretty pissed one.

Confused by her sudden change from prey into 500-pound death machine, his teeth clacked closed inches from her chin. He did a kind of doggy summersault, skidding on three, then four, legs spread wide to keep from toppling. It might have been funny in a dumb pet tricks video, except for the mortal danger she and the kid were still in. She kept the Bowie knife raised, but did not strike. She could not be sure of killing the creature and had an idea any pain might break the spell.

He looked at her. Rather, around her, up and down. Sniffing. Shifting his triangle-shaped head this way and that. He tried to make sense of the different things eyes and nose and ears were telling him.

She, too, could smell it, the angry musk of bear pee and bear sweat hotly clinging to fur. She exhaled not her own breath, but moist air tinged with the smell of digesting meat from deep down an omnivorous gullet. The wolf teetered between striking at what he saw or dodging the big-clawed paw that his nose told him was there and could snap his spine as easily as stepping on a twig.

His nose won. Gore-oozing tail stump between legs, the red wolf made a tactical retreat. For the next county, judging by his speed and pace.

Her arm, wrapped in thin jacket cloth, was stuck in an L-shaped formation in front of her. The Bowie was a steel icicle, steady despite the insensibility of the fist holding it. Safety Kid broke the spell, though it was quite a while before she could smell anything but bear.

"I don't hear no screamin'. I'm getting Triskit and telling Ma about you all."

"You do that, I'll be right behin—"

She shut up. Up on the ridge appeared another set of snaggly teeth framed by a hairy, blood-dripping snout.

"Glantzer!"

Darius Hofer Glantzer's lone eye looked down after the retreating wolf. He aimed the damnedest firearm. It looked to be a home-made blunderbuss. He had duct taped a Korean War vintage flare gun to a broken hockey stick. No doubt the chamber was filled with black powder, bolts, and rocks. It was more likely to perforate her and the kid—and blow Glantzer's hand off—than have any beneficial effect on the attitude of the wolf, who was long gone.

"Arrrh?" the scraggy man demanded.

"Don't you dare pull that trigger," Sienna shouted back up. At this time she noticed he was walking funnier than usual, a ragged cloth wrapped around his torn pants leg. "Thing ran off. Musta smelled you comin.'"

Glantzer spat brown baccy juice through his beard. His facial hair was nearly as bloody as the wolf's had been.

"Thanks I git."

Along with a new gimpy style of walking, Glantzer was dirtier than normal. Turned out, the red wolf had paid him a visit first. The rogue canine got in the first bite.

"On account of him comin' up on my bad side."

The wolf, taking unfair advantage of the 'billy hermit, had leaped without warning and chomped on his leather pants. These leggings were so crusty dirty they were like thick hide. By way of counterattack, Sienna's irregular warfare tutor, finding himself without his favorite knife, had half bitten, half twisted the wolf's tail off. He had it in his pocket and showed it to a clearly impressed Safety Kid.

"Can I have it?"

"I can sell it to ya. You know where your ma keeps her money?"

The boy, whose name was Kylie McNabb, was indeed Ellie's boy. He said that his own finances were sufficient to allow for the acquisition of this conversation-worthy local keepsake.

After performing the tailectomy, Glantzer claimed the wolf, having met his match, ran off. By the looks and smell of him, Sienna concluded it was more likely he rolled himself into the skunkweed swamp by his hootch and hid.

On their walk back to Ellie's, Glantzer kept gawking back.

"Once a critter git up in the blood like that, like that, I ain't never seen one turn." He looked at Sienna with suspicion, and maybe as much respect as his 'billy brain could muster. "Dog, coyote, wolf, don't matter. They don't stop till they's kilt."

"Don't worry. He's gone. And don't point that thing."

***

For reasons that had nothing to do with the red wolf, Sienna was glad to get to the McNabbs' place. Along the way she'd called Bryan. He was on his way with Mr. McNabb, who worked a cushy civilian job. They were accompanied by a medic to take a look at Glantzer's leg. If anyone needed rabies shots, it was the wolf.

"Shhh," Kylie cautioned them as the energetic kitten tried to climb his head. "Ma's resting. She got shot, but she's better now."

While riding in a convoy truck overseas, Mrs. McNabb had taken an AK round to her Kevlar helmet. This was a big Army base, but a small town. Everyone knew everyone's business. The hall table was filled with food neighbors had brought. Except for a small bandage, Ellie looked just like she always did. She seemed surprised to see them come in. By her still-concussed sense of time, only a minute had passed since she put Kylie in his room for a nap. She had enough wherewithal to ask Glantzer to stay on the porch, which could be hosed down.

Kylie looked intently at Sienna. "I know you."

"Told you I wasn't strange."

Kylie thought. He could tell it hadn't been an ordinary

walk in the woods. The sudden appearance of our man on the ridge, stinky and bloody head to toe, waving a home-built musket, these things had to have made some impression, even on a first grader. He just didn't know how unordinary it had been.

"When Triskit has kittens, you can have one. Your pick."

If Triskit has kittens, we'll enter him in the Raleigh science fair, she thought. "Thanks."

Without warning, Sienna needed some air. Right quick. She excused herself and dashed round the side of the house. Bracing herself on the siding, she felt she would pass out or puke. Her head shook of its own accord and she gulped for air not filled with bear musk.

Reverberating behind her eardrums were echoes of that weird thunderclap of fear. The one that saved her and Kylie from a bad mauling at the very least. The one that had connected her to the animal.

Soundlessly she heard it, nervelessly she felt it. She knew the red wolf. Knew that he had wanted to tear her up, and the boy, and the kitten. Destroy their carcasses until only scattered meat and random gristle was left. The wolf was sick. It could hunt and kill but could not satisfy its hunger. That made him crazy. Somehow her silent, half-second struggle with him had crushed his killing madness, and at the same time had broken his will to live. The wolf would go into a dark place and die. She knew this.

Those things were fading. Other things were rising. Later when she thought of the day, she would recognize the adrenal dump following acute stress response. It was her fight-or-flight system's revenge on her for discovering some strange third option. Sienna McKnight, just turned twelve, also grasped at memories her body and mind could not hold, then or ever. The memories of killing entire civilizations as casually as garden shears would snick the heads off inconvenient chickens. Mirages from a cold place at the base of her skull, *inside.* These clawed at her. She bent over and retched. Only clear drool and snot came out.

Through teared-up eyes, she saw Glantzer sidle around the corner. *Oh no.* If he said anything, or tried to help her…

He kept his distance and stood with his patch-eye side to her. As courteous as she'd ever seen the coot. After a while, she was done trying to hurl. She spat out and sucked in clean air. Glantzer had her knife. She never felt him take it.

"This ain't no proper gift for a girl."

What?

"I'mma take it back," he said. "An' fix it."

Which he did. He commandeered some no-slip paint from somewhere and lacquered the handle of Jane Bowie bright pink. Sometime between then and when she got it back, she decided a few things. She knew who she had to be. Sienna understood what she wanted more than not being afraid.

That day behind the McNabbs', Glantzer stuffed the long knife into one of the many hidden pockets of his raggedy woodman's outfit. As she squared up to him, his eye rolled over her, assessing her fitness to do something useful.

"If you're a'right now, you can go in and bring me some of that fried chicken I saw. And cornbread, and gravy, too. Rescuin' defenseless kids and their pets, it shore works up a ap'tite."

2

TEN MONTHS AGO
BENTLEY SUBGLACIAL TRENCH
ANTARCTICA

Second Lieutenant Sienna McKnight stared up from the bottom of the world. The midday sky was ethereal. It was dark and shrouded across half its horizon by Southern Lights of neon green. Glowing, feathery brush strokes on a canvas of deepest blue. To Sienna, the sky seemed hardly part of her planet. It seemed that from this point, there was no separation, or a feeble one at best, between her and the cosmic breath of the stars beyond.

She looked toward the heavens for any sign of Roger Halley. He was this mission's commanding officer and Sienna's boyfriend. She scanned for sight of supersonic combusting ramjet contrails from the plane that was scheduled to bring him over the drop zone.

"Now," Sienna said to her sergeant. She and Shetani Zeru Bryan stood on a glacier. Ice was a mile thick beneath their boots. Beside her in winter warfare gear, he was a familiar, solid presence. "They should have dropped him by now."

A single snowflake seemingly the size of her fist momentarily obscured her vision in the visor. It was on high magnification and the delicate crystal shape stuck on the lens. Wiping only smudged her view. Sarge Bryan's eyes were better than her gear. In the gloom of noon, they glinted like embers of molten gold out from a cloud of breath vapor around his head. His features, often so comforting for Sienna to see as a girl growing up in North Carolina, were lost in the pale haze.

"Say what you want about Air Force. They're most always on time. Let me take a look while you check on the storm front, Lieutenant McKnight."

Sienna noted pride in the older man's voice. Affectionately casual and reassuringly proprietary. In many ways, her family friend and mentor was responsible for her making it through four grueling years at West Point.

It was only weeks ago she and her cadet graduate classmates stoically tossed their hats in the air at Michie Stadium in New York. The most somber graduation there in living memory.

Only days ago she'd worn the formal mess uniform of a commissioned second lieutenant, with its distinct insignia: a rectangle of gold. Its likeness to a tiny metallic pat of butter gave rise to the slang: butterbar lieutenant. Here, out in the field, a stripe of matte aluminum under a flip tab indicated her rank. Snipers loved to pick off officers.

'Course the only shooting going on in this ice box was gripey lip from her small, tight-knit team of enlisteds. All about how the South Pole was damn cold and damn dark. Her lifelong ally knew how to handle them. She owed Sarge Bryan a lot. Right now she planned to repay him in part by not getting him frozen to death or otherwise killed on a supposedly simple rescue job.

The more she mulled on it, the more she suspected she hadn't been fully briefed before their triple-time departure from the Base.

Maybe Roger will have more information.

He was a ninja for Pentagon bureaucracy; his uncle was chairman of the Joint Chiefs.

Sarge Bryan squinted upwards. Sienna could only see his eyes and a curve of alabaster brow under his parka.

"Remind me why I left my porch recliner on a fine North Carolina evening to come to the South Pole just ahead of a winter storm."

"Sorry, Sarge, that's classified way above Enlisted-5 paygrade."

They'd had less than half an hour from roost to plane when they got the call. The request-for-forces brief had been routed to Sienna from the Pentagon through the commandant of the Base. That was standard procedure. Less standard had been the lack of vital details. The cryptic mission subheader, which ended up being pretty ironic, read:

```
RFF [immediate] Hazardous journey, threat
of  physical  harm  constant; NO  Imminent
Danger Pay (basic pay only); Bitter cold;
Long hours of complete darkness; Honor and
recognition from AEO Acting Assistant Deputy
Division Chief Perdix in event of success.
AFFIRM REQUIRED (EO 12356 classified).
```

The only other specifics were a takeoff time, projected in-flight time, and a note to bring milspec long underwear. Another odd thing: the mission was voluntary. She only had six minutes to decide. After that, the assignment would be offered to the Navy SEALs or Marine Force Recon. For graduate Lieutenant McKnight, accepting it would be a risk.

She'd just taken command of the tiny special-ops unit in their unique command post on the far side of the Base. After West Point, she chose the duty assignment that would let her return to Sarge, Annalies, home. Even though it was made clear to her the Pentagon powers that be expected her to take a more political position in DC. And those powers were used to getting what they wanted. Her career had begun on thin ice.

No one would have faulted her for declining the request for forces. She got the plum impression her immediate superior, a full bird colonel, wanted her to pass. If she screwed up and got all her people killed, it would look bad for him. Might even damage his prospects of becoming a general.

That made her accept the mission faster than a hare twitches its nose. She replied over SIPRNet "Heck yes!" The originator was Mr. Perdix at something called the Adaptive Execution Office, a branch of Defense Advanced Research Projects Agency in Virginia. *DARPA*. Inventing nutty ways to fight wars since 1958.

Months later, Sienna would meet Mr. Perdix. She would shake his slightly perspiring hand while forcing down the memory of the casually worded memo describing a mission she was not supposed to survive.

Back then, on thick ice, Sienna and Sarge Bryan shivered in grungy darkness relieved only by the aurora. It surged above like clouds made of pure light.

"What Adaptive Execution did tell us about the mission— once we were on the plane and it was too late not to accept it—is our only objective will be to pick up these distressed explorers and whatever they found."

"What'd they find?"

Sienna let out a spout of frozen breath so thick it looked almost solid. "We're gonna see, ain't we? Best guess is a digital optical module that got loose from the IceCube Neutrino Observatory. Years ago they put thousands of them deep under the ice to measure some science stuff in space."

"And one got loose."

"And popped up here. There's rivers under the glaciers, whole drainage systems all through the continent. This module, it's different. Changed. The super nerds inside DARPA want it. That's why we're here. And Sarge, when we get it, tell the guys, especially Whitebread, to be gentle. Don't break the darn thing."

"Got him," Bryan said, his eyes fixing on something above the highest clouds. "Roger snagged himself a real fancy scRamjet ride from DC. Too bad it's one way. He's in a single HALO pod and comin' down easy. Right on target for our camp."

Good thing too. Sienna looked at her weather map. Satellite images confirmed what ground stations across the continent were silently screaming about. First big ice storm of the season, headed right for them. This one was tagged Cyclone Skadi, after a Norse goddess of winter. A katabatic storm, fed as much by gravity as the rotation of the Earth, it packed winds of 198 mph and temperatures 100 below zero. In enviro science class she learned climatic change only made these vast weather systems more intense and unpredictable.

"Let's get these guys and get out of here." Sienna flipped her electronic visor away from her face. Over the ice flats, she could just make something out with her naked eyes, about three hundred meters away. She jabbed a mitt in that direction. "That's got to be them. Can you see it?" A faint glow came from under the ice.

Sarge Bryan shook his hood-covered head.

Jet afterburners must have dazzled his ocular implants when he zoomed in.

"I do. I see it." Sienna motioned forward and led the way. "Let's go."

Miles in front of them, but made not any less intimidating by the open distance, the storm front advanced. Skadi came toward Sienna and her people, obscuring the horizon's slim slash of day, swallowing the pinpricks of heavenly bodies and consuming the gossamer luminescence of the aurora australis in a curtain of cold fury.

3

TODAY – MARCH 19

VERNON J. BAKER NATIONAL MILITARY MEDICAL
CENTER

WASHINGTON DC

The medCorps captain stares at the eagle insignia on Sienna's casual dress uniform. There's a faint sheen of sweat on his upper lip. That's weird. She's the one under intense scrutiny. The physician's stare is full of suspicion, with a heaping side order of resentment. He looks at her with middle-aged man huff reserved for women half their age and twice their rank.

Sienna is getting used to it.

"Colonel McKnight," the pale, soft-featured doctor in front of her asks, "how do you feel about your parents?"

She hadn't been past the visitor's security gate of Baker Medical for even a minute when she got the page. The summons she hoped, just once, would get lost in the jumble of the Army's electron-based bureaucracy. The one that ordered her to report to the designated exam pod for a mandatory pre-mission psych eval. Baker Medical rivals the nearby Pentagon with its maze of complex corridors and tunnels. She found it easily enough, down a dead-end corridor in what looked to be the laundry wing, right across from a waste disposal unit.

It's been a week. Ever since Sienna got the intel on what a minor Khorasani criminal codenamed Sidewinder might know, she can only think about one thing: getting to Khorasan with her team, kicking in his door, and kidnapping the vile man. Then making sure Sidewinder's day goes downhill from there.

Tomorrow.

March 20.

This is March 19. She and Sarge Bryan should be strapped into a military scRamjet. Cold and noisy. Fast. Its trajectory will take it clear out of the Earth's atmosphere in its parabolic haste to chew up the 7,000 miles between North Carolina and the Gulf of Oman. Instead, she's sitting in an examination pod. Talking about her feelings. To an Army shrink.

OFM.

Sienna curses silently, keeping her thoughts steady. In preparation. Pointing right at her head is a Metcalf-Chang neural probe, fresh out of a DARPA labs packing crate. *This could suck mightily.*

The doctor taps his side of the diagnostic display. Sienna can't see the doctor's screens, but she knows they show dozens of diagnostic functions. The military mechBrain analyzes every input and tells the doctor what questions to ask.

The letters of his name panel glow on her side of the screen.

CAPT. W. JOFI, MD — DEPT. OF CLINICAL NEUROSCIENCE

Dr. Jofi is a real flesh-and-blood person, not a virtual physician. He's supposed to make patients feel more comfortable. Dr. Jofi, the pudgy tool of clinical neuroscience. But really, the machine is the one evaluating her. The machine will decide if she's fit to lead her people.

This is a reverse Turing test. The bad news is it's going to be her first frontal-lobe PET scan. The worse news is ever since she can remember, she's heard something. An unvoice. Sometimes. And it tells her to do awful things. Always terrible things.

Some of which I've most definitely done. Sienna feels the tension of being cornered and redirects it into a thin curving of her lips. She hopes it will be interpreted as a polite, collegial smile. *Oh yeah, Doc Jofi, when you stare into my brain, you might not be prepared for what's staring back.*

4

I can't even call it a voice. I know I'm not really hearing anything. It has to be my personal issued ration of crazy. What else could it be?

Mind probe. No biggie. Like in soccer when you forget about your foot and the ball and just think of the perfect spiral arc into the corner of the goal net. Past this psych exam is an aircraft carrier strike group. And Bryan and her team.

No silicon psychiatrist is getting in my way.

The mechBrain wants to know if she has the right mindset for command. Will she leave one of her people behind to get the mission done? Will she lie to her friends and comrades? Does she have what it takes to deliberately send them to their deaths to carry out orders, whether she agrees with them or not? Whether she even knows their purpose? The more human she is, the less chance she has of passing.

And she has to pass. Sienna needs to get to Khorasan as fast as jets and hovercopters can take her.

Jofi repeats his question. These psych exams. How many since Junior ROTC?

"My parents? I'll tell you about my parents. My birth

parents are both dead. I never met them. My surviving mom, Annalies, is a retired enlisted. If that's all you've got there, this interview is going to be short and sweet."

As if anything involving Army paperwork could be.

Jofi remains a blank. He stares at screens. Reflections jitter in the oval lenses of his glasses. Text and pictures and biometrics scroll in miniature mirror view. That's a whole Carolina peck of information about her.

"Short and sweet, uh uhmmm." Jofi waits to be told what to ask next.

He is just a sideshow, a prop. Like a cute dolly in a dentist's office meant to distract little patients from the stainless-steel instruments and the wickedly curved needle coming at them, jabbing into small open mouths to pierce tender gum flesh.

Inches in front of Sienna hang the bifocal eyes and ultrasonic ears of the Metcalf-Chang probe. It is powerful enough to decode and strip naked individual thoughts. But not all of them. Jofi can only monitor the neural oscillations in her frontal lobes. According to Sienna's West Point psyWar instructor, the older, deeper parts of the brain defy remote analysis.

"Oh, well, Colonel, I can't promise brevity. But we will be thorough. We will."

Piss!

Jofi's eyes again track down to Sienna's eagles.

"From second lieutenant to full bird colonel, O-6 pay grade. In under a year. By the tender age of twenty-three." Lips purse. "Must be some kind of record."

"Pretty average," Sienna says back. "The military seems to bring out the best in young people. A little slip of a girl became knight commander of the French Army. She smashed through English siege lines which had been dug in for seven months. She rescued the people of Orléans from death by starvation and disease. It took her nine days. She was seventeen."

She also heard voices. Probably not a good topic to bring up while trying to get declared mentally fit for duty by the most uptight psychoanalyst in uniform.

Jofi is not impressed. "Joan of Arc's adventuresome exploits all happened a while ago." He checks his monitor. "Are you feeling well, Colonel? Your stress index spiked."

Dang, this mind probe thing is sensitive.

She deflects. "As for the US Army, I only got dibs on the women's record. Union guy became a colonel at twenty during the Civil War. But yeah, as the youngest female Army colonel ever, I feel humbled and honored by Army Command's confidence in me."

Captain Jofi, O-3, studies his screen. Then, deliberately, he says: "Colonel Bitch."

5

If Sienna needs to suppress any reaction, it's a laugh.

Where does this guy get this crap?

More strange sweat collects on Jofi's upper lip. He's fiddling with his wedding band. He must do it a lot; his second knuckle is discolored.

"Colonel Bitch," Jofi says again. "That is your nickname in D Group, isn't it?"

"Yup," Sienna replies. "And I got the T-shirt to prove it."

"You allow your subordinates to disrespect you? How can you call yourself a leader?"

"A little thing called success." Boy, she could give Jofi some sweet nicknames of his own just now.

Instead she explains, just a little. "It was after my promotion was made permanent. Army Special Ops have a 'boys only' tree house thing. Some guys started talkin' trash. Just restless. Nothing I took personal. Sarge was gonna hurt 'em, before my ops unit, the Dogs, went and messed them up worse. It was more personal for them."

"And what about you?" Jofi asks. "How did you feel about these insults?"

"Big waste of energy. I down-riled everyone. And Ortiz sewed me a shirt."

And that is the most explaining, especially to a lower-ranked officer, she's done since Beast Barracks boot camp five years ago.

"This frustrates you, Colonel?" Jofi asks. "Having to sit here in this exam pod? You don't like talking to me?"

"You're cleared to evaluate me, not my mission," Sienna says. "There's a large mobile-weapons platform filled with angry service people. They can't proceed until the Dogs and I are on it. And we can't be on it until you green my psych update."

Her mission fob is a square piece of plastic. It contains her orders and permissions for Sidewinder. Three pinprick LEDs glow. Two yellow. One green. The head of Joint Special Ops Command in Washington transmitted approvals this morning.

"Normally you just input the results from my last physical," Sienna says.

She had planned to spend more time upstairs with Roger. The Sidewinder mission window is marked in hours and minutes. There's no time for dithering.

"You reassigned yourself suddenly. Away from Europe, to the Gulf," Jofi dithers.

"Last-minute target of opportunity."

"Your request for reassignment flagged this review. The one we're both enjoying so much."

She hates name-dropping, but she's in a hurry.

"Major Roger *Halley* is upstairs in the Executive Wing, holding off going into surgery until he can see me."

"I'm aware. I also know you and the son of General Halley are romantically involved."

So much for name-dropping.

"You see why my evaluation is so important. I'm the last independent link in the mission management chain. If you or one of your group is KIA… Well, I'd feel just as badly as if I'd made the fatal mistake myself."

"Probably not just as bad," Sienna says.

"Just as intensely, I assure you," Jofi says. "Likely worse. Because I have the burden of calm reflection and foresight. You and your soldiers can only carry out orders. Someone has to guide you. It's a terrible burden."

Maybe you should be in therapy.

"Did you say something?" Jofi asks.

Sienna's own voice stress analyzer, her ears, tell her two things. Jofi is browned off, and not just at her and her colonel's eagles. Something else is eating at him. And he's going to take out his own personal frustrations on her. Just because he can.

Jam this!

He reads his next question. "Do you have violent feelings toward others?"

Seriously. You're asking me that?

"It's kind of a job requirement, doctor."

"Some of these items are mandated. It's as much about your responses as your reactions."

"Which the mechBrain interprets," Sienna says.

On cue, Jofi bridles.

"I judge," the insecure paper pusher corrects. "Me. The machine observes. I am in control."

It's just like her mom, a career warrant officer, said: If you have to keep tellin' everyone you're in charge, you kind of ain't.

"Let me rephrase. Do you have *inappropriate* violent feelings toward others, or yourself?"

"No."

"Do you plan on killing anyone on this mission?"

"That's part of what you can't be told," Sienna says. "But, my rules of engagement do not require a fatality."

"Will you kill someone if the ROE allow it?"

"If they're armed and a clear and present threat to my team, I sure will, unless my team beats me to it," Sienna replies.

Jofi gets fed new questions.

"What if an unarmed civilian is threatening your mission?"

This is another crucial part of the mechBrain's test. Not enough empathy and they write you off as a psycho, or promote you to general or admiral, depending on the Pentagon's staffing requirements. On the other hand, too much empathy and you're put on administrative duty. You'd instantly go from soldier to desk jockey. Forever. Either way, you're out of the field.

"Not relevant."

"What do you mean?"

"No unarmed civilian can make my team choose between killing them and doing the job," Sienna says firmly.

"You haven't envisioned every scenario."

"You haven't envisioned my team."

"You have an unusual relationship with your sergeant," Jofi says, trying to get under her skin.

In a private part of her mind, Sienna is more concerned with what's gotten under Jofi's skin. Particularly his fingernails. They're gray, walking-dead gray. Something about that, besides the obvious grossness, reminds her of something.

Jofi does a double take at his display screen. "Your sergeant. He's an unusual-looking individual, isn't he?"

As Jofi slides so easily into racial prejudice, Sienna has feelings about hurting others. Namely this clown from clinical neuroscience.

"Sometimes he doesn't even have to shoot people. He just stares at them with his scary eyes and they fall down petrified."

"Petrified. Yes." Jofi squirms.

He's fat. But by now he should have found a chair that fits him or beaten a standard-issue one into submission with his flabby butt cheeks. He is uncomfortable. In pain. Goop under his nails, shaky hands, now this squirming.

This is the weirdest psych exam ever. Usually it's a few inkblots, pee in a cup, and you're squared away. Jofi's acting like he's covering his ass for a review later. Why?

"I'm going to give you a very specific scenario requiring a very specific answer."

"Shoot."

"You are in a burning building. Imagine Roger Halley is there, pinned down by debris. Your sergeant is there as well, similarly trapped. All things are equal. You can only save one. Which one do you rescue?"

Sienna knows this one.

"Sergeant Bryan," she says without hesitation.

"So," Jofi asks with satisfaction, "you value Sergeant Bryan's contribution to your mission more than a decorated senior officer?"

"That's not—"

"You feel closer to your mentor than your lover?" Jofi's

no longer reading from any prompts. "Do you have romantic feelings for the much older Sergeant Bryan? Do you desire him sexually?"

Jofi's baiting her into losing her shit. An impulse comes to Sienna. An impulse to ram Jofi's head into his console. And, it passes.

"All things being equal, I would first rescue Sergeant Bryan. Then together we'd save Major Halley."

"Not possible," Jofi snaps, checking his question list. "You can only save one of them."

"That's right. *I* can only save one. But it never said anything about what both of us, me and Sarge together, could do. Ain't that a Carolina peach?"

A no-win situation just means: try harder. Sienna truly believes that.

6

Jofi would be a truly disgusting person if he had an ounce of guts. Sienna has more respect for the mechBrain. Did some crusty fart in the subbasement of the Pentagon tell Jofi to deliberately scuttle Sidewinder? Just over some sort of petty revenge? *Whatever.* Sienna has to play this out. The second light on her mission fob is going to turn green. It is. It has to.

I wish I had some leverage on this goof.

The symptoms Jofi has could be from cheap antibiotics. But he's an MD. He works at Baker. He has access to all the top-line anti-microbial drugs he wants, unless…

Dr. Cadaver Nails interrupts. "It was Dr. Theodora McKnight who performed the emergency C-section that delivered you on a military base. You were the only infant born on that base and came into the world suffering from deep lacerations."

He must have dug up this part of her personal history on his own. That's just creepy.

"These wounds, the scars which still present on your body, they were the result of the abdominal stabbing of a young Khorasani woman. A girl, really, who was heavily pregnant. Your birth mother. You're fortunate someone with Dr. McKnight's surgical skill was there."

"Lucky me," Sienna says. "And yeah, I have scars. They've been there as long as I can remember. As you can see from my physical, they don't slow me down. And I don't have a breakdown when I see them in the mirror, if that's your next question."

"It wasn't."

It sure was, you weasel.

"And what's it got to do with my fitness to lead this mission?"

"Violence," Jofi says. "And not the organized sort the chain of command approves of. Helter-skelter violence seems to follow you around. And worse. You're a survivor."

He opens a file folder.

"It was the worst terrorist atrocity committed on US soil in thirty years," Jofi says. "And at the age of eighteen, you were in the middle of it. The Beast Barracks Cadet massacre."

"I think they ended up calling it the Battle of Beast March," Sienna corrects. "The first-year cadet column got ambushed. We were unarmed."

"Your classmate Ennis Reidt, he seems to have been the hero of that day."

Sienna looks at Jofi. He's talking like he was there. Like he wouldn't have crapped down his pants leg at the sound of automatic weapons fire aimed at him.

"He had a sword."

"And they made him first cadet."

"They did that," Sienna agrees. "After the shrinks let him out of the asylum. No offense, doc."

Jofi smiles. And trembles. His nails glisten dully. And he squirms in pain.

Weird. The way Jofi's antsing around you'd think someone's poking needles in his sack.

And then Squirming Needled Nuts goes too far.

"I'm intrigued." Jofi looks over his glasses. "Cadet Reidt's recounting of events is like yours. Up to the point you were knocked unconscious. Word for word, in fact. Would you mind talking…?"

And then Jofi's voice fades. Sienna hears another voice. One that makes a lot more sense.

It speaks to her from a part of her mind too ancient for the mechBrain to understand. It speaks so loudly it cannot be heard by men. Its heartbeat joins hers, hidden to everyone but her, stronger than her own. *Its* name is five runes long. One letter for each of the elongated scars on her adult body, one letter for each of the slashes she was born with, rent and bleeding. This she memorized before she was born. It is her own living dark recitation. It urges Sienna to

Kill the idiot, kill Jofi now.

It could be done quietly, cleanly. She has the tools, training, and opportunity to get away with a homicide of convenience. No one will even notice Jofi missing until Sienna is well over Khorasani airspace.

That voice, the one that issues from no living thing, tells her the small EMP device she carries can short circuit all the recording devices in the room. In the hall. It pushes images of the body-bag dispenser and the bio-waste hatch opposite this exam pod. Perfect for disposing of a pesky neuroscientist. Her palm tingles, wanting to feel the tough handle of her Bowie knife in it. The one at her hip.

No!

She tells the guardian inside her, her vǫrthr spirit.

I will not.

She fights against its healing spite and delicious venom. Silently, unseen by human or mechBrain, she struggles. The orphan girl born in blood with the birthright of pain and scars, she wins. The coiled thing inside retreats. The heart in Sienna's chest again resumes its solitary beats. The other remains. And remains itself. Silent.

Jofi continues jabbering, unaware how close he came to being in several eco-friendly disposal bags in Baker Medical's conveniently placed waste chute. Jane Bowie hangs against Sienna's thigh, honed sharp and unblemished by blood and gristly bits of clinical neuroscientist.

She has an inkling of a better idea. One not stewed up in the dark places of her brain, far beyond the reach of the mechBrain's frontal-lobe sensors. One that's crystalizing in a part of her own psyche she's been trying to cultivate: the sneaky part. She just about has it.

Jofi drops the bullshit diagnosis she should have seen coming.

"Your case file will have the distinction of being the first where I'm going to overrule the diagnostic apparatus and suspend you from active duty. Because *I'm* in charge.

"Your birth trauma has left you unbalanced.

"Secondly, you've suffered from an unusual upbringing in a non-traditional family setting. No disrespect, of course, to your mothers, but that's my opinion.

"Thirdly, you were victimized during the Beast March Massacre. And your years at West Point were far from normal.

"Finally, last year's horrific mission left you mentally and emotionally damaged. You are not fit for duty due to PTSD. I require you undergo further examinations including Likert bipolar scaling, EMDR therap—"

"Enough."

Sienna can't listen anymore. Jofi's mind was made up before she entered the pod. No. Scratch that. Jofi's mind was made up for him by the faceless ones at the Pentagon who, for whatever petty reasons, despise her and her people. If the neuroscientist had a spine, he would have demanded the number of pieces of silver they pay these days for a squirmy, weak little soul.

"Enough!" She reaches for the knife at her hip.

7

Her thumb flicks open the pommel of Jane Bowie and hits the switch of a small but powerful electromagnetic-pulse device.

The exam pod lights flicker.

Every device with a mechBrain reboots. The holographic display goes dark. Soothing flute music plays as a reassuring message appears.

Reinitializing in
-89 s
Thank you for your patience.
Find out if you qualify for a free hardware update at Eurolincx/licht

"Wha—?"

"Captain Jofi," Sienna says. "You have eighty-eight seconds to authorize my very important mission. You want to keep your mouth shut and listen up."

Thankfully, something in Sienna's tone makes Jofi keep his mouth shut. And listen.

"At first, I couldn't figure it," Sienna says. "Your hand tremors, some kind of groin-based discomfort, the weird color of your fingertips. Then it hit me, I've seen the symptoms before. On me.

"In Bangkok, after a jungle warfare training exercise, I got a somewhat ill-advised tattoo of a yellow rose hand-tapped onto my shoulder blade. I was too hammered at the time to insist the midget tattoo artist wash up before starting. So to cut a long story short, because we only have fifty-six seconds left in our brief but memorable time together. The local Thai doc, really more of a combo hairdresser/dentist, he gives me loads of cheap, over-the-counter antibiotics for the infection around the tattoo. Which actually turned out pretty good, once the swelling went down. Fluoroquinolones. The same ones you are taking to secretly treat your venereal disease."

Jofi sits, shaking quietly.

"My money's on gonorrhea," Sienna continues. "And from the looks of you, it's a pretty tough strain. Nothing you're gonna knock out with off-the-books meds. No way. But they're the only thing you can take and hide your infection from your boss and your wife. Both of whom really have a 'need to know', especially Mrs. Jofi.

"The bruises on both sides of your ring finger made everything fall into place. It looks like you yanked your wedding band off and then jammed it back on. Regulations state you have to report any serious domestic discord to your CO. Bet you kept that quiet, along with your drippy spout."

The look on Jofi's face! *This is too much fun. But only twenty-nine seconds left for this guy to do the right thing, for a change.*

"Now seeing as we're friends and all, as well as fellow Army officers, I'll do you a solid to seal the deal," Sienna says, winding up. "I'll get my corpsman Whitebread to hook you up with Acremonium compound, just the thing to give that godawful infection of yours a wuppin'. JSOC med stocks are classified, totally off the books. So, doc, does that sound like something to clap about?"

***

Eleven seconds later, Sienna exits the exam pod. The second light on the mission fob glows green faintly in the brighter lighting of the corridor of Baker Medical. She leans against the wall, asking herself if she really just did that.

Yup, I just flat-out blackmailed my assigned Army shrink. If I'm really cracked, maybe I shouldn't be leading my people. Maybe I'll go see Dr. Metcalf, when this is all over.

The Dogs, her team, must be rubbing off on her. Snakelips, Nobu, T-Rex, and Whitebread are basically grown-up versions of the kids in high school who dressed all in black. The ones security guards at the metal detectors would never turn their backs on. Now they're grown up, and the government has issued them flamethrowers and explosives. And her. As their commanding officer. That's something they are not going to take away, not with some bought-and-paid for, sorry excuse for a neuroscientist.

Bet Jofi never saw that one comin'. I do enjoy exceeding expectations.

Sienna's steps feel a little lighter leaving the exam pod than they did walking to it. Blackmail may be wrong, but it sure saves time. She double-checks the clocks. She is nearly twenty minutes ahead of schedule. Down the spotless hallway is an elevator. She hits UP. Roger is waiting.

8

Sienna hits the floor button harder than she has to.

Jofi, you...

A half-second pause makes sure the mini mechBrain controlling the elevator logs her rank tab ID. Then she scans her mission fob. Roger rates the Executive Wing, where they take the president. There are extra layers of security and luxury. Like in fancy Charlotte office buildings, this elevator is high speed/low drag. She barely feels it moving. The passage of floors is marked by a muted chime. *Ding.*

What a dick.

Sienna can forgive him for his personal attacks. She can overlook his thinly veiled prejudice against Sarge. But she'll never forgive him for trying to scuttle Sidewinder. And the slimy way he tried to do it, a fake PTSD diagnosis. *WTAF!*

The medCorps captain was blindly following, if not orders, then unequivocal suggestions. Ones made by people in the Pentagon who just wanted to screw with her and her team.

"How do you feel about your parents?"

What an ass—

Ding

She resents the near miss by her enemies. Still, had the toady Dr. Jofi inadvertently hit on something? This Sidewinder mission, her career, her obsessions, all do relate to her birth parents. The story of how she was adopted is improbable. What came before seems inescapable.

A female military couple took in a wounded Khorasani orphan. A foundling who started life at the edge of the Wandering Desert, one who should have died without ever having been born. Yet, what little she knows of the story of her birth parents—Hamida Qazi and a British boy—is as fantastic as it is tragic. At least the parts of her parents' story which Sienna learned or guessed over the years. The story of two teenagers, both now dead, which played out more than two decades ago.

Before first term at West Point, Sienna visited Kelley Oliphant Langton's grave in Scotland. He was just twenty-one years old when he died, younger than Sienna is now. Kelley probably had no idea he was her birth father. It was her birth mother, Hamida Qazi, who really showed brassiness by not lying down in a muddy ditch and quietly bleeding to death.

Instead she crawled, wounded and leaking her heart's blood, *their* hearts' blood, into the sands. Hamida dragged herself over muddy hardpack through the night right up to the gates of UN Base 90-CH. The results were the twisted miracle of Sienna's birth, and the more or less standard-issue childhood in North Carolina on a special-forces enclave known as the Base.

Ding

She thumbs the mission fob.

One more green light to go. Then it could all end. Asrah's silent years of horror. Some measure of justice for a teenager who bled and died on the edge of the Wandering Desert without ever seeing the baby girl she gave birth to. Everything can change, I can change everything...

Once Roger inputs his codes, things will move fast. A long-range transport jet waits at Andrews. It will take her and Sarge from DC to the Base. The same plane will take them all from NC to the Gulf of Oman. A HALO-pod jump later and all six of them will be standing on the deck of the CVN 108. The USS *Lee*. The aircraft carrier she used all her powers of persuasion to enlist in the final battle of a private war. A war she was born fighting. In Khorasan.

Ding

Sienna will return. To Khorasan. For justice. For Hamida. For vengeance's sake. Hamida Qazi's silent strife would finally have a voice. Sienna's answer would be justice tempered with no mercy. The killer would know the futility of his crimes. The murderer will face her and see he had brought pain and suffering, but had also failed. If the Sidewinder mission succeeds, a curse named Asrah Qazi will finally be lifted. And then?

Ding

Doors hiss open. A ceiling-to-floor curtain of reinforced transparent aluminum blocks a fan of wide corridors. One of those layers of POTUS-level security looks at her with suspicion.

"*Colonel* McKnight, is it?" A thin hospital corpsman studies the pictures of her on his screen. And eyeballs her eagles.

Sienna is getting used to it.

9

During the weapons and explosives scan she's forced to part with Jane Bowie. Explosive-resistant doors open to spacious corridors. Utility robots keep to the sides. A cleaning bot meets a delivery bot. Optic sensor to optic sensor, they pause. Salutations are exchanged. With a slight whirring, the two mechanoids pirouette. Two metal and plastic ballerinas brush past each other on their way to different stages inside the huge building.

Sienna stands in front of Roger's room, mindful of her West Point class ring. The ring winds thickly around her finger. It is plenty tough, despite the feathery-lettered engraving spelling out her grad year's motto. The dark stone flashes dimly under halogens. She doesn't want to put a ding in the door. Like everything else in Baker's Executive Wing, the wood looks mighty expensive. Sienna's just about to knock when the damnedest shouting comes from around the corner.

"Come back here, you coward!"

Huh? Sienna angles her head, and her hair swings to the side. It's sometimes impractical, but does not impair her hearing. Along with the shouts, she tries to make sense of an ominous, low rumbling. It gets louder, and closer. More shouting. She knows that voice, saturated with the Carolinas accent of her youth. An ironic smile pulls at her lips. *Of all the places and all the people...*

"I've got ya now!"

"Ennis freaken Reidt." *What the—*

A bot runs away from something, its small propulsion unit revs to maximum. With arms folded it comes only to her knees. The ungainly cylinder, painted hospital white, careens around the corner. Small wheels drift-skid across polished floor. Visual and sonic sensors click. After checking for humans and other obstacles, it comes straight at her. Or rather, the cat-flap style hatch in the wall.

The bot is being chased by someone joyfully destructive to enemy humans and mechanoids alike. Curses get drowned out by another sound—the engine percussion of an M1 Abrams main battle tank chugging its favorite beverage, jet fuel. This growling competes with a classic rock song belted out with excessive bass. She can only imagine what he's riding this time.

"Ennis!" Sienna yells over the rising noise.

Thirty yards away, a pimped-out Hawking wheelchair follows the line of the smaller robot around the corner. Three gurneys could fit end to end across the hall intersection. Good thing, because the heavier pursuer drifts on four—then two—wheels and nearly topples over. Ennis's one-seater is kept upright by miniaturized suspension suited to a Formula 0 car. Narrowly missing the wall, he continues the hunt.

"I got..."

Crunch

"YOU."

Spines of a vicious mine plow jut from the front of Ennis's wheelchair. Inches from safety, the bot gets impaled.

To call Ennis's chair modified is a big understatement. Its operator can only move his head and right shoulder. His teeth clench a controller stick. A pad of toggles hangs on his chest. Dangling from the chair's front is a functional replica of the digging teeth battlefield tanks use to clear mines. From its desert camo painted body, at least six stereo speakers point outwards. These look like M18 Claymores antipersonnel mines. On top of each speaker grille is a stencil:

FRONT
TOWARD ENEMY

They play music and recorded tank motor sounds in a bizarre harmony. A damn loud one.

"Turn that off. You'll wake the dead."

The twenty-five-year-old quadriplegic toggles a switch and quiets his ride.

"Now, colonel, would that be all and about such a terrible thing? As long as the undead follow orders and stick to an approved meal plan, we can use everyone in the fight." Ennis grins. His facial scars twist into a strangely appropriate combination of chronicled pain and present mirth.

Caught between surprise and laughter, Sienna also feels duty bound to play a prank on her school mate. He cannot see it, but the service bot is still alive. The mechanoid looks up at Sienna with six eyes. Its tiny mechBrain probably recognizes Sienna as human. These bots do the endless hours of grunt-work in the vast complex. Driven by self-preservation software, it silently struggles to get through the robot flap to the safety of the service conduits. If Ennis notices, he'll keep grinding on the wounded little fellow until it's all nuts and bolts.

Ennis needs distracting. A hospital worker passes. Sienna clucks. "Man, I thought it was dress code for nurses to wear bras."

Predictably, Ennis looks in the direction of healthcare cleavage. Sienna's foot flicks off the stricken bot's power. It plays dead.

"Another notch on your scabbard. You've killed it. What are you doing at Baker? This place is for soldiers who are badly hurt."

"Harrr," Ennis says with ruthless good humor. "That joke's as funny as the first fifty times you told it."

With the controller, he looks like Franklin Roosevelt puffing a cigarette holder. An FDR with a blond crew cut, one eyebrow, and a homicidal twinkle in his eyes. She and Ennis are both from the Carolinas, but time and travel have only made his accent more pronounced. Especially when he talks fancy.

"How the fates mock me. A year ago we were butterbars fresh out of Academy. Then you get a free trip to the South Pole, a full bird colonel field commission. And me? I get blown up by my own tank, issued a lousy wheelchair, and my deeds are etched in memory only by a snapshot on the Wall of Heroes stashed behind the children's clothing section in Bonworthy's discount department store in Charleston."

Sienna thinks. "Don't your folks own all the Bonworthy's stores?"

"Indeed they do." Ennis rolls his eyes. "My humiliation is complete. Bury me now!"

From the side of the chair, a bas-relief gold disc flashes.

It's the helm of Athena, goddess of wisdom and war strategy, patron of West Point, on the hilt of a sword.

"What? They let you keep that? In here?"

"I told the guard it was just a really long scalpel."

"Man, they searched me for toothpicks. You handicappers get all the breaks and the best parking spots."

Ennis's sword had been present at nearly every West Point graduation ceremony since its founding. Sienna does not know how many lives had been ended by that weapon in its history; she only knows for sure it killed people during the Battle of Beast March.

She checks out the many features of her friend's ride. It ain't no Army-issue quad. "I'm surprised they noticed it, with all your new rig's got goin' on."

From the back of the carbon-fiber body, a traffic safety flag whips around dangerously. It features the mascot of Ennis's battalion, a monstrous Hellcat, ripping the heads off Nazi zombies. The pennant reads:

Treat 'Em Rough!

This is the last place she expected to see Ennis. "I heard you were in Charleston giving talks and all." His drawl is infectious.

"I was, but then I heard my second-best chum on Earth had recovered sufficiently enough that the surgeons could mess him up again for his own good. Couldn't miss that." Ennis leans forward as conspiratorially as anyone in his position can. "I also wanted to get the low-down on what y'all brought back. Scuttle is they're blueprinting weapons with it, includin' a 120-ton MBT with a railgun—"

"Dammit, Reidt," Sienna hisses at him. She looks around.

Baker Medical is a secure facility, but there are some things you just can't go flapping your gums about. Anywhere. "You know that's all classified. We signed treaties with everyone saying we'd only use the Ansible for peaceful inventions. Even the commander-in-chief is on a 'don't ask, don't tell' basis with the DARPA."

"Sorry." Ennis shrugs a shoulder apologetically. "But really, like they'd ever discover something new and not try to blow stuff up with it. Peace always seems to break out when we have the biggest guns."

As well as being a jabber-mouth, Ennis perpetually needs to see other kids' toys. "Hey, let me see it," he says eagerly. "I know you got your ring. You're jaybird naked without it."

Her short fingernail finds the switch at the side of her class ring. A holograph of all her commendations appears. She flicks to the last one.

"Pretty, huh, Ennis?"

The Antarctica Service Medal, with its multicolored ribbon, floats a few inches over her hand. Skin graft scars and general paralysis notwithstanding, Ennis looks pretty darn jealous.

"Is that the Wintered Over bar clasp?"

"Sure is," Sienna says. "Technically, we weren't there long enough. But my warrant officer, T-Rex, wrote his congressman and said it was damned dark and damned cold down there and if that didn't qualify as wintering over, he had no idea what would." Sienna cuts power to the hologram. Mementos of her Army career since Junior ROTC flicker and vanish. "So they gave in," Sienna says. "I suspect they wanted to keep the whole thing quiet."

"Yeah," Ennis guffaws. "Like everyone doesn't know you took on a mechanized battalion of Russians. Just your squad and some jury-rigged air support. You were on the cover of *Stars and Stripes,* for Pete's sake."

"All they talked about was Beast, the hostage rescue years ago, and my hair."

"True. Remind me, what was the headline?" Ennis pauses to rub it in. "Oh, right: 'Youngest Army Colonel Since Civil War Redefines the Combat Coiffure.' To be fair, they couldn't say much about the beatin' you put on those bushwhackers."

Sienna watches Ennis's eyes grow bright as he imagines the frozen carnage. It's the type of fun he is now forced to miss out on. He jerks his head sideways, which Sienna interprets as halfway between a fist pound to her and the flashing of a middle finger in the general direction of Moscow.

"Boy, were those Russians tore up when you took that weird blob of whatever it is out from under their noses," he says. "They thought they had you dead to rights. Using a big ol' ice cyclone as cover for their heavy Arctic cyborg-warfare unit out of Bellingshausen."

And don't forget Roger getting hurt so bad he had to hand off command before he passed out.

"In the end it worked out okay," Sienna allows. "Just not for the enemy."

Just saying it makes her wonder who the real enemy was, or is.

10

Antarctica was a set-up. She should have known it going in. The mission was her "welcome to the Army, you uppity base-trash hillbilly" gift from the tubby men and brittle crones in the subbasements of the Pentagon. From the moment she graduated, they'd been pissed at her. They wanted their new Second Lieutenant McKnight, cadet brigade commander, winner of the Attucks Medal for Scholarship and Athletics, for their own. They wanted Sienna to become a walking recruitment ad for military gender and racial equality.

In an all-volunteer Army, Don Draper has replaced Sergeant York. PR is the fast track to the top. She was supposed to become their multi-cultural, photogenic-from-most-angles, safe-to-let-talk-in-front-of-cameras shill. The career path aggressively offered to her featured blue-ribbon recruitment drives, Lincoln Center lunches, and dinners at the White House.

OMFG! Like that was gonna happen.

Butterbars get to request their first duty assignments. In the olden days, after they let girls into West Point, folders were tabbed blue for boys and pink for girls. Now duty binders are unisex. But, like the fine print on the enlistment form says, for five years you are property of the US Army. Sienna was pleasantly surprised to get the billet that took her back home. She should have known there was a hook.

A year ago, Sarge Bryan and his squad were grounded. Declared inactive because no commanding officer of at least second lieutenant rank was willing to be responsible for them. The joy of being assigned to lead them was tempered right quick. Her brand-new command post was a decommissioned latrine. The message could not have been more clear had they texted her: mess with the Pentagon powers, and your career ends in the crapper.

They made the best out of what they got handed and ended up calling their unique CP Whiskey Charlie for water closet. The worst part was having to endure T-Rex's toilet jokes. He kept coming up with new ones long past the point of funny. She should have known that hook would have a split shank to it. They hadn't been there hardly a week when Antarctica was dropped on them.

Eleven months is a good long time to cogitate. The plan was obvious. After she led her team to shame and ruin, even the Army's Air Defense Artillery would be too good for her. ADA had for years been a decent haven for women soldiers who just had to join men in combat roles.

Once Sienna failed, if she survived, then the bureaucrats would be free to relegate her to ever more obscure and ever more crushingly humiliating postings, the military equivalent of the typing pool. And there she would stay until she could legally quit.

Too bad for them, she and her team exceeded expectations.

"And," Sienna continues to Ennis, "this is Roger's last big surgery. None of the others got seriously hurt. Though Whitebread had to have some frostbite treatments on a part of his body I can't discuss in polite mixed company."

"You just watch yourself over in Europe, Sie. While you're guarding the thing, and the Dogs are all together," Ennis cautions. "When you rub the Ivans' nose in it, like you did, and make them wear their tin asses as hats, like you did, they'll come at you sideways. Without the vaguest pretext of honor."

Sienna does not have time to explain. She's used every ounce of influence and cashed in every favor to get out of going to Europe. At her feet, the damaged service bot plays possum. Its head dangles by some wires. Sometimes her own head feels like that. Ennis is the only one who knows her. The only one who's seen what she can do if *it* takes over. They've never talked about that particular subject. Now is not the time. But Sienna needs something, some kind of reassurance that she's doing right by Sarge Bryan and her team.

"Say, Ennis," she starts, trying to figure how to ask something no one can tell her, "you remember in Tolkien, where the little hairy guy has to carry the evil ring to the volcano of doom?"

"Besides Twain and Faulkner, I'm really more of a *Road Rage Cataclysm Online* man." His one eyebrow raises in casual mystification. "But I saw the movies."

"Well…" Sienna feels stupid but keeps talking, "how did Frodo know it was him deciding to do things? And not the ring?"

Ennis's eyebrow squirms. He cogitates. "Sie, in a case like that… well, as long as Frodo felt he was following orders and sticking to an approved meal plan, Middle Earth needed everyone in the fight."

That's enough. Thanks, Lt. Reidt.

Sienna points at the broken bot. "Speaking of enemy hostilities, what did this little fellow ever do to you?"

"That mechanized miscreant affronted me with untrammeled provocation that required a swift and violent response." Ennis looks down at the presumed robocorpse gored by his wheelchair. "It was supposed to bring me my food tray after a pool rehab session. Instead, this little bugger brought me a bedpan."

"Okay. That's not so—"

"It wasn't exactly empty," Ennis huffs. He takes up his mouth stick and nudges his chair forward with the idea of further punishing his victim. The tines of the miniature mine plough shear off a section of the robot's metal skin. It is no longer pinned. "And that's as detailed as I can be about the episode in polite mixed company."

"I think it has learned its lesson. You killed it good." Sienna looks down the hallway. Sarge is supposed to meet her. "You didn't see Bryan, did you?"

Those two always had a friendly but intense rivalry, which rarely came to blows. Though Ennis's blood is up and Sarge would be advised to mind his manners or risk falling victim to possibly the deadliest mod of a Hawking chair ever.

"Now, mmm, let me think," Ennis says. "Two-fifty, six-one, with glowing eyes that look like they fell out of a pinball machine and into his head?"

"That's our man."

"Ain't seen him." Ennis's shoulder twitches like he wants to check his six. "Say, the rest of your people, they around? Nobu or T-Rex?"

"Nope, they're all in NC. You're thinking someone rigged the poopbot as a joke?"

"Now that you mention it…"

Sienna shakes her head. "If it was T-Rex, you'd be wearing what was in the bedpan," Sienna says and grins in the easy way she can with Ennis and perhaps no one else. "You remember what he and Nobu did after that Navy commander refused to help Sarge during Ess Alüm? They hacked the central rations supply system and everyone got something extra in their meal packs."

"Those swabbies are never going to forget that one." A smile creases the shrapnel scars on his cheeks. "For weeks every ready-to-eat meal the sailors and Marines got had a big gummy candy treats in the shape… the shape of, uh…"

"Of a cock."

"Sie!"

"What? We're in a hospital, and I'm pretty sure that's the medical term," Sienna says as she sees Ennis's face is actually getting flushed. "There's nothing to be ashamed about, Ennis. Nearly half the population has one."

"Sie!" His face is getting redder by the second.

They've made huge advances for people with spinal cord injuries. Ennis looks nearly as fit as he did at graduation. Robotic physio machines keep his muscles toned. His brain just can't use those muscles. For anything. For someone as aggressively physical as Ennis had been all his life, the sudden change must be devastating. At least his vicious sense of humor hasn't been paralyzed.

"And using robots in a prank, that kind of engineering's more Whitebread's field."

Ennis's cheeks puff in a silent whistle. "That is one scary mother—"

"Can't be him, neither. He's in stockade," Sienna says. "That's the other reason I'm here. The secretary of the Army wanted me to see him in person and promise if they let Whitebread out of the can I'd put him back in when the mission's done."

"That old politician just wanted your autograph."

"Y'think? He did have me sign two glossy pictures. Said they were for his daughter."

"Just accept it, Sie. You're the most famous active soldier we've got and no one can actually talk about what you did." Ennis considers the list of suspects. "If I had completely inadvertently done something to get Snakelips annoyed, she wouldn't send a bot. She'd just shoot me."

"Delicia's not known for subtlety," Sienna says. "She would probably peg you off from up top of the Washington Monument. It's got a good view of every window here and most entrances."

Sienna checks the time. She wants to ask how he has been. After he was wounded, Sienna tried to see him at the Reidt estate. His parents told her he was resting. For five days. Each morning, she sat on their broad, sunny porch. Maids came by with lemonade and all-butter pie. Ennis would not see her. Sienna understood. Still, on the last day, she left a note. With Jane Bowie, she carved a mild obscenity in the wood railing of the porch where a person in a wheelchair was most likely to read it.

Asking how he is would just make him mad. And those

tines on the front of his wheelchair look pretty sharp. Besides, what can she say? What can he say? They know each other. No one has to tell them to suck it up. No one has to urge them to endure. They know. They do.

"Good seeing you, Ennis," she says simply. "Hooah?"

"Hooah, Sie," he replies. "Always."

She needs to go. And so does Ennis.

"Well, Lieutenant, when a retired southern gentleman like yourself can find the time, drop by the Base. That is, if you haven't replaced this mine plow with a shuffleboard paddle."

Sienna uses the R word on purpose, just to yank her friend's chain.

"What? Retired? Because of this?" Ennis looks down at his inert body as though he's just sprained his ankle. "This ain't nothing. I'm a 22nd century warrior. I do physio every day and twice on Sundays. I have the body fat and muscle tone of a champion triathlete. I'm the star of the Walk Again program. I only use this chair after anaerobic physio. You wait until they hook me up with my milspec ATLAS suit. I'll be back in a real tank and… hey!"

Sienna kicks the sleeping bot's power on. It dashes off.

"Would you look at that," Sienna says in her best surprised voice. "It ain't all dead."

Ennis is instantly incensed. "Out of the way. That miscreant bot has to pay!"

She blocks him. The jagged extension of the wheelchair threatens her ankles.

"Don't think I won't, Sie!" Ennis warns as he twists his mouth controller.

"Now, that'd be striking a superior officer, lieutenant. I'll make sure they put you in with Whitebread," Sienna taunts back. "I'm just giving the little guy a head start. It's one of the principles this nation was founded on. Everyone deserves a fair chance."

Scraping along the far wall, he gets past her with a roar of recorded tank noise.

Through teeth he says, "Sie, I'm damn sure the Founding Fathers did not include dumb excrement-bearing bots when framing mankind's preeminent clarion blast of freedom and liberty."

His chair handles the corner well but the next corridor is narrower. Sienna hears a crash. A tray rolls out.

"Oh, I truly am sorry. Just charge that to my room, please."

Sienna knocks and enters.

11

The door whispers shut. Sienna winces. She thought they were going to hold off re-fracturing Roger's skull and mandible until after his other surgeries. Some doctors jumped the gun. Some doctors armed with precision bone saws and surgical chisels. The parts of her boyfriend's face not covered with bandages are splotched with bruises and the stain of persistent silver disinfectant gel. His right leg and hip are shrouded by a hyperbaric tent. Underneath, metal rings of Ilizarov arrays hold mending pieces of bones in place.

"Hey, Roger." Sienna forgets about kissing him. His face is a minefield of potential pain. "You're…"

"I know." Roger's mild Boston accent filters through his wire-locked jaw. "A sight for sore eyes. And sore everything else."

Sienna takes his hand. It is warm and welcoming.

"Guess who I met outside."

"Ennis the Menace. The whole hospital wing heard."

The room's window frames the Lincoln Memorial and Reflecting Pool. Early tourists are out. Except for the wake wash of a few ducks, the rectangular lake is pristinely smooth.

"At least you got a nice view," Sienna says.

A chill crawls down her spine. It's been nearly a year. But damn. Seeing Roger's damaged body. The snowy whiteness of the sheets. It brings back horrors of Bentley Trench. Their fight in the frozen wilderness against a relentless enemy over something no one really understood then or understands now. The glowy thing. The Ansible. Despite Roger's training and education and breeding, as ground commander, he made mistakes. Bad ones.

Roger tries to smile. He gives up. "Pretty gross, huh?"

"Compared to back then…" Sienna stops herself. Roger is a male in uniform with a senior officer's ration of pride. She has no blame for him. Roger's dark eyes reveal inner pain.

"Sienna, I know I aced up. Real bad. I nearly got everyone killed. I had no business, no right, insisting on leading Antarctica."

"If you hadn't HALOed in, we never would have known what we were up against." Sienna tries to stem the tide of self-recrimination. "Enemy mechanized would have bushwhacked us."

"What I had to tell you, it's not something I could have put in a text. Still…"

Sienna searches for a tactic to lighten his mood. Even attended by the best doctors in the nation's capital, there is danger. And the only weapon Roger has now to fight with is heart.

"I'm serious. Don't beat yourself up. We all made it back. Without that fancy jump pod you came in we couldn't have jury-rigged Ansible comms and gotten air support." She mimes polishing her rank insignia. "And I wouldn't have this tom turkey if you hadn't hacked the command and control mechBrains."

Her encouraging words have the opposite effect. Bedside manner has never been her thing, despite having the last name of a famous surgeon.

Roger's hand trembles. "I even managed to screw that up."

Maybe the autoinjector registers his mental distress as physical pain and is pumping meds. *Man, I hope it's not Red Mist, or conversation is gonna get real strange in a hurry.*

"…even managed to screw that up," Roger repeats. "I gave Sarge Bryan the command. I just wanted… wanted you guys to make it back even if I couldn't. I thought Bryan was best, best chance.

"Hey, just rest."

"Sarge," Roger continues. "Good ol' Bryan, he did the right thing, Sarge did. Soon as they iced me. He gave you the field bump to colonel. It was the best decision of my career, and I was out cold when I made it. Get it? Out cold?"

"Still, you made it stick afterwards. It wasn't just a coincidence the senator from North Carolina put pictures of himself and the local girl made good on all his re-election posters, was it? After that, they had to make the battlefield promotion permanent."

That was huge. She gets twice as much money to send home and way less people are able to tell her no.

"Just occurred to me." The anesthetic makes him talkative. "Command of D Group, heck, even commandant of the Base, those are full bird colonel's billets."

True. With a West Point diploma and eagles on her lapels, Sienna could move up from leadership of her tiny detachment right up to garrison commander. Roger's mention of this possibility and his manner instantly puts a small knot in Sienna's gut. Commandant is a full-time, on-base position. With an office. And a desk. And a real steno-typist who is not a kleptomaniac killing machine. T-Rex would be out of a job. And there would be no more field deployments.

The symbol of her rank is a struttin' badass eagle, wings spread, ready to drop fiery arrows on the enemy. *Why would you make someone a full bird then clip their wings?* A silence drags.

From under fast-drooping eyelids, Roger looks at the mission fob. Two pinpricks of green and one of amber glow on matte-black casing.

"Are you sure about Sidewinder?"

Sienna nods. Roger's meds kick in. He talks with an endearing three-martini slur.

"Just in case they didn't let you out of Europe, CENTCOM's… a Plan B with some SEALs. They're on the *Lee*. Team leader's Ty Denbow, Ty, great record. Ready to go."

Roger's hoping she'll back off? That he won't have to green the last mission fob light? Sienna wants to say: *Not on your damn life! This is my fight. I'm gonna finish it.*

Instead she says, "And let SEAL swabbies take credit? Don't let Ennis hear. You know what he thinks about Navy, and his new wheelchair is a weapon of mass destruction."

It's about time for a reunion with her cousin. "With what's in Sidewinder's head, we can get him. We can save lives."

Roger's gaze drifts to the lake and the monument. "Go."

Roger activates the mission module. Three lights green. The mission clock starts ticking. MechBrains flex the steel muscles of the nation's military. Part of Sienna wants to stay. But the most powerful part becomes activated at the same time as the fob. Dozens of logistical and tactical factors spring into her mind.

"And after?" Roger says, dreamily staring at the ceiling. "You think there'll be time? For us, I mean. To live like normal people?"

No words immediately come to Sienna. She does not know if there is a reply inside her. The place where it might come from seems empty and hollow. It is guarded by a vǫrthr spirit in the darkness there. A watcher who never blinks. She's about to respond, some quip about no one ever having accused her of normalcy.

Then she sees a reflection in a water jug. Something is under the bedsheet by Roger's good hand. A square, black box. At first she thinks it's Roger's rumored Brigadier stars. But why hide those? Suddenly she realizes what the box must hold. Weeks ago she'd noticed a big charge to a jewelry store on top of his desk. Something for his aunt, the DC socialite, she thought. It ain't that.

Oh, Roger. If you pull out an engagement ring, here, now, like this…

Sienna's left hand tightens around the fat band of her class ring.

A knock on the door is accompanied by a familiar bass-tinged voice.

"Colonels, hope I'm not interrupting."

You are. And thank you, Sarge.

"Never, Bryan," Roger says through metal and plastic retainers. "Just take care of our girl. You've got the *Lee*'s battlegroup. Captain's kind of odd. Odd bird. But the air group commander is a friend. He'll make sure, all covered, covered. Black-bag op or not."

Bryan's eyes beam. Literally. His albino pigmentation gave him extraordinary night-vision. But eventually the eyes he was born with needed augmentation. Since Sienna was about sixteen, Bryan has watched over her through one or another set of ocular cybernetic implants. The current versions look like binary stars of liquid gold. They shine at her.

Roger's own black-box op is put on hold. The object, which she's now certain is what she thought, gets pushed back under the covers.

Bryan can see the mission fob lights through her pocket. They settle into their shared mindset. Sidewinder is only scheduled for a few hours total. A single, low-value target who has no idea they're coming. Doesn't get simpler. Those few hours could change everything. She and Roger will have time to talk later.

"Were you able to square Whitebread's release?"

"Yup. He's got to learn," she says, like she's repeating a backwoods adage. "If you go out for moose with a grenade launcher, civilian hunters always complain."

Bryan stares out the window to the front entrance. He squints. "Do my eyes need an overhaul, or is that Ennis Reidt down there being escorted out of the hospital by four security guards?"

A nurse and a surgery prep bot appear in the doorway. Both seem impatient. Sienna and Sarge promise to check in when they can. Before she leaves, Sienna risks giving Roger a light kiss on a patch of cheek that is relatively free of bruising.

12

Sienna and the Dogs arrive on the aircraft carrier *Lee* in a cloud of steam issuing from monopropellant landing thrusters. Their multi-personnel HALO pod is basically an eight-passenger tin can attached to a big silk hanky. While still on the scRamjet, Sienna checked out the descender rig. It was a similar spec to the one they used in Antarctica. This one had space for a small dune buggy, which fit Specialist Whitebread perfectly.

Once the pod was ejected from the jet, she had a great view of the Gulf. At first, the *Lee* was only the largest dot trailing a dash of white. The most significant cipher among smaller groups of Morse code engraved on rippled metallic water. As they glided down, the Howard-class *Lee* got hella larger. Despite these most modern ships of the line belonging to the Navy and being filled with sailors and Marines, Sienna always feels something special about being on one of them. These are

71

floating islands of USA sovereignty and whupass. What's not to like?

Before the deck crew has completely subdued the parasail, Sienna pops the hatch. Ear-splitting roars of catapults and hot blasts of engine backwash greet her. Contrails of departing aircraft extend from the bow. Temporary scars in the sky, pale streaks bleeding into deeper shades of dusk. The metal deck feels as solid as any ground. Long enough to land a fair-sized transport plane, it is firmament on a liquid infinity. She feels the vast presence of the sea.

Sienna checks her people. All of them want to get going on the next leg of Sidewinder.

T-Rex warms his gripe engines. "They coulda slowed down for us. My man Nobu-san had to bang us around just so we didn't end up ditching."

Whitebread unfurls his massive frame from the pod's cargo bay. "Not their fault." He tosses his oxygen mask and speaks quietly. "Fixed-wing craft need about thirty knots across the deck to help liftoff. A good flattop skipper will follow trade winds. They have the most predictable isopleths."

T-Rex decides to remain indignant. "Trade winds? Isocraps? My ass! Downright unhospitable, them zig-zaggin' for no reason when they know we're comin'."

Things go well. At first. The carrier strike group was officially rerouted out of its Pacific Command zone into Central Command's Arabian Sea backyard for a joint training exercise. The real reason is her covert op. And her captain didn't cotton to that, not at all.

The *Lee*'s captain, Nestor Stahlback, is the acting flag officer of the whole Navy strike group. A dozen other ships sail beside the *Lee* like asteroids around a comet. Among the guided-missile cruiser, two anti-submarine destroyers, and smaller vessels is a large, odd-shaped replenishment ship known as an oiler. Its long snout latches onto the *Lee*, feeding it fuel and supplies. The oiler is named *Aardvark*. T-Rex wastes no time spouting off rude jokes about intership copulation.

Instead of greeting them personally, Stahlback sends his exec officer, Matt Bianchi, down from the bridge tower. During the plane ride, she and Bryan reviewed key *Lee* personnel: Stahlback, the ship's XO Bianchi, and Amman Kanin, the Carrier Air Wing commander. Known as the CAG, he is in charge of everything that lifts off the deck under its own power.

Bianchi is an able-looking man in his late thirties. He's got that starched quality some career Navy guys get. As her squad sorts out equipment on the flight deck, he introduces himself.

"Welcome, Colonel." Bianchi doesn't stare at the eagles, which make her his interservice superior. He's obviously studied up on her and the Dogs. That could be a good thing. Or not. When he looks the other way, Sienna makes sure her flight suit completely covers what's underneath.

"Commander, thanks in advance for accommodating us." They are playing on Navy's turf for now, and her parents always taught her to be a polite guest. "I assume the captain will want to debrief us. We've got a narrow window—"

Bianchi holds up his hand. "You are good to go. Captain had some last-minute ship's business," the XO says in a way that tells her Stahlback had no last-minute business and Bianchi is glad his superior is not here. "He's approved the briefing package and flight plans. There's no contingency for search and rescue. If anything happens, you're officially on your own.

That's not uncommon in these, well, these types of operations."

You mean underhanded, lower-than-a-snake's-belly, deniable, black-bag op.

Sienna gives the XO props for not saying it. Still, it is bad form for Stahlback not to even come over and meet them. Maybe he thinks that's part of deniability in case the mission goes south. Fat chance. The Dogs and Bryan are a tried and tested machine. The *Lee* is just their thousand-foot taxi ride.

On the other side of the deck lurks a line of metal manta rays sheathed in stealth carbon black. No windows or cockpit. These robotic cicadas seem alien to the *Lee*. Their wings are studded with cluster bombs hanging like dark, jagged jewels.

"Stymphalian drones? I thought DoD grounded them after those complications."

Complications in which semi-autonomous systems overrode remote pilot inputs in reaction to a perceived threat. A Stymph mechBrain eliminated guerillas aiming a SAM battery at it. Then, pretty logically for a machine, it decided since those hostiles were not in uniform, everyone was a combatant. Those drones returned to their floating roost empty of ordnance. Behind them were terrible friendly casualties. Maybe Bianchi gives Sienna props for not saying "negligent Navy blue-on-blue massacre." She cannot tell. The executive officer of the *Lee* has a game poker face.

"Captain got permission to do some test runs with the Stymphs while they work the bugs out," Bianchi says. "He loves these birds. If you need fire support, I'm sure I could talk him into loaning you one."

"Thanks, but we're here for intel, not random body parts."

***

While Sienna is up in the steel oak tree of the bridge island to file their final flight plan, she passes by the captain's ready room and catches sight of perhaps the flat-out freakiest thing she's ever seen in her military career.

Stahlback takes no notice of her. He's taking care of his urgent business: yelling about the mess menu. A cook in a laundry-fresh chef's apron stands at attention in front of him. Behind his big leather chair is the thing that strikes Sienna as being off-the-chain weird.

The wall of the captain's private study has custom-made cherry-wood shelves. These hold about fifty major-league baseball figurines. Antiques. Team names date them back to the 1960s. Despite being vintage, they all work. They are nodders. Their heads bob up and down and sideways behind Stahlback. With each sway of the ship, fifty plastic heads nod.

After that peck of abnormal, Sienna decides she's fortunate to be dealing exclusively with Bianchi. What a tightrope the *Lee*'s executive officer must be walking.

Sienna's sense of reality becomes more grounded the closer she gets to being with her team on their assigned stealth copter. It wears the same non-reflective skin as the Stymphalians, but is flown by two very solid pilots.

She puts on her HUD visor. As she's getting feedback on the aircraft's readiness, the mission fob updates itself. The little piece of plastic reports an unspecified delay.

Naturally.

Nothing to do but wait through their optimum launch window. Sienna spends the downtime making sure Sarge

Bryan is making sure the Dogs are staying out of trouble.

Without preamble, the mechBrain signals pre-takeoff flight checks. She climbs the gantry into the aircraft's midsection, glad to be leaving all that Navy drama junk behind. Nearly. Stahlback has arranged one last parting shot.

A man runs toward them. A set of really white teeth flash underneath a just-been-to-the-ship's-barber crew cut. The square-jawed man with broad shoulders and fractional body fat saunters up.

"Colonel McKnight? Lieutenant Denbow, ma'am."

He holds out a stylus-sized order scroll. A moment later, Sienna gets Captain Stahlback's punchline. And doesn't laugh.

"Okay everyone, listen up!" Sienna says.

Her words instantly silence a low baritone of grumbling which underpinned the high-pitched whine of warming plasma rotors. They have been waiting nearly two hours past median launch time. The reason why is Denbow.

"While I did not put in an RFF for any additional personnel," Sienna explains, "Central Command and the *Lee*'s captain have graciously sent one of their most capable officers to assist. This is our chaperone." Sienna flicks her head to the SEAL. "Lieutenant Commander Tyler Denbow. Formerly with the Marines' MARSOC, he moved laterally to the Navy."

"Can't take that one back now, sailor boy." Snakelips takes a sidelong measure of the new guy. "You got yourself squidinked." Denbow's SEAL trident tattoo goes up from his wrist to the back of his forearm.

Denbow stares at Snakelips. She just keeps polishing the mahogany body of her customized sniper rifle. Maybe he's not used to enlisteds side-talking while their CO is speaking.

Tough for him. That's how it is with them. Denbow will only have to endure it for a few hours. Then he can go back to Qatar and tell his buddies all about the most boring Army-led mission ever.

Denbow's move from Marines to Navy is curious. The Marines and the Navy are separate. Going MARSOC first did have one advantage: trigger time. Because of the type of deployments they get, Marine operators spend more time actually engaging enemies in sustained firefights than all the others combined. But at the end of the day, they are still Jarheads. SEALs get access to the highest-level missions, equipment, and intelligence. A transfer like that would have taken a lot of approvals and was a risk. If you washed out of BUD/S, you could spend the next five years scrubbing potatoes on the *Aardvark*. Denbow seems to have cherry-picked the best of all possible covert ops postings for himself.

"As you will notice from the commander's op sheet, which is in your HUDs," Sienna continues, ignoring T-Rex's eye rolling and Whitebread's disaffected foot scraping, "he's a highly decorated US Navy SEAL and qualified medic. He will be providing oversight for Central Command, in whose backyard we have graciously been allowed to play. On the flight in, he's operations officer in charge. After landing, he'll be second in command according to his rank."

"So, you're a Hinge?" T-Rex's close-to-the-red-line comment makes Sienna cringe. The slang term refers to the mythical lobotomy performed on sailors when promoted to lieutenant commander. Supposedly, they have a hinged skull flap through which half their brain can be removed. This procedure is said to be essential to the smooth running of the Navy's chain of command. Denbow does not know it, but insubordinate rudeness from the Compton native means T-Rex is trying to make friends.

Sienna looks at T-Rex. "You *will* extend him every courtesy as a member of our team. Right?" Sienna follows the rhetorical question with, "Hooah?"

Snakelips Delicia Ortiz, Geronimo Nobu, T-Rex, and a glowering hulk slumped in the shadows in the last seat, Petr Whitebread Whitbrodsniewski, all look at the newbie. Denbow's face and gear could have been copied from the military's manual on the grooming and outfitting standard. He even smells like Navy-issue shaving cream and night-ops camo grease paint. Everyone instantly dislikes him.

But their "**Hooah!**" in reply is genuine. Despite the interloper, they are together again. They are the Dogs of D Group again. After what seemed like a strung-out layoff waiting for Army couriers to deliver commendations, they are on the hunt. To Sienna, it feels better than good.

Their pilot, codenamed Nightjar, squawks in. "*Wheels up.*"

Bryan adds, "Final prep. Watch personal illums. We don't want to break stealth until the last possible moment. Okay, gather in."

It was their year-old ritual, from back when it really looked like some or all of them would be frozen morguesicles left for another team to pick up off the South Polar glacier.

"Seven out…" he begins to the grouped-up hands.

"…seven home," everyone finishes.

The copter lifts lightly off the *Lee*'s deck. Sienna feels a measure of relief. Something's just off about Stahlback. During mission planning, Roger mentioned his nickname. It finally makes sense.

Captain Bobblehead.

13

Sienna's pilot takes ten tons of hovercopter sideways and lets it drop off the deck of the *Lee* elevator-with-the-cables-cut style. Her partially digested Air Force MRE lunch rises. That sensation is interrupted not by splashdown, but by a sideways, kidney-jamming g-force lurch. He is either warming up or showing off. Either way is cool as long as no one hurls. Sienna's glad she has Nightjar on the stick tonight. He's crazy, but he's the Dogs' kind of crazy.

An exterior monitor shows the copter's skin. Its surface polarizes and they become invisible above the darkness-shrouded water. The Dogs check each other's gear. T-Rex does his duty as Sienna's secretary. He syncs up Denbow's mission scroll to update the data cache.

T-Rex has received more pardons than a Catholic sinner with OCD. His persistent boundary issues center on private property belonging to people who own way too much stuff. Growing up in L.A. hadn't helped. Technically, all members of Army Special Forces units have to be enlisted paygrade 6 or higher. The Dogs are exempt because they are a reserve (pronounced 'refuse') section. Before Sienna, when Delta and Green Berets got called away for real missions, their active duty included teaching PT drills and occasionally visiting local schools to urge kids to say "no" to whatever parents feared kids were saying "more, please" to.

Even so, DoD has standards and the only way T-Rex can even have a job in the military anymore is as a specially commissioned steno-typist. He is Sienna's personal secretary, Military Occupation Specialty Code #2115. As a colonel, she rates one. Rex even carries a dictation pad in his webbing next to a hook-bladed knife.

Not only does he have a flexible sense of property rights, but he can't keep his mouth shut. When he is around his best friend, Nobu, sometimes Sienna feels she's in charge of delinquents. Ones playing with explosives, automatic weapons, and monofilament tomahawk axes that can hack the arm off a cyborg. Despite his promise to behave, it doesn't take T-Rex long to start in on the new guy.

"Say Mr. SEAL frogman, sir," T-Rex says. "You realizin' this a two-hour op at most. Looks like you packed a week's worth of lunches."

Nobu gives his friend's boot a small kick.

"Uh, Lieutenant, sir."

Sienna noticed Denbow's baggage. A stuffed three-day pack lies in regulation configuration under his jump seat.

Denbow remains unfazed. "I like to be prepared." He looks at the warrant officer's name tag. "Mister... T-Rex?"

The trickiest of the Dogs flashes Denbow a polite smile. For the L.A. native, manners are inverse. The more polite T-Rex is, the worse trouble you are in with him. "Have a nice day" is the equivalent of a death threat. She figures this quirk of his is an inversion of linguistics a much younger T-Rex learned from years dealing with foster-care bureaucrats and bleary-eyed, nicotine-vapor-inhaling, don't-give-a-damn-anymore social workers. For T-Rex, politeness equates to apathy and the violence of the hateful, grinding neglect he experienced as a boy. He's probably too downright shifty to pursue a career as a gypsy repo man. For some reason, he wants to be in the Army. Sienna and Bryan's Army.

"That's one of the fly things about being the admin officer," T-Rex replies. "I gets to be in charge of the stencil maker."

He waves a thumb toward the dark corner of the hovercopter. "See that big fellow over there? His folks came to America from Po-Land. And they were so po' when they got off the boat they couldn't afford no vowels for their name. So they got all consonants and stuff just jumbled together on their immigration papers. We call him Whitebread. Even signs that to re-up."

The specialist filling the corner of the copter takes the ribbing in stride. He reads a paperback by his helmet light.

When the Rex mouth train gets going, it has nearly infinite track. Sienna could have put a cork in it with a small gesture, one an outsider like Denbow wouldn't notice. For now, it's okay for them to settle back into their rhythms.

They have not all been together since Antarctica. Their return was followed by weeks of debriefing and reams of non-disclosure forms. Then, just when her team thought they were getting a cushy assignment in Europe, Sienna told them to pack kit for a fast smash and grab. The Dogs' relaxing tour of France, Switzerland, and the strange little country in between has been pre-empted by desert camo, sand, and the possibility of bullets flying at them. Sienna didn't hear a single gripe. So let them pick on the Navy man, or each other.

T-Rex zeroes in on his favorite victim. "Say Whitebread, wassu readin'? You finish all the comic books? Now you into novels and shiet? Man, I liked it better when you were all dyslexic illiterate." T-Rex leans over and checks the cover. "KooYo?"

"That's pronounced Koo-Joe," Sienna says. "It's by a much under-appreciated military strategist, Stephen King." Whitebread's bulk and quiet nature hide a voracious intellect. He looks up like he has an idea and might as well have said it out loud. "And no, Petr. We are not getting a dog."

"But, we're called the Dogs."

Snakelips says, "Alpha Dogs, por favor. We have company."

"Just don't let Petr get started on George Martin," Nobu says. "We'll all be issued big-assed wolves."

Whitebread continues to argue for a pet. "So I thought, just a little one?" But seeing his idea is not gaining traction, the specialist slumps back in his seat.

T-Rex offers advice. "Think a minute, Whitebread. Who gonna look after a pooch when you're in stockade? Nobu? I mean, yeah, both sides of his gene pool likes dogs—well done and beside some coleslaw!"

Geronimo "Gerry" Nobu is Sienna's radio telephone operator and electronics expert. He has a Japanese-American father and Apache mother. As far as Sienna knows, he is no more prone to feasting on canine flesh than the rest of them. Besides sporting desperately spiky black hair and maintaining a Zen-like calm when dealing with malfunctioning equipment, he expresses his dual heritage by carrying both a short samurai sword and a modern tomahawk.

Snakelips shakes her head. "Yo guys, time to target. Remember? The whole Sidewinder mission thing?"

The woman who reminds the others they are not on a frat house field trip is Corporal Delicia Magdalena Ortiz. Somehow T-Rex found out the nickname her sharp tongue and occasional foul language earned her in Catholic girls' school. *Boca de la serpiente* had, after a slightly bent translation, become "Snakelips." It's not a moniker someone who sports non-regulation knuckle tattoos reading "Who's Next?" can really complain about.

The Ortiz family was displaced and her father killed during the construction of the Nicaraguan Canal. A lack of patience, not lack of talent, makes Snakelips the second-best sniper on the team, after Sienna. Snakelips has perhaps the most common sense and certainly the largest heart of them all.

"Good point, Snakelips." Sarge Bryan checks the master displays. They are studded with electronics that control light-bending panels on the exterior. Through cameras and sensors they can watch a whole battlefield day or night and remain nearly undetectable. They need to maintain maximum stealth. They're flying through airspace which is officially neutral but will change to hostile in a hurry if local air defense tags them.

Denbow has some distinct habits. At some seminar or briefing, those may not have stuck in her mind. Here, next to her trusted team, their Navy chaperone is definitely the odd man out. The SEAL keeps his eyes focused front. On nothing in particular. Denbow's file says he is six years her senior. The tight skin drawn over his jagged cheekbones makes him look older. She has a feeling that whatever his qualifications, he is no Dog.

Then Denbow notices her, noticing him noticing nothing. Maybe the only reason he pipes up is to not appear awkward. "Full bird, huh?" the lieutenant remarks as he looks at her eagles.

Sienna nods in his direction. *If I only had a dollar...*

Bryan's albino skin makes him a white shadow in the dark interior. His liquid-gold eyes probe the newcomer. "Hell yes, Lieutenant," he says with pride. "Our CO's the youngest Army colonel since Gettysburg."

She shrugs. "Technically, it was a battlefield bump. A jump-step after the regional Antarctic base commander he, well, he was unable to fulfill his duties on an ongoing basis." *Being frozen in a block of ice will do that.* "And Roger was badly wounded. He had to take himself out of the fight." *Being nearly eaten by... something impossible will do that. Roger! Damn that was close.*

"Army mechBrains, those stubborn little buggers," Sienna says shaking her head as though recalling a kid who just would not eat her peas. "You can't bribe 'em, can't scare 'em. Sometimes they just reject inputs from lower ranks without uplink override. Which we didn't have on account of some annoying jamming."

"Right, the winterized cyborg hostiles," Denbow says. "That was in your after-action report. The parts they let us see. But then the Pentagon brass confirmed you from butterbar to full bird. Unusual."

"They did," Sienna returns. "And unusual is pretty much what we specialize in."

Sienna tries to figure out what's underneath Denbow's so-far blank exterior. The SEAL is probably reporting back to Stahlback, or tattling on them to some two-star fidget in Qatar. Not a problem. Once they are on the ground she will have full control. Until then, she has to play it cool. In the air, Denbow can scrub the mission for any reason or no reason at all. They'd have to return to the *Lee*. They'd lose their window.

And let Asrah slip away again.

Nobu, probably the calmest and most intuitive member of the Dogs, senses the need to humor their Navy babysitter.

"Lieutenant, heard your SEAL element just got back from Africa," Nobu says. "Some local gangster took over a clinic in Djoboro. Threatened to hack up the doctors and feed them to crocs if they didn't get a ransom. Bet you SEAL guys sorted them out."

Denbow does not reply immediately. It's like he's mulling over what to say, or struggling with some horrific memory. Heck, in their jobs they all have enough of those to last a lifetime. Maybe Denbow just has a stick up his ass, and sans said stick, he might be a good guy. Maybe. But if how he reacts under pressure can get them all killed, maybe just isn't enough. Not today.

"Right. You heard that," Denbow finally says, his voice barely audible over the whine of the engines to either side of the cabin. "What you didn't hear, 'cause it was kept real quiet, is that the place in Djoboro they decided to hit was a Worldwide Help International facility."

That tidbit causes everyone to perk up and listen.

"Oy, cagada."

"You're joking."

"For reals, boss?"
Even Whitebread grunts in surprise.

14

Speaking of the unusual. Someone trying to raid a Worldwide Help International facility is almost unheard of. For good reason. They are the colossal humanitarian charity that, when threatened, bites back.

"Must have been some new terrorist kids on the block," Sarge Bryan says. "Everyone knows you don't screw with WWHI. Maybe they thought the hospital was an independent NGO flying fake banners to scare people. Or figured Worldwide Help headquarters wouldn't notice before the local government paid up."

"The Serpens banners were real," Denbow says. "And WWHI HQ noticed. Right away. Three of their doctors and eight infectious-disease technicians were taken out of their cots. The Dengue fever patients, just locals with no cash value, were the stars of the ransom-demand video. They got hacked up and fed to crocs."

"Don't they teach these people anything in terrorism school these days?" T-Rex is indignant at the falling standards in insurgent education. "First class on the first day should be: Don't mess with Colonel McKnight's Dogs. In fact, don't mess with anyone from North Carolina. Second: no matter how cute they is, forget about kidnapping any nurses from Worldwide Help. They'll always jam you up before you know what's up."

"So, Lieutenant, what happened? Did you and your squad sort them out?" Nobu asks. "Was it pretty hairy?"

Denbow looks at Nobu, then at Sarge, then out the virtual window. "It wasn't anything," he says flatly. "A WWHI contractor went in before SOCOM even got the call. By the time we dropped in, it was all over. They used a microSwarm with lethal effect."

"Just lots of bodies, huh?"

Sienna sees a weird look crawl across Denbow's chiseled features. Like he's happy and creeped at the same time.

"No. No bodies. A few smashed drones, and these divots in the dirt. Shallow, man-sized holes lined with muck. Lots of them, these... patches. Most had weapons lying beside them, nothing else. No *bones*. No DNA, either. We tried to ID who's who, assuming these were remains of the guys who raided the hospital camp. We wanted to make sure the warlord was dead."

Denbow shakes his head. "No dice. The swabs just came up with random protein strings. It was like the bad guys and anyone not tagged WWHI personnel were digested and spat out. For a mile around. Exact. As if it was laser ranged. Inside, every military-aged person, even livestock and jungle animals, all got stung. Worldwide Help sorted it out. And they wanted to send a message."

"Worldwide Help contractors," Bryan acknowledges grimly. "They work solo and sort hard."

Denbow's face shows Sienna that he's not finished. He's deciding whether he wants to share something else.

"And y'know," Denbow adds deliberately. "That wasn't the best part of that freak show."

Not even T-Rex has anything to say.

"Our team was sent to recon. One boy from a village nearby said there was *music* playing during the, uh, activity. When the music stopped, so did the screaming."

Sienna knows about microSwarm drones. Each bot is about the size of a fat bumblebee. They are used to deliver medicine to remote communities and wild animals. Immunizing herds of reindeer against anthrax in Siberia, stuff like that. They could also be weaponized.

The Base has an inventory of systems adapted to put down smokescreens; they work even in high winds. The Geneva Conventions outlaw use of swarms as offensive ordnance because they can deliver targeted pathogens and precision-guided chemical weapons. Of course, what really stops armies from using them to kill and maim is cost. Drone swarm modules are extremely expensive to manufacture and maintain.

WWHI can afford them. The interplaited Serpens banner is the loved and feared and respected and resented symbol of a massive charity. In one form or another it had been around for centuries. In the last fifteen years it has gathered together more volunteers and staff than the Red Cross and Red Crescent movements put together. Its budget seems to rival the Pentagon's. Worldwide Help is the unofficial government in the refugee safety zones in southern Khorasan.

Normally WWHI immunologists use microSwarm devices to help small outlying villages stricken with malaria. In this case—and Sienna has no reason to doubt Denbow's story—the microSwarm was programmed to kill and wipe out all traces of the incident. No bodies, no war crime. The central government of Djoboro, whoever that is this week, is not going to complain about the retaliation. They would have done something similar, if less elaborately brutal, to anyone who jeopardized their lucrative relationship with WWHI.

The drones' individual, bee-sized mechBrains coordinate their activities through sound. They network. As a swarm, the flying bots become a much more intelligent mechanical organism. Typically, they use ultrasonic bands out of the range of human ears. The contractor who was behind this "message" had to have one very sick, twisted mind to come up with an audible soundtrack for a mass execution.

"I didn't believe the local kid," Denbow says. "Not about the music. Not at first. He didn't seem too bright. Then he showed me a video he caught on his junky old phone. It was pretty low res. It showed some real old guy waving to the kid and his friends to run away out of the kill zone, then getting hit by a small object flying at medium speed. Then falling over. Then dissolving. The phone recorded sound, too. There *was* music. After it was over and the microSwarm stopped stinging, the kid says he went in. He followed the inactive drones as they flew back to their hive. Stupid kid."

"Gutsy kid," Snakelips corrects Denbow.

He continues like he didn't hear. "When he got to the middle, there was one person and a small chopper in the camp. Kid must have been seeing things. He told me the deadly gray bees flew into the pilot's helmet. There was nobody else. The WWHI hostages were gone, probably exfilled by truck. The pilot. The kid couldn't say—or was too freaked out to remember—if it was a man or a woman. The pilot listened to him complain about his dead grandpa.

"The village kid told the contractor that they were just farmers and herders and they didn't have anything to do with the kidnappers. One day the bad guys just showed up on their land. The pilot pointed to the ransom of gemstones. A fortune was just lying there. Said the kid and the other survivors could have it. Then the contractor took off.

"Kid showed me a diamond. It was laser-holo etched with the WWHI logo, certified conflict-free and legal to sell anywhere in the world." Denbow takes off his glove. "Here it is. Ain't it pretty?" A swirling crocodile casting holds the looted jewel firmly in an open maw. Broad facets flash cold, dark fire.

"Damn," T-Rex says, scratching the tribal symbol he's growing on the side of his head.

For a few moments, the wail of plasma nacelles to either side is the only sound.

Finally, Whitebread asks, "What was it? What music did the microSwarm play?"

"It was Elvis," Denbow says. "Suspicious Minds."

15

OVER THE WANDERING DESERT
KHORASAN

Sienna and Bryan exchange glances. WWHI contractors.
Deadly musical drones. Been there, done that. *At least this
mission won't be badgered by that level of strange.*

At the command console, her gloved hand pushes a
trackball. After checking location and heading, she turns an
exterior cam to the ground. Ambient-light view shows wispy
outlines of rock and dune. Thermal and infrared views reveal
more. Plasma rotor wash bleeds magenta into a corner of the
screen. They don't spin like old-style rotors. Wide plasma-
induction turbines give the aircraft lift. Thin wires hold captive
lightning. Sienna's always found them hella cool and considers
them one of the few reasons pilots are not complete dorks.

Telling them about the heavy-handed actions of
Worldwide Help's contractors makes Denbow more talkative.
In the worst way possible. He gloms at Sienna's insignia. His
tone smacks of complacent resentment and testosterone-laced
condescension.

I'll never get used to that.

"Goes without saying, I never have any problem taking orders from female officers. Or with women in combat generally. In the field. Naturally." He glances at Snakelips and wipes a slick of perspiration off his neck.

The Navy man stretches his arms over his head, looking more like a surfer than a soldier. He eyeballs Sienna's body with an undisguised hotshot expression. "But really, being realistic, a woman can never be as strong as a man. I mean, heh, you compare someone who's one hundred and thirty, thirty-five to, well, a man like your boy Whitebread over there. He's got to clock in at three eighty in a towel."

Denbow looks around. The Dogs stare back. Either Denbow thinks he's being smart or he's distracting them.

"In a fight. I'm talking about a real close quarters H2H throw-down. Not long-range standoff shit. Hand to hand, y'know? If it came to that. She's a skid mark. This theoretical buck thirty-five female soldier we're talking about. I mean anyone is, with those odds, right? I mean, it's just physics."

Denbow looks at Nobu. Maybe he thinks the half-Asian will be receptive to his logic. Sienna watches as the SEAL finds an Apache warrior staring back at him. Nobu looks disappointed. Maybe he's thinking what a stingy war-belt trophy would be made by Denbow's crew-cut scalp.

Ortiz's knuckle tattoos blanch. There is little question of Who will be Next if Sienna lets her off the chain just then.

Sergeant Bryan grinds his foot in the deck. Denbow is a commissioned officer and, most annoying of all, able to scrub their mission at will. Her mission. He is Central Command's boy. The whole region is USA CENTCOM's backyard, from Egypt to Mongolia. And Khorasan's government has not authorized the incursion into their airspace or the planned kidnapping of one of their residents. In flight, they are in Denbow's hands.

T-Rex is getting ready to get ugly and throw things into a tailspin.

"Our esteemed Navy colleague may be articulating a valid viewpoint," he says, very politely, while fingering a frag grenade.

The SEAL does not know the Dogs well enough to be afraid. If her team figures he's a real danger to their mission or their teammates' safety, consequences would ensue. Denbow would find himself foam maced, cocooned in two dozen yards of duct tape, and stuffed in the mobile crapper unit for the duration of Sidewinder. Clusterjam back on the *Lee* be damned. And if the Navy man was determined to be a dangerous liability or turncoat spy, a retro M67 grenade stuffed into Denbow's jockstrap and an impromptu skydiving lesson would not be entirely off the table.

Sienna notes, with a sense of accomplishment, T-Rex limit himself to verbal barbs. Just as the tension rises to match the million-wasps-in-a-plastic-bag sound coming from the engines to either side of the now cramped and airless cabin, it is Whitebread who throws cold water on the dispute.

"Energy."

The word comes in a baritone rumble from the slice of shadow cutting the far corner of the aircraft cabin.

"Fill something that looks smaller with enough energy," Whitebread says with patient menace. "That makes it exactly the same as something bigger. Exactly."

Sienna suppresses a smile. Perhaps no explanation of

relativity has ever been delivered with such a homicidal undertone. Whitebread concludes his brief science lecture in a way that does not invite follow up.

"Exactly the same," he says. "Mass–energy equivalence. Einstein. Physics."

***

Half an hour later, they speed over modest low-rise Khorasani houses and sleeping livestock. Light-bending skin keeps them invisible. Broad, opposing plasma rotors spread downforce wash wide. Acoustic monitors tell Sienna their passage makes hardly a sound in the night sky. At the rear of the wide-body cabin, Bryan helps Sienna double and triple check a last-minute borrow from the Base's experimental arsenal.

The RAPTEK weapons unit. She's been wearing it since getting into the HALO pod for the descent from the scRamjet onto the *Lee*. The letters stand for "Railgun: Ansible Powered Test Kit". Its magnetic flux can push projectiles to phenomenal speeds. Basically, the thing strapped to her shoulders is a linear accelerator. It doesn't affect her gloves or her class ring. The ring is ceramic with a tourmaline stone dating back to 1835, courtesy of Ennis Reidt.

"You sure about this thing?"

The shoulder-mounted mayhem-dispensing device hugs her trapezoids like a neoprene yoke. Being one of the few people in the world cleared to know about the Ansible artifact has its advantages. One of them is trying out inventions based on its peculiar qualities—future weapons the military's research arm, DARPA, is feverishly and secretively developing.

Gadgets all governments promised each other never to build.

"Tried it out enough in the lab," she assures him. "Time for a field shakedown."

"I'm surprised they let you sign it out of the armory," Bryan says, suspicious.

Sienna pretends to fix a wrist strap on the RAPTEK.

He lets out a short sigh. "They did let you borrow it, didn't they?"

"Well, it's Friday and everyone who's cleared to be in that section is away till Monday. No one will ever know it's been gone."

"Sienna, colonel," Bryan says with mild exasperation. "They're away because the Ansible tests are happening in Europe. All the new comm systems are offline. Is this here thing even gonna work?"

Sienna flexes her arms. A flick of her wrist deploys a mean, two-pronged fléchette into her palm. Green and IR-aiming lasers flash on. The system syncs to her helmet visor.

"You bet it works," Sienna assures Bryan. "The juice comes from a cold-fusion beryllium source. They just touched the chip to the exterior of the Ansible one time and it started vibrating like a quartz crystal, except millions of times more powerful. No moving parts. What can go wrong in one day?"

All the same, Sienna quadruple-checks the weapons system's controls. As the RAPTEK warms up, she feels a small vibration in the base of her spine where the power plant is. *That's normal*, she guesses. For a prototype system powered by a possibly alien artifact. All function lights are green. Check. If used properly, it probably won't take her fingers off. Check.

That's all the science she cares to learn from the guy who delivered it.

***

Weeks ago, an ultra-geek from the DARPA's Adaptive Execution Office showed up with a box. It was the size of a footlocker. He flashed an order scroll that unnerved the commandant. Ignoring everyone, he made a bee-line for Sienna. Above a shimmering hologram barcode, his name tag read "Perdix, AEO."

He presided over the unboxing of the RAPTEK like a young preacher performing his first baptism. Perdix and Nobu nearly had nerdgasms as they went over its features. She only half listened to the lecture delivered by the intense boy from Cheyenne Mountain. He looked like he hated sharing his toys.

To ensure it stayed in place, there were several points of contact between her skin and a sort of hydrostatic gel. This gel looked and felt wet, but was not. The knowledgeable and attentive Perdix was about her age but seemed younger and older at the same time, in some bizarre, scientist way. As the RAPTEK latched on, Perdix stroked the interlocking scales of the personal railgun's armored exterior.

"He seems to like you." Perdix's manner was close enough to creepy to irritate. If Sienna thought he was being degen, she'd have punched him. He seemed much more interested in the weapons system. He didn't even notice her scars.

"You talk about it like it's alive."

Perdix—and Sienna quickly came to the conclusion that was not his real name—met her eyes with a watery gray gaze through glasses which weren't corrective at all. His little white hands pressed on her wrists, elbows, and shoulder blades to make sure the fit was perfect.

"There are many things we don't know," Perdix replied with eerie excitement. "About the An... I mean, the artifact. And that includes all related tech. There are many things we can't fathom. Yet. Not really." Perdix almost purred as he stroked the RAPTEK. "And it's all thanks to you and your group of brave soldiers that we have it at all." As if she and the Dogs had dragged the Ark of the Covenant back from the South Pole just for him. "An unexpectedly optimal outcome. You were not my first pick to lead the retrieval mission. I was overruled."

What a shocker. "Well, we're happy to have exceeded expectations."

Just like that, Perdix's interest for the humans in the room dissipated. "As I said, he seems to—"

"Yeah, seems to like me." She flexed her arms, dropped her visor, and sighted in on a demo target.

"Careful. It is designed for field testing, eventually. But there's only the one. The Navy tried for years to make their electromagnetic railgun system work. Never could. Not enough energy. And they didn't ask us to help. They called the project *Veloticas Eradico*." Perdix mouthed the Latin in a highfalutin way.

"I, who am become speed, kill."

"Precisely. The RAPTEK you wear is basically DARPA's update on the ancient sling. The original mass-driving weapon. Besides the obvious biblical reference to the David and Goliath sortie, the Greeks used lead sling bullets extensively in the Peloponnesian War. The effective range of specially cast projectiles was four hundred meters, about twice that of the contemporary bow and arrow. They even inscribed taunts to the enemy on the missiles."

Perdix smiled at how naïve the ancient Greeks and Romans were, or she was, or both. "They even believed the best slingers could throw so fast the speed of their shots through air would melt the metal before it struck the target. An interesting, if completely misguided, inkling of hypersonic aerodynamic heating. Thanks to our RAPTEK, you, Colonel McKnight, are the first foot soldier slinger in history of whom that's scientifically accurate."

She knew all that. West Point's curriculum featured the classics, especially where they were connected to historical warfare. Perdix would have known that if he'd bothered to look at her academic record.

He just thinks of me as a grunt, an animated mannequin.

She flexed her hand in the glove module. One of the practice projectiles lying on the table flew into her hand. Perdix looked perplexed. Sienna cheated him out of some more mansplaining about how the thing worked. As she fingered the metal ball inside invisible lines of magnetic force, she made a mental note to look up the relevant lines of the *Aeneid*.

Later, in a dog-eared text, she found them:
His lance laid by, thrice whirling round his head
The whistling thong, Mezentius took his aim.
Clean through the temples hissed a bolt of molten lead,
And prostrate in the dust, the gallant youth lay dead.

Inside the Base's underground test firing range, she gained confidence. Perdix fussed.

"It's a little tricky—"

"I got it."

The scientist gawked anxiously, but he wisely stayed out of her way. The guy's attitude, his dumbed-down tech babble, his soft hands, they all bugged her. Also his name. *Damn.* He probably picked it out himself and was arrogant enough to think workaday soldiers like her and her team wouldn't know.

In Greek mythology, Perdix was the student of master builder Daedalus. His apprenticeship ended in a fit of ancient nerd jealousy. The older man booted Perdix off the Acropolis. Legends say he transformed into a dorky partridge. In real life he probably just went *splat.*

Shutting the vault-sized doorway on him, she told him she'd be a while and not to wait up for her. "And Perdix, I've been to Athens. Watch your step on the Acropolis—it's a nasty drop."

***

Maybe she borrowed the RAPTEK because she wanted to give Perdix the finger. Under her flight suit, it looks like the imprint of some kind of custom body armor. But unlike ceramic scale armor, it is more flexible and doesn't chafe. Maybe it does like her.

Images of hills, small and cruel, dash past virtual window screens. Sienna goes over a final team readiness check.

"No biggie," Sienna assures a worried-looking Sarge. "I'll have it back before they know it's been halfway around the world without them. Just wait until we all get one."

She holds the hovering fléchette up to Bryan's metallic eyes.

"More firepower than any assault rifle. Only caseless ammo to carry. Never overheats. I can switch between antipersonnel, non-lethal, and troop support ordnance instantly. Face it, Sarge." She pounds him lightly on the shoulder. "Guns and bullets are so over."

She carefully sets down the small projectile. Sienna definitely does not want to send it blasting around inside the copter. Its outsides are plenty tough, but designers no doubt assumed no gunfights would be taking place inside the cabin.

16

They are close. The Navy guy's window to screw things up is closing. As though on cue, a burst of static in her ear precedes the update from the cockpit:

"Target structure in two-five seconds."

"Solid copy, Nightjar. Snakecharmer actual out," Sienna replies to the pilot, using the Dogs' mission call sign.

Sienna gives the Dogs a hand signal to confirm everyone heard that. Nobu nods as he checks out the SEAL's communications system. Her RTO tends to the newbie first, so he can then set their chaperone safely by the door. That way Denbow can't get into any mischief.

Like the specially purposed wing feathers of owls, their plasma rotors break turbulence into smaller currents. The stealth craft floats over the target village like a low-flying cloud. An elderly man walks steadily down an unpaved street. They pass over. Sienna imagines he only feels a brief, warm rush of air. If he were to look up, there might be a shimmer, then it would be gone. The non-combatant does not look up. They proceed to the designated structures.

The six of them have their own way of doing things. Able

as his file says he is, the tagalong SEAL operator is not part of it. Nobu finishes with Denbow and moves on. Their team stenographer typist is next up for comm check.

"Man, I just got used to this here newfangled relay," T-Rex protests as Nobu yanks some unneeded wires from his gear.

"Suck it up, Rex," his friend says. "Just don't play any gangster rap over the common channel. Maybe we get this done before breakfast is over on the ship."

"Gangsta what?" T-Rex shakes his head. "Man, why you always gots to be all culturally insensitive?"

As they gripe, they efficiently sync gear and locators. Sienna takes them through the breaching scenarios in their specialized shorthand. No one minds Denbow.

Following standard procedure, the doorway is wide open. This spec of aircraft is designed to fly that way. As long as interior lights remain off, they can be spotted only by someone with sensitive NVG gear.

Sienna stands with Bryan, looking at the command monitoring panels. These dimly lit multiple screens face away from the sliding exit. In one rectangle, she sees Whitebread's 360 heads up display feed. The resolution is good enough to notice he's got some kind of rash on his arm. Sienna makes a mental note to ask Sarge to ask Whitebread about it. It could be some kind of men's problem with potential to embarrass her hard-working specialist.

The rest of the Dogs' cam feeds and vital-sign monitors wink on one by one. She'll be on the ground with them and wants to make sure their data is feeding into the mechBrains okay. They're programmed to alert her if there are any problems.

"What the..." Snakelips gasps, looking into the central monitor.

Sienna looks. Snakelips rarely goes off without cause. She definitely has cause.

A big frame has just flickered on in the main display. It is circular, not rectangular like the others. The image which resolves into focus is of the ground as seen through Ortiz's custom sniper rifle. The weapon's scope is a battle-environment monitor as well as a straight-line optic. When switched on, it always defaults to the widest input setting. It shows three concentric ring bands, giving Snakelips multiple battlefield views without her having to take her eyes off a target.

The first ring is a warped schematic of the whole area of engagement. It takes practice to make sense of the squashed digital map. All her team can do it. The next ring is a wraparound view from the chopper's belly cam, showing any immediate threats closing in. There are none. The center is the traditional sniper crosshairs and ranging tools. This is zooming in on a live target just under the hovercopter.

The problem is, Snakelips is standing to Sienna's left, nowhere near the weapon. She curses. They realize what's happened.

Denbow has grabbed the rifle off the rack. The scope cam shows the crosshairs lining up on the sinus cavity of a Khorasani boy of no more than twelve. The friend-foe designator of the mechBrain paints him yellow because he is standing next to a rifle leaning against a wall. The mechBrain recognizes him as possible threat because he is near a weapon. The kid is only a potential threat, which is why he is painted yellow not red. And Denbow is about to blow his head off.

Sienna leaps the distance between herself and the SEAL operator. She smacks down on the barrel of the high-powered precision rifle. The SEAL's gloved finger touches the finely tuned trigger. It fires.

The integrated suppressor shoots a single sabot-sheathed armor-piercing round. It impacts the doorframe of the aircraft with a *whunk.*

"Hey!" Denbow barks at Sienna.

She doesn't let the weapon go. She jams it back into Denbow's chest and pushes him back into a flight seat.

"*What* are you doing?"

"Clearing enemy opposition," Denbow returns aggressively. "They're in the sanctioned target zone, Colonel."

Sienna feels her face flush. If someone were to look at her through IR vision, her head would be glowing like a magnesium flare. She's burning with anger at this homicidal idiot. She wants to knock him senseless.

"This is *not* a goddamn free-fire zone." Sienna flicks the safety on and pulls the rifle out of Denbow's hands. "Rules of engagement are up to me, Lieutenant Denbow. And they are *weapons hold.*"

As Sienna tries to get a look at the damage to their ride, Denbow comes back with more lip. "Colonel, with all respect," he starts off, with enough lack of respect he's in danger of not needing a rope to exit the copter, "in a couple years that will be a military-aged male. Whether this future combatant eats a bullet now or in five years, what's the difference?"

Sienna wants to tell Denbow that five years, five months, even five days can make all the difference in the world. She needs to believe that. And she's seen that sometimes it's actually true. But as surely as she knows she's glad she stopped a kid who had no choice but to grow up in a war zone from having every choice taken away from him by a bullet to the temple, Sienna knows Denbow would not hear her. He certainly would not understand. So instead of saying any more, she kicks the fast rope over the edge of the open hatchway.

"Rope's on the ground," Sienna says. "My mission. My call. Back off."

Before Denbow can reply, there is more movement on the ground. A second figure comes out near Denbow's preteen target. In the frame of the doorway, a thuggish man walks up, smoking the butt end of a cigarette. He swats at the boy, who deftly ducks. Then the adult picks up the rifle. The mechBrain target designator paints him red. The outline of the boy turns green as he makes a local obscene gesture to the militia man's back.

Still fuming, but wary of yelling loud enough to give away their position, Sienna walks over to Snakelips. She pushes the mahogany stock of the rifle sideways into her body armor.

"Here. And Corporal Ortiz," Sienna says, "keep control of your weapon."

"Yes, Colonel."

She only ever uses real names and ranks with the Dogs when she is pissed. Everyone knows that. Sienna almost feels sorry for Snakelips. She will take the minor rebuke hard. Sienna is still not through being angry at the homicidal idiot she's been saddled with. Denbow is the same kind of fool that opens fire on kids playing on the decades-old, disabled wreck of a tank. She turns to the Dogs; they snap to.

"Everyone got that? Weapons hold," Sienna repeats. "Use

EEL rounds as primary ordnance, but don't take any chances defending yourselves or each other. Get me?"

Their response is drowned out by the pilot cutting in on comms.

"*Snakecharmer, we have a little situation brewing directly portside, eight o'clock.*"

He does not have to elaborate. The thug, outlined in red in the monitor, points at them, shouting. Right at their formerly invisible ride. The stray bullet fired by Denbow knocked out the stealth field on one side. From the ground it must have looked far-out alien and slapstick stupid all at the same time. Half a copter appearing in mid-air just like that. You don't see that every day.

"Go go go," Sienna says and kicks the second fast rope out of the gaping doorway. Denbow reaches for the rope. Her RAPTEK-clad forearm halts him.

"Not you," Sienna says firmly. "Until we're back on the deck of the *Lee,* it's my mission. You stay here. See if you can fix your screw-up."

Sienna points to the big gouge in a critical panel torn by the tungsten-core bullet. The aircraft is not designed to be shot at with SLAP rounds from the inside. The light-bending array is completely buggered.

Snakelips aims her reclaimed rifle out the doorway. She quickly switches to antipersonnel rounds and zeroes in on the armed hostile just as he is raising his rifle to shoot at the floating apparition. Delicia Snakelips Ortiz takes him out. Her single round to center mass is instantly incapacitating and instantly fatal. A clean, necessary kill.

17

Multiple 3D frames in her visor track Sarge and the others as they quickly secure the poorly fortified mud-brick dwelling. Here is where their best intel placed a local creep codenamed Sidewinder. He has one thing of value: a nugget in his brain. Sienna needs to dig it out. She re-checks everyone's progress. Ready to jump in if crap happens.

Resolved to never show it, she always worries about any of them getting hurt. Tonight that weight is heavy. This is her fight. Her birthright battle. At least they have the best equipment military budgets can afford. And one visiting team advantage—personalized stealth.

Historically, foot soldiering was always about armor versus speed. It was always rock / scissors / rock. From ancient Greek hoplites weighed down by half their body weight in bronze to Genghis Khan issuing all his horsemen arrow-trapping silk vests. Modern material innovations brought in a third option: active camouflage. If the enemy can't see you, they can't shoot you.

Sienna flips her visor down to meet her cheekpieces. As she presses herself against a wall, her outer cover reads the closest background color and projects it out. So does the transparent ceramic of her helmet. Totally chameleon. In fact, DARPA stole the guanine nanocrystal mechanisms from that tricky little lizard. They use advanced photon physics to change colors. It's not perfect. Sienna's experienced eye can still see who's who without HUD-enhanced view. But in darkness, coming up on an unsuspecting enemy, the effect this night is total, awesome shock.

The lower-floor guards are neutralized before anyone else notices their now very unstealthy stealth copter. Sienna starts to relax. Late breakfast on the aircraft carrier might happen.

The upper floor of Sidewinder's crib is one big bedroom. It would have been nice to scout the place with a mini drone. Their tagalong SEAL fixed it otherwise. She has to assume news of their arrival is getting out through militia channels. Checkout time has been moved up.

Sienna taps her mic. "Everyone, sound off when main floor is cleared. Then proceed up. I've got the cellar. Snakecharmer actual out."

As soon as she mutes her mic, she stops. In front of her, a rusty rifle muzzle pokes out of the next doorway. It trembles. With one hand, Sienna grabs it, aiming it down and away. Her other hand sends an EEL around the corner. The written manual for the M588 Electrostatic Enveloping Ligature round, and common sense, both hold that touching something in contact with someone receiving fifty thousand volts is not a good idea. Sienna feels a small shock. The combatant gets a hella bigger one. There's a thud, followed by a groan. The metal barrel sticks to her palm for a second. *Magnetic attraction.* She shakes it loose. This is a new talent for her RAPTEK.

Interesting, not important.

She shoots a fléchette into the weapon's ancient breech. It shatters. Holding to cover, she flicks her head. The mechBrain in her visor understands. A holographic scanning mirror appears in the air. It gives her a view around the corner. The hostile is down, and alone.

A pimply faced male of about sixteen lies on the floor in silent spasms. As soon as the EEL struck, he tried to wipe it off. Both the youth's hands are enmeshed in a clear epoxy resin. In a few seconds, the electric shocks will stop. If he tries to move, the bio sensor chip will shock him again until he learns or passes out.

Sienna is impressed by the hands-free utility of the RAPTEK. Normally she'd have to sling her main weapon and be conscious of muzzle direction. Now her hands are two muzzles when she wants them to be. And she has the only one in the world. It is a little heavy, like an extra SAPI plate. But heck, so were the first cell phones. Now they have ones that are injectable.

Nobu's calm voice cuts through occasional updates from their pilot. *"Wirehead to Snakecharmer actual, we have subject. He has hostage and is cornered on second level. We are holding. Over."*

Okay. Complications. Sienna bounds up the stairs. *Bring 'em!*

***

The complication waiting for her on the second floor doesn't worry her. She is still so much more chafed up at Denbow for damaging their ride. And most of all, for playing fast and loose with the rules of engagement. Her rules.

Outside of very specific parameters, the use of deadly force is simply murder. There is a line. One thinly engraved on a world which too often mocks the concept of sanity. She needs to locate herself on the side of that line that defines the good guys. The line that separates her from havoc.

Contrary to what most people think, "havoc" was not shouted at the opening of ancient battles. Hundreds of years before Shakespeare's *Julius Caesar* made the term famous, it appeared in *The Black Book of the Admiralty* and again in *Grose's Military Antiquities*:

Likewise be all manner of beasts, when they be brought into the field and cried Havoke, then every man to take his part.

Cry Havoc, and let slip…

Since the dawn of warfare, Havoc has given soldiers of armies license to loot and pillage, permission to rape and kill the helpless.

Havoc urged soldiers to let loose their inner beasts on the innocent.

Havoc called during battle without authority was punishable by death.

Sienna has always had a unique perspective on inner beasts and the sinews of will holding them back. If anything gives her quest and her struggle meaning, it is those rules. They sanctify righteous struggle. To Sienna, they are the consecration of her battlefields. They are hallowed.

She reaches the top floor under the crooked roof. "What we got?"

She has a pretty good idea. The schematics of Sidewinder's

hideout are etched in her mind. A small motion dismisses her personal mechBrain's offer of an interior diagram. Sienna slides along the second-floor wall to where T-Rex, Sarge, and Nobu have their main objective at bay. He's close, shuffling around the corner. Nearly close enough to touch.

"One hostile. With one pint-sized hostage," reports T-Rex. "Can't try an EEL. Girl's all, like, *pint-sized* as sheit."

Nobu crouches on the other side of the doorway. He's using an old-school dental mirror to keep an eye on the scene inside. All ways out are covered. Sidewinder is trapped. Sienna flicks through her team's POV displays to her sniper's scope view. Snakelips watches through the window. She has no shot. Sienna takes off her helmet and visor. They need Sidewinder alive. She hopes the price won't be too high.

Her belt drops. The webbing holding a sidearm and Jane Bowie falls to the wooden planks. She keeps the RAPTEK. No way is he going to recognize the shoulder-mounted mass driver. There is only one. That's her play. She exhales.

Careful to use polite intonations, Sienna speaks standard Dari. "I am not armed."

She inches out into plain view.

"And I would like to speak with you, kind sir."

Her words and her gloved, empty hands are not to Sidewinder's liking. He shows his disapproval by firing wildly. Sienna ducks back to hard cover. The door-frame splinters. Small chunks of plaster and wood fly. Her team reacts to assess the threat and any damage, then instantly revert to normal stance. Though no one normal likes being shot at, it's nice to see the band is still in tune after a long layoff. Inside the room, glass falls.

"Wassrongwifyou?" T-Rex hisses around the corner, outraged by the terrorist's inhospitable act.

Sienna stands on the balls of her feet. She's in the best spot to tackle the guy if he makes a break for it. A few tense seconds pass. Sidewinder stays put. She'll give appeasement another try.

Before the badly aimed shots were fired, she got a look into the room. The hostage is a small girl. Burning in Sienna's brain is the image of the twin orbs of the kid's eyes. She has to be only five or six years old. Her violet eyes are underscored by the glinting edge of Sidewinder's knife under her chin. If Delicia has no incapacitating shot, they can't risk a frontal breach.

Scratch that.

Even if Ortiz had the perfect shot, Sienna would stand her down. Sidewinder is the frayed end of a thread she needs to reel in. Asrah Qazi, the Scythe of Heaven, is on the other end of that thread. She can't let it break. Not now. Not after all she's gone through to get here. No one else *has* to die here. And despite Sidewinder's best efforts, she's not gonna let him.

She tries to smile. Army psychologists say people can hear you smile in the tone of your voice. *Whatever.* Sienna just needs this jerk to do nothing for a few more seconds.

"Kind sir, we are not here to kill you." *You lucky mook.* "Only talk. There is a way we can both get what we want. There is a bargain here. But if you shoot again, no bargain. We roll in a stun grenade, and if you wake, you will be in chains."

Sidewinder fires back, this time verbally. "Don't speak nonsense, woman," he yaps in rough street Dari. "It's the *girl* you want! She will die in blood and pain. I will roll her head out to you if I do not get what *I* want."

His voice does not have a smile.

Sienna decides it's time for her to risk getting shot. Any more chitchat and Sidewinder will think they are delaying and tricking him. Which they are. What did he mean they are after his hostage? They've come for him. For one small fact inside his squirrely brain. Sienna knows nothing about a girl.

She walks straight past Sarge Bryan's disapproval and around the corner. Into the line of fire. Bed clothing lies in disarray. Money and jewels spill out of motorcycle saddle bags, signs of a hasty escape plan abandoned.

Sienna takes in the whole scene like a fresh snapshot. A fish tank sits in a corner, shattered. Hit by a ricocheting bullet. No water inside. Only sand. It is the same color as the desert. Multiple dark shapes crawl over the mess. Scorpions.

Hands empty and raised, Sienna takes a few deliberate steps toward Sidewinder.

"Kind and wise sir, I am unarmed," Sienna says and turns thirty degrees either way to prove the fib. "Please do not shoot your humble servant." Dari has a lot of polite and respectful terms, especially for addressing a male elder.

She confronts a man close to sixty. He looks a lot more spry in person than in his surveillance pictures. He is not large, but his captive, a slim-boned girl, makes him and the wickedly curved blade he holds to her neck seem huge. Sidewinder's left hand holds a pistol. His file says he's right-handed. That could be an advantage. It's hard to shoot off-handed under pressure.

Sidewinder's bloodshot eyes look at her. Dark pinpricks of hate pause momentarily on the outline of the RAPTEK. Then they continue over the rest of her. She can almost hear his mind writhing. Sidewinder is figuring his best chance to come out of this tight spot. Like he has come out of every other one before.

Even without her visor, Sienna has a naturally wide range of vision. When she was small, she was self-conscious and thought her eyes were bulgy, like a frog's. In her periphery, Bryan's expression silently shouts to her: *What the hell are you doing?*

She tries to cheer him. A slight inclination of her head lets him know. *Don't worry, I got this.*

"You! You are but a female. Send in your superior officer. I will talk only to him. Now get out of my sight, you worthless bitch!"

Sienna starts to worry. Maybe she made a mistake exposing herself. The word translating as bitch is particularly foul and insulting. It denotes the base smell and filth imputed to female dogs as well as the animal itself.

Sienna smiles meekly. She keeps her eyes downcast, unthreatening, while still being aware of the man's every move. Some greasy gray hairs poke through his sleeping robe, hairs which sprout from a patch of crackly, dry skin. Below hang the disheveled curls of his hostage. A mop of dark hair frames the girl's upturned face.

"Yes, kind and wise sir, I am but a female," Sienna admits. "I am here only to translate your words. You can see I am no threat."

She is well into the room. Sidewinder's belief that they are after his hostage is snarling things up. Threatening their ultimate goal. Her first idea had been to reason with the unpleasant but historically very businesslike fellow. Time to improvise. Sidewinder has to live, but Sienna cannot let the girl hostage die.

The RAPTEK system generates two distinct types of electromagnetic fields. A primary repulsor used to accelerate fléchette darts—the ones hidden on her wrist magazine. It's overkill. Bolts from a big railgun can sink a battleship. All she faces here is a mangy coward. A second, weaker RAPTEK field pulls ammo into place. Sienna's improvisation depends on this feature of the experimental system.

She edges in.

"NO CLOSER!" Sidewinder snarls. Sienna can smell his breath. "I will cut her head off!"

The girl hostage's strange eyes are nearly as uncanny as Sarge Bryan's bio-engineered ones. They watch the activities of the adults closely. The girl is upset. You'd expect her to be with a blade the size of her own arm at her windpipe. But she is not hysterical. She does not struggle, seems to know what is coming before…

"I *will* cut—"

Sienna flexes the palm of her magnetic glove and feels a distant tug. Got something.

Now or never.

"No," she says calmly. "You won't."

Before Sidewinder can flinch, his knife's blade is enmeshed in the electromagnetic field. It rips out of his sweaty grasp and flies into Sienna's hand. At the same time, she flicks her right wrist three times and sends as many wickedly forked projectiles into and through Sidewinder's gun hand. The impacts back him against a wall.

Free, the girl runs forward. Sienna nudges her to the side

and behind, out of harm's way, toward Bryan and the other people who always have her back.

And just for calling me names...

Sienna wings the dagger at Sidewinder. It pins his robe to the wall and even draws a little blood. Bloody staples through cartilage pin the hand holding the gun to Sidewinder's left shoulder. She walks forward.

"I lied. I am a threat," she says. "Let's start over. My name is *Colonel* Bitch, and you are my prisoner."

She pushes the slide release button on the ruined pistol. Its magazine drops out, accompanied by a gratifying howl of agony.

18

"Man, how many of these things are there?" T-Rex flicks a small scorpion off his pants leg.

"What kind of a weirdo keeps crazy mierda like that in his bedroom?" Snakelips has gathered up the girl and holds her aloft, clear of the arachnid-infested floor.

The girl looks local. Judging from her features and clothes, she could be Hazara tribe. On the other hand, Sidewinder may have grabbed her from south Khorasan, from the big refugee safe zones. In that case, she could have come from anywhere and been brought up speaking the local language. The girl has fast figured out that these odd new people are friendly. She tugs her minder's facial piercings as though a nose ring is the most fascinating toy in the world.

"Ow, girl," Snakelips says mildly and gently pries small fingers off her facial jewelry. "Hey, Sarge, she's got a hell of a grip on her."

"Give her a juice box. I'm busy." Bryan holds Sidewinder by the neck. Nobu employs pliers to pull the metal nails out of the prisoner's shoulder bones. He covers the wounds with pressure bandages so Sidewinder does not bleed to death and thereby waste their time.

Bryan looks at Sienna, his eyes wide like twin golden moons. "Nice one, boss. But please, never, ever do that again. I tell the new cadet classes I didn't raise no cowboys."

She grins back. "Far as I can tell, you raised nothing but."

Bryan turns to her and studies the glove apparatus on her hands.

"How'd you do that? With the knife?" Bryan asks. "I thought the RAPTEK only shoots metal fléchettes."

She cocks her wrist back and feels the energy of the electromagnets. "It's the loader. How do you think the projectiles get in my hand? There's a shaped mag field that pulls them up. It's way less powerful than the one for shooting. I had to get close to be sure I had the knife blade."

Sienna looks at the distraught and defeated Sidewinder. "Was totally worth the millions they spent developing it, just for the look on this guy's face."

Bryan shakes his head, quietly mouthing, *Never, ever, please.*

There's a limited window to get what she wants. Denbow's screw-up disabled part of their hovercopter's stealth. That makes exfiltration before sunrise urgent.

Snakelips balances the former hostage on her waist ammo pouches and helps search the rooms. T-Rex, always multitasking, needles her.

"I wonder if they have one of those kangaroo baby carriers in olive drab."

Nobu snorts. "Rex, requisition a milspec Bjorn. NATO code M-NANNY."

T-Rex slaps his best friend's hand.

While the Dogs have an informal command structure, it is the sergeant's job to deal with most operational details that come up during a mission. Including six-year-olds.

"Sarge," T-Rex asks, "what we gonna do with the miniature non-com?"

"The *Lee*'s captain seemed like a tightwad," Bryan says. "Standing orders from the ship are to leave 'em behind. Only exceptions are for urgent medical conditions directly caused by our op."

"Y'know… when she's not all screaming in terror or has a knife to her throat," their warrant officer observes, "she kinda looks like them old pictures of the Colonel you gots in your office, Sarge." He can't resist piling on. "Yeah, just like her spittin' image if you axe me. Round about the time her mom, Dr. Theodora McKnight, was KIA helping out earthquake victims."

Sienna watches Bryan's bio-mechanical eyes meet the astonishing violet eyes of the girl. He has made up his mind. Wordlessly, she affirms Sarge's plan.

"Okay, okay," Bryan says. "Nobu, write it up as suspected dysentery and shock caused by all the racket we made. We take her to the *Lee*. If she has family, Worldwide Help can get her back to them." Using his drill-instructor voice, Bryan shouts down from the second-floor landing. "Now mop this up!"

As all the men leave, Snakelips realizes what's happening.

"Hey! Where you all going?" she calls after them. "You know this is totally sexist, right? I'm a cold-blooded, hard-as-nails killing machine, not a malada nanny!"

The girl, who doubtless does not speak their language and whose name no one yet knows, yawns. She hugs the female assassin and rests her head on neoprene-covered armor. Still in chameleon stealth mode, the uniform projects the color of the girl's hair.

From upstairs Nobu says, "Hey, Whitebread. Help me sort and bag intel in this room. And watch out for the scorpions. They're all over."

The specialist heaves himself up the stairs. They creak under his weight. He checks out the master suite.

"They must like kids a lot here," Whitebread says casually. "There's kids' clothes and toys all over. They gave her the biggest room."

Sienna leads the patched-up Sidewinder down to a cubbyhole on the ground floor beneath the stairs. It looks like this space has been used for drinking tea and smoking chillum pipes. If she hadn't been so intent on figuring out how to get what she needs out of their prisoner, she might have anticipated the next disaster that was about to drop. All 382 pounds of it.

"Whitebread," Nobu says sympathetically, "you are a strong warrior, but your buffalo not always run in the same direction. See all the guy's clothes and crap here? It's Sidewinder's room. And there is only one bed."

Sienna nearly has Sidewinder into the tea room. Her team cleared it out to serve as a makeshift interrogation cell. The first sign of a problem upstairs is Nobu gasping.

"Oh crap…"

The next is a rumbling, like a herd of bison coming down the stairs. All of them are moving in one direction. Sienna has just enough time to kick herself for not anticipating Whitebread's possible reaction.

Whitebread came to the Base from a Wyoming Junior Reserve Training program. Despite his very high IQ, he had no drive to attend college and always tried to hide his intellect. Something very evil had driven him away from his home. Whitebread's mother was committed to a public mental hospital. According to county sheriff's records, his father and older brother were killed in a propane explosion on their farm. Sienna always suspected there was more to the story. She hasn't pried.

Petr always takes harm and cruelty inflicted on innocents very personally. Most times, that is consistent with their mission, and commendable. However, in this case it threatens to ruin the whole Sidewinder operation. The point of the large and complex undertaking is nearly scotched by the point of a serrated blade that drives right at her prisoner's head. Sidewinder would have stood there like a goof and gotten the worst nose job ever had Sienna not pushed him out of the way.

"Specialist! Stand down!" she yells. "We NEED him!"

But words no longer have any restraining effect. Whitebread is in a blood rage. He wants only to kill. The giant yells and prepares to slash at Sidewinder again with his foot-long knife.

"My... *brother*, Dom, he was only trying to *protect* me... you whupped him until his ribs showed... you son of a bitch... gonna *skin* you like I SHOULDA!"

Thankfully, the rest of her team is just as fast. Bryan and T-Rex grab Whitebread, but only succeed in preventing his forward motion. The blade, with its slick blood groove and sturdy ridges on the heel, custom designed for severing joints and limbs, hovers inches from Sidewinder's face.

Sienna grabs the big man's elbow and wrist. She jabs pressure on specific nerve clusters. The weapon slips from numb fingers and clatters to the tile floor. Sienna kicks it away before Sidewinder gets any ideas that will get him frustratingly dead. Sienna puts her face close to Petr's ear and whispers something the others cannot hear.

She stands back. "Let him go. We're good here."

Without a backward glance, she turns to the cowering Sidewinder. "All right. Playtime is over. Where were we?"

19

The room is bare. Sienna pushes Sidewinder's good shoulder. He goes in. Her people have tossed out everything except two plastic chairs and a card table. Its surface is worn and stained with sepia-colored rings. Harsh light flares from a stupid elephant-shaped lamp. It sits way up on its shelf. There is no chance the prisoner can use it as a bludgeon or try to set a fire. This guy is not a scrapper. He is a talker. And an aspiring decapitator of kids.

Sienna sits opposite Sidewinder. There's no time for the whole gradual breakdown of resistance thing.

On the ship, Langley spooks will be all over him and the squirming rotten things in his head.

Not that Sienna is expecting a holiday basket from the CIA. Agencies rarely have the stomach for a real grab mission. They're messy. These days, for them, at CENTCOM's Doha base and others, it's all about robot-dropped missiles and thermal gun sight camera videos of cars and houses silently exploding. "We got him!" they would shout. Never mind questioning a charred body is problematic, and the guilty are sometimes hard to find among collateral damage.

That's why Sienna used all of her influence to get here. Had she used Roger? Probably. But he knows how much getting the man behind Sidewinder means to her. Right here and now she will do anything, use anyone, to get what she came for.

So close now. She pushes a scroll screen at Sidewinder. A double tap enlarges the picture, a grainy long-range photograph of him in an open 4x4. A younger man beside him is a blurry menace behind the steering wheel.

"Asrah Qazi. You call him the Scythe of Heaven," Sienna says flatly. "I've been after him for a while." Her fingers idly feel for scars beneath the shoulder ridges of the RAPTEK. She stops. The motion feels too personal. *Irrational.* This guy has no idea who she is or who Asrah is to her.

She watches her prisoner carefully. He watches back. Tough old bird. He is in restraints and in pain but not beaten or broken, not yet. When he looks at the picture, a spark of recognition flickers in dead fish eyes. It's a glimpse of what's rattling around in his vulture-like head.

An evil, wicked hope. Perfect. He'll sell out anyone.

Sienna gives the prisoner a few seconds. Kerosene combustion in the mantle lamp throws off stark light and discomforting heat. The trumpeting elephant figure hisses like it's permanently winding up a pachyderm sneeze. Their time's running out. By the book, their prisoner should be on the copter and on his way to disappearing forever into the black-ops bureaucratic garbage disposal.

Sidewinder exhales, as though expelling a long drag on an imaginary water pipe. He's stowed his open contempt for her and seems almost humble. He switches from English back to Dari. He's up to something.

"We are alone?" Sidewinder says. "You have no one listening? None of your people understands our language, uh huh?"

"No one's listening. If you help me, maybe I can help you."

Sidewinder licks his lips. His eyes lower but keep flicking, left, right, left. "I know I am not so smart, not so exalted. I am not so notorious. Uh huh?"

He leans back until his shoulder wounds make him flinch. *He's crafty. He might know we're running on a short fuse.*

"I have to ask myself: am I worth all this?" Sidewinder rolls his eyes at his wrecked house and the wreckers busy wrecking it some more. "This is a neutral country. One it took much effort to create. Khorasan is a new start for a troubled land. A place to hide away the unwanted. We are deep within United Nations-recognized boundaries. No quick dash over a disputed border, uh uh. Why? My business activities?" He smiles, recalling a decades-long list of murders, extortions, and violent corruption.

"I do not think so. I only killed my own people. Never Americans. Not one," he says proudly, like a car salesman bragging about his dealer warranty. "The transaction I am handling would not concern your government at all. So I ask, then I look, and I see. I see you. That is what I see. I see the look in your eyes."

"Well, look closer," Sienna invites him. "Your ICC finding says dead *or* alive."

Sidewinder does not flinch. "I would be, as the teenagers put it, out-stressed. If you were here for me. Or my precious little jewel."

Sienna has a sick feeling he's not talking about his treasure stash of black opals.

Sidewinder shakes his head. "You are different. You have another *need* in you entirely. Something is empty. It is something you are wanting."

Sienna leans forward. "You know where HE is. TALK!"

Tied hands brush a short, thick beard. The movement pains him. It signals a shift in initiative. In his favor. *Damn.*

"I know my time in Khorasan is over." Sidewinder exhales moist, spice-smelling breath. "Even if you release me, I would not anymore have my people's trust. They see you come, see you go, and leave me. They will think I have become a spy. You should not have caused such a disturbance. Everything I have is for sale. I cannot stay. And if you take me to your ship, or land transport, or high air station, I will never leave your cages."

As if he were sketching out a map on the tabletop, the prisoner's fingers scratch and poke. Somehow Sidewinder does see into her. "A ship. Yes." *Creepily insightful bastard.*

"That is good. It must be in the Gulf. Also very good."

Sienna fumes. *I know I didn't give anything away. This guy is hella slick and on his home turf.*

"Between here," Sidewinder says. "Where we are, and the coast where you must go, is a place. Here."

His mottled index finger jabs down, making a soft *pok* sound.

"A fishing village. I am blood-bound to their chief. Take me there. Inside the jail of that town, is a man. Farid. A disgusting man of abhorrent perversions." Sidewinder makes to spit but has no saliva, or none he wants to spare.

"This man Farid is wanted for a bombing in Madrid.

Tourists died. Foreigners. Americans. Farid is a much bigger prize. You take him, you let me go."

This thread is going somewhere. Sidewinder's life and lifestyle are too precious to him for him to be yanking her chain. Incoming militia will just as soon kill him for being a collaborator as try to fight the Dogs.

"And they are going to hand over Farid?"

"Ach!" Sidewinder releases a bit of precious spittle at last. "He is in jail for being khawal. A womanly man, uh huh. No one will miss him. His own father put him in jail for his unnatural crimes of man loving."

The house is crawling with scorpions. Large and small, they have found every crack and hole. One tentatively crawls onto the card table. It is only about half a finger's length in size, but bold. Its movements are elegantly alien. Pausing to groom itself, its tail pulses steadily.

"Right," she says, rejecting the pig-in-a-poke trade. "Next you're going to tell me that I have to trust you. After you give me Scythe's location, we'll have only minutes. As soon as we leave, your information turns out to be garbage and you're gone. Uh huh?"

Sidewinder contemplates their tiny cold-blooded observer. A third silent party to their parlay. He points his bound hands at the scorpion.

"The young are born not out of eggs, but living. Like people. They can live for a year without eating. Three days without taking a breath."

Sidewinder puts his hands on his chest. "My heart. I keep them for their poison. It heals the heart and has, shall we say, other uses. Fascinating, isn't it? How a little venom can keep one alive. Whereas too much…"

Enough of the Nature Channel rerun. Sienna wants to skip to the good part. Where the lioness rips the jackal's spine in half and has a snooze in the shade. "Give me what you have. If—*if* we get Scythe, maybe we can do something."

"Ha!" Sidewinder slaps his hand on the table. The scorpion's tail twitches. It dives under the tabletop, scorning gravity.

"I know lady-colonel is smarter than that. You can have him, your Scythe of Heaven"—he glances at the clock in the side of the elephant lamp—"in less than an hour. Thirty minutes, if you are quick. Your country's operatives are very close to him, though they have no awareness of this."

"Hogwash." This guy might as well have pulled five aces out of a deck. A sinking feeling scrabbles at her midsection. *This is all for nothing!* "For twenty years he's been a ghost who knows how to stay hidden. You're telling me you can just reach out and drop him in our laps? In thirty minutes?" Sienna stands and grabs him. "We're out of here!"

"No no no!" he squeals. "Leave me in the village until Scythe's capture. The chieftain will fear your stealth drones. If I lie, he will give me back."

Her experience tells her to get more. Some small truth that will color the rest. The astute concierge of horrors anticipates her.

"He is in France."

Her pupils react. Sidewinder notices. She doesn't care.

"Why there?" he asks, squirming his shoulders in a painful half shrug. "His end of the game he keeps to himself. They needed my help. As usual, I know more than anyone supposes.

Asrah Qazi is out of his natural waters, working on something big. Working with new people. He takes chances for something he desires above all else."

Something icy hits at the back of her brain. *France— Europe. We were supposed to be there. Coincidence?*

"Agreed," Sienna says. *Got to go for it.* "With conditions. My government—"

"No! Not with any government." Wounded and bound, he feels in control enough to cut Sienna off. He looks up boldly. Now he is the man he was when they were introduced. The man with a sharp knife to a girl's throat. The one who saw in front of him only a worthless bitch.

"I am dealing with you. And *I* will set my condition. Only one. And you will give it. You are here for yourself. This deal I make, it is between us, like a special friendship, uh huh? Your codename is Snakecharmer. I am the snake and you have been so very charming to me. But I know you... Colonel Sienna Iðunn McKnight."

Before she realizes it, Sienna has Sidewinder by the throat with her left hand. Hovering in her right palm is a charged fléchette aimed at the man's temple. Carbon-steel tines float on waves of electromagnetism.

"I could make you tell me now, save an hour."

Alarm and cold fury compete inside Sienna. *Stupid breach of protocol.* If he's an accomplice of Asrah's, maybe he knows her face from a picture. Just before, when he saw the photograph. It wasn't recognition of Asrah she saw in Sidewinder's face. The thought of those two discussing her disturbs Sienna more than she wants to admit.

"Yes, you could try brute violence," he admits while getting a closer look at the RAPTEK, "but I am an old man. My heart, it may give out. Then you would be back to the square one?"

Sienna decides. "If you're lying, we'll see how much your heart can stand. What is it? What do you want?"

"A nothing. A trifle." Sidewinder's eyes, haggard, bloodshot, triumphant, meet Sienna's once more. "The girl. She is called Anis. She has no relatives, not any longer. No one will miss her. I want her. She stays with me or no deal."

20

Sidewinder's demand hits her like a boot in the guts. Bartering the girl, Anis... Sienna didn't even know her name until now. Trading Anis just like that goes against every single value Annalies and Bryan tried to instill in a wild, headstrong, often angry girl. It would defile the memory she has of Theodora McKnight. It would attaint Hamida's sacrifices.

It is easy for Sidewinder to think his offer is a great bargain. The lives of innocents, especially children, are traded and bartered and used here every day. The creation of Khorasan itself, for example. How many people starved and died of dehydration and heatstroke in the region before the powers built the *TYR Lens* desalination plant? How many thousands of refugees worldwide have been saved since? Here, individual lives are the lowest denomination of currency. Sienna can do nothing about that. But the girl. She is different. Sienna and the Dogs wrenched her out of this fiend's grasp only minutes ago. Sidewinder expects them to put Anis back in his clutches.

Sienna thinks fast. And decides.

"If I thought for a moment you were what my man thinks you are, I'd try out rapid fire on this rig right here and now," Sienna says, prodding his forehead with the hovering projectile. "Or better yet, leave you in a room with Petr."

That gets his attention. The only sound is the hissing kerosene lamp. The only movement is a trickle of blood from the end of Sidewinder's nose. Whitebread's evisceration tool must have just nicked it. Like a razor's cut he probably doesn't even feel. A fat droplet, colored extra red, wells up from an invisible fissure. It mixes with oily sweat. The globule grows fat, dilutes, and falls on the tabletop.

"You're sick. But not in that way. You are twisted. But not toward sexual depravity. Anis sleeps in a basket in your room because she's valuable. You don't trust anyone to watch her. Who is she? A hostage? An opium warlord's daughter?"

Sidewinder scoffs, "You know nothing. A girl before childbearing years, even from the wealthiest families, isn't worth a herd of sickly goats. To you she is nothing. The little darling is all I have left. Since we are friends, even short-term partners, uh huh? I will tell you."

Sidewinder relaxes. Coming up is some version of the truth. Maybe there's a third way.

"In this pond called Khorasan, I am not the largest frog," Sidewinder continues. "I am an old and smart one. Nothing occurs without word reaching my ear. For as long as I can remember, scientists have been looking for people, young people. Through DNA mapping. As they were stealing bits of blood and skin, I was waiting like the beautiful horned viper of my home country. They were close. But I got her first."

The fingernails of Sidewinder's uninjured hand scrape the worn surface of the table.

"Her parents are dead. Her future is greater than anything

you could give her. Think of yourself. Only you can stop the mayhem your cousin Asrah is planning. We both know his ambition for atrocity has no bounds. What is one girl against all those lives? It may already be too late."

Sienna fingers the pouch of black opals.

"Pah. If you offered me everything you have, it is not a tenth of a tenth of Anis's price to the right parties. Make up your mind. In the Wandering Desert, all is sand and time. You do not belong here. Your time is running out."

Sienna's head sinks between her shoulders.

"Okay," she hears her own ragged voice say.

Sidewinder savors triumph. The old critter has the brass to say, "I think it is customary to shake on it."

21

A minute later, Sienna motions to T-Rex. "All yours."

"Another satisfied customer." He grabs Sidewinder's collar. "Please step right this way, suh. Would y'all care fo' some dessert now?"

Not waiting for a response, T-Rex zip-ties a black hood over Sidewinder's head with practiced ease. Their prisoner inhales dust, coughs, but is otherwise as complacent as someone resigned to flying coach.

Sidewinder thinks he's won. Good. Have to keep it that way.

Sienna looks around, checks everyone. It's been a decent op. Not a scratch on her people. No collateral damage. They got exactly what they came for. A damn near perfect mission. Her throat feels rough. *Damn desert air.*

"Listen up!" Sienna says. "Let's exfil this craphole, double-time!"

As Sienna steps outside, a burst of static makes her wince. It's Nightjar. That's never good. The best pilots act like limo drivers in Mickey Spillane novels, you hardly know they are there.

"Snakecharmer, this is Nightjar actual, we are engaged by hostiles. Stealth still thirty or forty percent non-functional. Fast

movers a few klicks off and trying to paint us. My orders are not to return fire under any circumstances..."

Then, the normally impassive pilot loses it.

"Oh, shank it! Get out of there. This shit is getting real!"

Sienna nods to Nobu. Her RTO replies, "Solid copy, Nightjar. Deploy countermeasures and jamming. We can exfil in 6-0 seconds. Snakecharmer, out."

"...and we can be broiled Spam in ten seconds if that doesn't work," the pilot mutters under his breath before he remembers to turn off his mic.

With a small motion in her HUD, Sienna indicates a move to pick up zone Bravo. It's a trickier spot for the copter, but more defensible if ground elements come looking for a fight. Sienna checks the RAPTEK. Magnetic fields feel like invisible squeeze balls in her palms.

The Dogs, their hood-wearing guest Sidewinder, and the wide-eyed girl move out. Sienna curses Denbow under her breath as she sees half their ride hanging in the air. Only for a second. Then the hovercopter veers off rapidly. The pilot dashes straight away from them. In confusion, the girl Anis lets out a small cry.

Sienna speaks Dari. She tells her the pilot is just playing a game and will come back shortly. *He better.*

Her visor shows what Nightjar is up to. The copter opens its engine vents wide. In thermal view, heat rays scatter against stars winking on the horizon. The trail leads away from the new pickup zone. Nightjar baits the oncoming jets. And gets fast mover love.

Two Khorasani birds, JF-17s or Eurofighters, come in low out of the horizon. Nightjar releases flares and metallic chaff.

Like some early-morning mirage on the horizon, Nightjar and his big old hovercopter disappear. Their pilot has closed the craft's heat sinks and veered off. Enemy missile mechBrains are completely taken in by the ruse. A string of orange and crimson pearls light up distant, dark hills, like match heads flaring one after the other.

Moving sideways and keeping the jammed open door at a downward angle, the dragonfly-agile craft returns.

"Gotta go, gotta go," Nightjar squawks. *"Fast movers coming in for another run."*

Wash from plasma nacelles rolls warmly through Sienna's and Anis's hair. They climb in. She scans the command console feeds. Nothing moves in the streets. Everyone knows what's happening and all are staying out of it. Had Sienna and the Dogs come in heavier with a bigger show of force, village elders might have taken it personally. In Khorasan, showing weakness means death. Here, warfare is life.

This is the land where, in 1842, British General Elphinstone led 16,000 into a valley pass. Days later only one European, a badly wounded surgeon, rode out. Sienna is glad not to have to engage motivated local ground fighters on their home turf. One less complication standing between her and getting her people back home from a messed-up world.

Denbow greets Sienna and the Dogs with a smug look. Their tagalong SEAL is way too pleased with himself, especially for someone whose screw-up nearly got him blown up by an air-to-air missile. He glances at the hooded Sidewinder, then goes back to looking at nothing in particular.

Sienna makes a mental note to sort Denbow out. Later.

Her job is getting her team to safe airspace and back to the *Lee*. After one stopover.

She taps Bryan's helmet.

"I got a full count. Plus trip package. Plus…" Sienna pauses a second, looking down. The girl has latched onto her leg, probably because she is the only one who speaks the local language. "Plus a humanitarian medical refugee."

"Strap in, everyone," Nightjar says calmly. *"Not only is half of my helo's stealth field offline, but my main hatchway will not close. Enjoy your flight!"*

Despite Bryan and Whitebread's muscle power and Nobu's tinkering, the doorway damaged by the errant bullet remains stuck open. Wind whistles through the cabin as the aircraft flies evasive patterns. Sienna learns that more hostile but untouchable local aircraft have joined the search for them. Thankfully, they are looking in the wrong direction. As long as their ride does not slow down, they will be fine.

Sienna walks into the cockpit. She has a short and intense chat with the pilots. It takes some convincing, but being a colonel with a direct line to top-tier command at the Pentagon has its perks. The aircraft quietly veers away from its direct course back to the *Lee*. They are now headed to a place on the coast which does not have a name on their maps. It is a small fishing village.

Inside the cabin, T-Rex stares at Snakelips's back. She leans sideways toward a seated Anis, making certain the five-point harness fits the small girl.

"Hey, woman," T-Rex says. "You got cooties."

"Rex," Snakelips says over her shoulder, "I've had just about enough—"

Nobu interjects. "For a change, Rex is right." Using a pair of metal throwing spikes like chopsticks, Nobu picks a baby scorpion off the back of the woman's vest. "Gratz Corporal!" he says, grinning at her. "It's a boy!"

Snakelips is out of her seatbelts in a flash. She scowls and shakes down her uniform. With the hatch stuck open and the copter maneuvering, she makes sure to keep a grip on the webbing behind the row of seats.

All we need, poisonous hitchhikers. Sienna looks sideways at Denbow. He's tucked into his corner, away from everyone, watching the show. Sienna says to the others, "Those things were all through the house. Everyone check yourselves and each other."

Nobu flicks the eight-legged stowaway out the open door.

"Not hungry?" T-Rex asks as he checks his friend's kit.

Sienna stands near a handhold on the other side of the wide central compartment. She feels something uncomfortable and prickling on her back and neck, like a throbbing and a tingling all at once.

No way it's a scorpion. It might be the gel adhesive of the RAPTEK. She's never worn it for so long. She ignores it. There's enough to think about. It'd be a misstep to reveal any weakness, even fear of stinging arachnids, in front of strangers. Denbow. Sidewinder. Even with his head covered by a blackout hood, the Khorasani thug seems to be staring right at her.

Everyone's keeping an eye on Denbow. Truth be told, the SEAL creeps her out just a little. She doesn't know exactly why. He's an arrogant blockhead, but outside of her own hand-picked team, there is no shortage of those in the military.

It's more. Since they re-boarded the copter, Denbow has

eyeballed all of them, including the hood-wearing Sidewinder. But he has not even glanced at the girl. Not even out of curiosity at an unexpected juvenile passenger accompanying the special operators home. Intentional disinterest? Probably nothing, just a feeling.

Speaking of which... That creeping clammy feeling on Sienna's back and arms really starts getting to her. It's hot and cold at the same time. It's probably sweat from the extra weight on her back. She cannot take it off with the hatch open. If this priceless hunk of DARPA hardware went whipping out into the dark rush just outside the door, she'd never hear the end of it.

She disregards the sources of irritation and walks over to where Anis sits strapped in her seat. Bryan catches her arm before she gets there. He whispers. Which is strange. Normally for covert communications he'd text her wrist unit. Unless he doesn't want a record in the system.

"Pilot's off course," Sarge tells her. Sienna should have figured he'd notice. Bryan's visual augments have some kind of built-in compass. "Said you ordered it."

Sienna coolly meets his questing, metallic-gold eyes. She does not even flinch in Sidewinder's direction. Denbow is straight-up staring at them. "I'll explain. Later," she tells him firmly. "I have to do something."

Sarge goes back to his seat.

The itching feeling on Sienna's back gets stronger. And stranger. It's all she can do not to reach under her flight suit and tug at the conductive gel. In a sec she'll go forward into the cockpit to remove the experimental weapon. This is no normal discomfort. It's like something that's not quite there yet. A memory of a sensation… one that's about to happen in the near future. Sienna flexes her back. She'll deal. And get this thing off. First she has to have a chat with the girl.

She kneels down and says in Dari, "Anis-chan, you okay?"

The girl with the strange eyes nods. Sienna takes off her own RFID dog tags and puts them around Anis's neck. Sienna tries to keep her hand steady. She feels like her own body is vibrating.

What the heck is it? An attack of hypothermia? In ninety-degree heat? She struggles to look composed so Anis won't be scared.

"Here," Sienna says, patting the dog tags down inside Anis's clothes. "Keep these on, always."

Sienna glances over at Sidewinder. His posture is upright and cocky. The murderous old scavenger has sharp ears.

"You have to go with some people for a while," Sienna says kindly, but firmly.

The girl looks a little confused and shoots a glance at the hooded prisoner. "But I want to stay with you."

Sienna cannot say any more. She wants to. She decides. She was wrong. *This is wrong. It's not worth it. The girl is scared. What was I thinking? I'll turn the copter back to the* Lee. *Once he's there, Sidewinder will talk. We'll get Asrah another way.*

Sienna wants to tell Anis she doesn't have to go anywhere she doesn't want to. That she's safe now. In her mind she holds the intercom button down and tells Nightjar to make for the *Lee* at best speed. But she cannot.

She really cannot say anything. With growing alarm, Sienna realizes her muscles are not doing what her brain tells them. Not a one of 'em. Her vision suddenly blots out, as though her visor—the one she's not wearing—has lost power. She's facing a big, dull, empty screen. The inside of the copter, heck, the whole world, has gone blank. No. Not quite blank. The huge orb right in front of her face will not budge.

Is that some kind of eye?

Sienna's vision snaps back on, but it's different now. It's more. In her new 360-degree periphery, Sienna can still see the copter cabin and the people in it. A girl looking at a woman. The woman has rad but impractical hair.

Oh yeah, that's me.

The girl is Anis. She seems more frightened now than when she was being held hostage with a knife to her neck. Anis starts to scream. Or just opens her mouth in silent astonishment at something. There is a sound and the Sienna who looks down at Colonel McKnight hears it: a high-pitched squeal made by her own skull vibrating a million times a second.

Sienna fights hard against blacking out. She tries to keep her remote body upright. A fainting spell in front of Denbow. *That would suck mightily.* Sienna is a puppeteer in the roof of the hovercopter cabin, looking down, willing Colonel McKnight's body not to collapse. She's definitely having an out-of-body hallucination while feeling everything.

Sienna is kind of glad the feet of her body are frozen in place, as if by some kind of electric current holding her not just to the metal floor of the copter, but in a separate pocket of space which just happens to be traveling at a hundred miles per hour in the same direction as the aircraft. Sienna finds herself seeing too much. Too suddenly. She can see from a dozen angles. And it's damn strange.

With an undramatic burst of brain static, the big 360

perception of many views collapses into one. Now Sienna finds her consciousness on a precarious perch on the back of her own right shoulder. She's a tiny thing standing on Colonel McKnight, near the tattoo of a yellow rose. She sees through the vision of a creature whose entire body carapace is an infrared sensor. A creature about half as long as her index finger. A scorpion. The one from the interrogation room. Calmly, as an arachnid would, Sienna sees through the ten eyes of the scorpion and observes that there is a fire. Coming out of Colonel McKnight's body.

Blue-white glowing fire spews a pulsating aurora up and out of her uniform. To her mind, it is an electric dawn as she sees her old world through the new eyes of the arachnid. From a distant point where logic holds truths, her intellect warns her the only rational explanation is the copter's plasma jets have malfunctioned and turned the cabin into a blast furnace.

Sienna tells her intellect to *shut the hell up*. Colonel McKnight's body is the only thing on fire and the flames feel like a cool breeze. Sienna is still connected to her drifting, floating body with eight spiny, gripping, night-vision-seeing legs. Skin and the fat underneath is not crisping, charring, or vaporizing. Not yet.

Next, reason tells her the cool fire bursting out of her could be some atmospheric effect, coronal plasma discharge. St. Elmo's fire. A strange combination of the malfunctioning stealth field and ionizing atmospherics could have created for Colonel McKnight's body a cocoon of corrugated light.

It really is all *her*. At some point in time, time, which is becoming a more meaningless measure by the...

Sienna tries to clear her head. Hard to do because she's

looking at the back of her head from the outside. One thing she's pretty convinced of: St. Elmo's fire does not lift things into the air. And that's what the unknown effect starts doing to her. Colonel McKnight levitates in the wide-body cabin of the hovercopter. If no one else saw the human spark plug thing she was doing, this they gotta notice.

They do. The last thing she experiences of this suddenly unreal real world are Anis's small hands reaching out to her. Other, larger hands, maybe Bryan's or Whitebread's, also try to grab her. These only propel her faster toward the open hatch. Her private, tiny cosmos obeys an exclusive inertia. She drifts. Sienna, the mind of a woman hitchhiking on the scorpion, the scorpion hitchhiking on the body of woman, and that woman bathed in a snug green-blue aurora, all drift into the rush of dark air framed by the gaping doorway.

Sienna falls into darkness, and she dreams.

Ever dream you were falling?

What if you really were

Falling

Into an endless blackness

What then

would you dream of?

22

INSIDE A DREAM OF FALLING
ABOVE THE WANDERING DESERT

A DAUGHTER

The dark brick wall of wind hits them like a ton of downy feathers. Still traveling, they are in freefall.

The scorpion is the first to recover his wits. He tests the air. Clean. He inhales for the first time in an hour. He bids goodbye to the big, noisy hot-bodies and their moving caves that spew foul air. With eight legs, he pushes off.

A daughter's body frets with gravity and drifts down.

A daughter's mind follows.

***

She is returned by the sky to this land. Not even knowing her own name yet, she knows this. Long departed, grown and changed, but remembered. Here. Remembered for innocence annihilated, blessings of purest hate bestowed through jagged iron's kiss. Remembered here by taste of unborn blood, rain adulterated, sand savored, ceded and accepted as sacrifice, all a lifetime and a stony pulse-beat ago. She falls now, back to the place of her first tenuous birth, pulled in, pulled down, by a force stranger and filled with more mystery than fate.

A daughter comes home to be reborn. And she will be.

When she wakes.

Until then, she dreams of falling and relearns stories as they are whispered to her by wraiths of dusk and sand.

***

A daughter falls like a single raindrop, one trailing comet fire. Reaching up for her is a miles-wide embrace. It makes her feel small, and find herself as part of everything that almost exists.

A decades-quiet part of her mind gains a voice. Truths rise like the fruit of millions of seeds lying dormant under desert sands. After a rain, silvery-green tasseled grasses will sprout and rise and sway with each gyre of warm air. A daughter can feel each new sprouted grass blade as its seed's promise in the future. This promise holds through a thousand generations.

***

With a dash, their downward momentum stops. She rolls down a hillside bedded by windblown dunes and bounded by sharp rocks. Cuts open. She bleeds a quiet greeting. Her throat coughs out sand. She tastes the earth and breathes.

She receives the land's ferocious welcome. One for a daughter who has returned. It watches her and knows her. She feels the land smile.

***

Older than names of nations, older than the tribes. This roving desert is littered with the carcasses of war machines. Naked, rusting ribcages thrust up through dust, remains of titanic battles no one remembers.

Still, this land has not had its fill.

Its appetite is endless.

***

People.

The scorpion senses them. With a flick of his stinger and a droplet of venom, he severs their last tie. A daughter is on her own.

They come, attracted by the strange light of the slow-falling comet.

Closer now, she sees their lives. Sees their factions fight, infants swaddled in dusty rags, flies buzzing and landing and breeding. Fires tended behind thick-walled houses send smoke into a hard blue sky. Old men drink tea and talk and stare out at an unflinching horizon.

She sees herself among them. They should be frightened.

***

They collect a rag doll and drag her off. A daughter's mind follows. The men, indeed, are frightened. Not of her. They offer their prize to a white-beard whose scarred hands clutch an ironwood staff. It is decorated with the skull fragments of his enemies. Wraiths whisper his name—it has no substance where she is, the name of the white-beard.

He recognizes the remains of her uniform and decides to add her to his living inventory. Because she is a foreigner, she's to be given the largest cell. He has a notion of inviting debased opium lords and greedy Jamiates to view and bid on her. Too early for business thoughts. Time for tea at his eldest son's house.

The limp body of a daughter gets carried and dragged. Executions of the defiant and unransomed have left many vacancies in the white-beard's underground prison. From one cell comes shuffling and faint wheezing. From another, lacerated, prayer-like muttering seeps through mold-crusted grating.

They toss her in.

Where her head and shoulders hit the floor, where shackles latch on tight, new bruises swell and rise. She will feel them later.

For now, she is a weightless shadow. Alone with herself. A memory draws her. It pulls a daughter on a journey no human mind can take.

**

Out where her body is, words are being spoken at her. The pauses between syllables might last a day. She has time.

**

There are four spaces in front of her. The same number of

chambers that make up the human heart. Three atriums hold things for a daughter to see. The fourth is the unpast and nonfuture. She must choose.

She chooses all of them.

She has been and is in all of these places. In order to again become for herself and for those in the life which awaits: daughter, leader, friend, warrior, lover, protector, she must find things in this maze. The four rooms in front of her hold who a daughter was and who she will be. The journey's end is understanding.

With her mind, she steps forward.

***

The first atrium is peacefully dim. She is alone, but not isolated. Two hearts beat. This is a pre-birth memory. Everything she studied about physiology and psychology dictate it should not exist. Yet it does. It exists with a simple certainty and clarity that she cannot deny, as much as she might want to.

Because if she could deny it, she could stop the shattering violation that takes place next. The one that forms the inner core of this first impossible memory. The tranquil darkness in which her unborn body floats is torn asunder by a merciless invader. Cold and sharp, it cuts through her world and her body. Once, twice, three times, then again and again, leaving bright daggers of terrible pain, like flashes of lightning seared onto eyes that have yet to open for the first time. The pain threatens to tear a scream out of lungs which have never drawn breath. Ragged cuts leave her small body floating in her own blood. Red rivulets mix with her mother's. And a tiny heart pumps faster and faster in distress, each beat having less fluid to push than the last.

Infant heartbeats become a rush of thunder and air. She must go. She must!

The image of an animal's five terrible claws is etched in her mind. Images that match wounds on her body. Wounds she will be born with and which will form the scars she will carry forever. In those few moments, a scripture of earnest pain, true hurt, and undying hate is inscribed upon her body. And she has yet to be born.

She wants to leave this place. But she cannot, truly. This place is her. She can only live within its confines. But they are as large as mind and spirit can make them. Practice and faith and discipline and love have made its frontiers large.

She moves on to the next chamber.

***

Words are being spoken. The pauses between syllables might last hours. She has time.

***

The infant who was dying in her mother's womb is alone. Really alone now. Out. She tries to cry with sodden lungs. She is too weak to open her eyes. She can hear only one heartbeat. Weak. Failing. Hers. The other is separated from her, though she feels slickly covered with that heart's last issuance of blood.

She is newborn. Trying to see, unseeing. She is surrounded by air. She wants to breathe in, unbreathing. She is new to life, unmoving. Dying.

Years from now, a girl will run soap-wet fingers over her own scars. A young woman will read them with her touch and yearn to feel the history they hold. What is new is the clarity this unique seeing gives a daughter who has returned. For the first time, she sees she was not born alone. For the first time, she discerns the other. Her vǫrthr, her racht. She witnesses the precise moment it clambered aboard an unborn girl.

Rust-corrupted iron delivered pain and wounds. And more. This rough blade infixed the other. So intense was Scythe's frenzy, so receptive her unborn mind, it passed into her. The coiled passenger crawled across a gangplank of warped metal to board a tiny vessel of bleeding flesh.

As a daughter watches the past unfold, the dark spark sliver wriggles into the cozy space of her most ancient brain. No sooner has the partitioned segment of the distal tendril taken root than it finds itself insulted. This vestige spark feels its tiny infant host dying.

For the first time, she sees the other's essence. It is made up of a few twitching ethereal nerve cells. Her vǫrthr is a strange life form. Its embodiment is quantum resonance dermis sloughed off from a severed tentacle of an incomprehensibly vast being. A master parasite mind which eons ago tore itself into existence.

This other was injected into her through the five wounds on her body. This shade of a shade of a brutal, disembodied consciousness cannot leave its host. It is trapped within a newborn. The other senses her weakness. It is disgusted.

With the reflex convulsion of the cut tip of a snake's tail thrown into simmering coals, it gives her a selfish gift. From the cold, deep pillars of the universe, it speaks to her, the newborn daughter. A soundless word no conscious human mind could ever understand reverberates inside the torn body of an orphan girl lying unmoving above the blood-stained plastic floor of a combat hospital on the edge of the Wandering Desert.

Hate.

The cold vibration pulses out from the dark passenger. The giver serves only itself, according to its nature. These vibrations are the only evidence this other is alive and has a frightful will to stay that way. It lends its stark life force to the alien child.

It gives her the energy and the will to sustain life when no other human could have survived. Through this twisted miracle, an infant girl endures. They are born together. It will become known to her as her racht, which means "sudden surge" in a language she never learned.

Tháinig racht feirge uirthi, bhuail taom feirge í.

Through this rancid mercy, a daughter lives. Just long enough for caring, skilled hands to sew up terrible wounds and fill veins with enough blood for a tiny heart to pump. She moves. She breathes. She opens her eyes and looks into the face of someone she will soon recognize as Theodora McKnight.

***

The second chamber fades. She is Sienna Iðunn McKnight, daughter of Hamida, Theodora, and Annalies.

***

Words spoken. Pauses last minutes. She has time.

***

SIENNA

The third chamber envelops Sienna's mind. This one is not memories. At least if these are memories, they are not her own. Sienna considers them ideas, images recorded by a far-seeing eye.

They confuse her. The knowledge they hold has no reference to any time or place she knows. Her practical mind struggles to find something real, something she can use in the fight that awaits her the moment she decides to awake and face the critter who holds her actual head under real, wet, drowning water. Her body's mundane needs, like breathing, must wait. Sienna needs to sort this. Here, in this between.

The most rhythmic and, indeed, prettiest images in this third atrium coalesce first. A ballerina in front of a mirror. No. These are two dancers—twins, definitely twins. Their grace is only exceeded by their speed. A variation is completed before a hummingbird's wing has time to thrum a single beat. Glittering back at her with four cat eyes, the white-clad twins twirl. Red drops fling at her from elongated needle-nails.

Before these strike her face, Sienna blinks. The pair are gone.

Next, out of time and out of place, comes a rolling cloud. But no cloud ever hugged the ground so greedily. No storm ever spread from horizon to horizon like this enshrouding mass. It moves like a smoke cliff miles high. It obliterates the horizon and has no end. For it is its own end. From the midst of the undulating blackness comes a five-taloned demon. Metal-clad bone spikes hew down, down through rock armor into loamy earth. Above those terrible claws hang eyes that tear into her own with their gaze. They are a screeching nothingness that sees all in their own image.

With an effort, she turns away toward the final coherent image of this atrium. Three modest, curved horns crown a stone devil. He leers. Not exactly. He does not leer, he stares. His face is unable to reflect the kindness he harbors inside his stony chest. Despite the sharpness of alligator teeth overflowing his broad mouth, Sienna is not afraid. Quite the opposite. Somehow she feels the impulse to pity him, though she cannot even guess why that might be.

Gentle eyes of agate search hers. The round stones are polished so brightly they seem to be wet with tears. This peaceful demon spreads wings which were hidden behind his back. Just as she has the impulse to ask him to take her with him, he simply vanishes.

She is left alone in a hall of mirrors that have run out of things to reflect. Sienna leaves the place she made by wishing it away.

***

BETWEEN A DREAM AND SURFACING

Sienna approaches the realm of sense. A shimmering membrane bounds a fourth and final atrium. It is the last step before wakefulness and the world she must return to. The water surrounding her head is there. Her need to inhale her next breath looms there. She decides she *does* want to go back. Despite the pain. Despite the impending misery intended for her.

She has many things to do, many things to put right and something important to say. Something to tell the idiot whose grip on her hair feels like it is pulling her scalp off. The one who holds her head under some kind of putrid goop. It makes her retch and heave as much as fight not to drown.

The ephemeral wall rushes toward Sienna. The bleak promise of this place assaults her reawakening mind. There is physical pain, blood-pounding breathlessness, and the looming threats of madness and violent death. It is familiar. This place she can understand and accept. Arriving here is like coming home.

Sienna's hands are bound. She is in some form of hostile captivity. She expects the people who have her prisoner to be proud of their skills in humiliation and torture. Who are they? Doesn't matter. They cannot hurt her.

Sienna McKnight has a high tolerance for pain. Perhaps it's natural. There is a pain scale medics often ask patients to use to rate their level of discomfort after some injury or illness. The highest she's ever admitted to has been a seven. Once when she was a girl messing around on a Green Beret obstacle course on the Base, she fell. The wrenching, twisting impact resulted in the compound fracture of her shin. Jagged, curious pieces of bone came poking through the tanned skin a few inches under her kneecap. It was not something you could rub dirt on and walk off. Her main sources of distress at the time had been fear of being banned from the obstacle course and not wanting to upset her widowed mom with the sight of the injury. Theodora McKnight had been the Army's top trauma surgeon. She was the one who was used to blood. But she was gone. Pain-wise, teenage Sienna's broken shin was only that. A seven. No more.

The men out there, at least two, waiting for her just across the boundary of consciousness, they cannot hurt her.

She is tough and resilient. Sarge Bryan enlisted a knife-fighting tutor. A tortured madman, who lived in the North Carolina woods, ate roadkill, and shaved his face with broken glass. From him, she learned how to take a beating. They cannot break her. She has been taught she can always find a way to win.

But there is a more essential reason why her current captors' attempts to inflict soul-crushing torment upon her will fail. Their petty tortures are something she was born immunized against. As the sun blots out the light of any earthly candle, the hurt she suffered at the hands of the Five-clawed Beast, a true master of anguish, these will surely drown out the persecutions of any aspiring sadist. As she finds her way back, this one thing is certain.

The ones waiting for her up there cannot hurt her. Silently, Sienna's reawakening mind tells them why.

You don't know how.

23

MARCH 20
SIX HILLS VILLAGE
KHORASAN

What Sienna's captors can do is curse. She returns to the realm of her own bruised and battered senses. Sounds gain meaning. Nagging from an abusive alarm clock prods her toward wakefulness.

"Upeeech!"

"Upeeech!"

Words are grubby sonic puffs heard through sodden eardrums. Her head gets pulled up. Her hair is bunched inside the vise grip of a big fist. Snorting and coughing nasty liquid, she draws in the air her lungs are burning for.

"I said for you to wake up," a man says. "Beeeatch!" He has a very distinct accent.

Sienna blinks and tries to shake her eyes clear. One is swollen. The other works okay, assuming the light here is lousy. She gets a first look at her tormenter.

This, this here must be real. Not in my wildest dreams could I make up a stupid-lookin' piece of crap like him.

By speaking, he's already told Sienna where he's from. And his status as an outlander in Khorasan. Her captor's place in the local food chain? Near the bottom.

Snips of memories jab at her like a damaged camcorder she can't turn off. She tries to piece together what happened. Some sequence of events after the fall from the hovercopter didn't kill her.

That last bit, that will take more figuring.

Though she's been treated to more than enough moisture in the wide bucket, her lips feel dry and cracked. A tongue, hers, thick and fuzzy, fills her mouth.

And who is this guy calling bitch?

She hacks out slimy water. Her windpipe makes sounds.

"Hey, bud," she wheezes. "To you, that's *Colonel* Bit—"

That may not have been the best howdy. With reactions faster than you'd expect from a man with a protruding gut and bleary, dissipated gaze, the man from the Chechen Republic grabs her jaw. Compared to her face, his hand is large. Two dirty fingers jam into her mouth. Unfortunately, not at a very good angle to bite. Sienna gives up the idea. Let them think she's only making a show of defiance.

Two fingers are the least you're going to lose when I get loose. If I get loose.

Her neck torques sideways. She squints at manacles on her wrists. Chains latch them to the floor. Suitable for restraining a bull camel. The reality of confinement slams home.

How the heck am I gonna get loose?

The Chechen's fingers slither out of her mouth and find a better grip on her neck. She tries to mock her tormenter with a devil-may-care grin. With her swollen features, it's probably only a grimace with a slightly protruding tongue. Her audience reacts as expected, with a snarl of outrage and a tightening of thick fingers.

"Ha!" Slack lips smack over splayed, rotten teeth. "Heih, Ghazan. She has up wake."

The first thing that hits her as her senses come back is the tomblike rankness of the air. It's mixed with the body and breath smells of the guy holding her. He pulls her head up. She gets a better look around the small cinderblock room.

Judging by the wall undulations, she's in a basement. Rock and sand, the creeping bowels of the Wandering Desert, move like thorax segments of a vast thing alive. They press in on the man-made cavern. For some dumb reason she thinks she can perceive the movement of the earth.

Boy, that fall must have rung my bell.

The Chechen looms closer. Goo drips from her hair into swollen lips. They won't close right. Inner-ear vertigo spins the room. Sienna fights to keep from vomiting.

"I don't know how you do," the Chechen growls. "But in my country, this is how we salute bullshitting bullshit Colonel!"

The second thing that hits her is the Chechen's fist.

Sienna can feel her assailant's body tense as he brings his hands together like an overgrown monkey playing cymbals. Her head makes a lousy instrument. The sodden *thwock* sound would add nothing to the percussion element of the little three-piece band they could have going. As the leader of misery's orchestra, the Chechen has his own rhythm. Sienna braces herself for another gut-wrenching impact. In the moment her eyes focus, she scans the other side of the dark room.

No other prisoners. Not here, anyway.

None of her people are here. Her team got away. These

mooks tend to group captives. They beat the crap out of one, hoping bravery or cowardice will get others to talk. Just being dead did not get you any slack time. They will pull KIA soldiers' bodies in, mutilate them, and leave them in prisoners' cells.

There's the Chechen drummer and another, thinner guy. Her vision clears during the rest in the music featuring her jaw and cheekbone. She makes out a college-aged man wearing spectacles. Ghazan. He sits on a bench near a partly disassembled AK-47. Unlike his buddy, Ghazan could be local. The way he shaves the sides of his beard and the flimsy look of his wire-rimmed glasses make Sienna think of someone more at home in a student lounge than a torture chamber.

"Rasul, a moment, comrade, please," Ghazan says. "What are you doing? She has just come round. Would you send her to sleep again? Artuk said watch her, not beat her unconscious."

He speaks English. And is way too polite for his job. Sienna's ear for languages in this part of the world is good enough to recognize a distinct Pashtun accent. Definitely local, likely from an upper-class family. Ghazan's vowel intonation reminds her of France, the real one, not the fake one in Canada.

Reluctantly, Rasul releases her hair. Sienna's head droops. On the muck-crusted floor lies the body of a mouse, explosively disemboweled, boot heel stamped on matted gray fur.

Have to call housekeeping about that.

She had been half expecting to wake up in the med bay of the aircraft carrier. But unless the Navy has really changed the décor and staff…

Last thing Sienna can recall, the copter was taking fire. They were being pursued. Airspeed must have been over 100 knots. Somehow, she's nearly in one piece.

Bryan must be trying to mount a rescue. But her dog tags and their homing chip are not around her neck. They are somewhere more important. It is a damn big desert to find something the locals want to keep hidden. Outside assistance is not likely. This mess she's gotten herself into—she's got to get herself out of it. Somehow.

Maybe it is all my fault. Maybe I deserve this. I lied and cheated to make the Sidewinder mission happen. And worse, when offered a deal by a devil, I shook his hand.

Sienna inhales through one side of her mouth. The deeper breath sparks deeper pains in her ribcage. She stays hunched over. Past the mouse corpse, a shallow gutter runs along the wall. It empties into a larger runnel in the hallway. The way out. She pushes doubts and recrimination out of her mind. Those thoughts have no place here on the edge of the fight for survival.

Sienna's mouth is freshly bloody. Little drips, black colored in the stark shadows, fall into the bucket. She peers in. The viscous oval ripples and morphs. Sienna's reflection twists in the murky water.

Her knees grind numbly into the stone floor. Sienna absorbs the pain. Pretending to writhe and whimper in discomfort, she angles this way and that. Bit by bit, she gets circulation and feeling back into her lower limbs. She'll need those lower limbs if there is any chance to escape. She systematically takes in the throbbing from various parts of her body, including her jaw, where the Chechen laid a good one on her. Something in her cheek feels squishy and loose.

No biggie, I have premium O-6 dental now. Main thing, nothing critical is broken or dislocated. I'm not getting dizzier

or blacking out. Serious internal bleeding likely not happening.
Sweet!

Now if I could just get moved to a room with a view. Too
bad it's only in movies they leave high-value prisoners alone.

Along with pain and poor hospitality, Sienna soaks up as
much knowledge as she can. These two are not hard to figure
out. Chechen Rasul sulks against the far wall. Having been
asked to stop striking their captive with blunt objects and
refrain from drowning her in sewage, he is at wit's end. On
a bench sits what looks to be a genuine Kalashnikov rifle, a
true classic. It's partially disassembled to clean out desert grit.
Rasul pretends to wipe down the worn, greasy parts and waits
to be allowed to continue his pastime. That's all she is to him,
a rag doll that makes gratifying sounds when you damage it.

Ghazan is local, at least in appearance. From his grooming
and general manners she concludes Ghazan's parents had
money, enough to send him to a foreign school. That must
have been a shock for him. Leaving a place where everyone
bowed and scraped in front of him and his family to live in
a European metropolis. In Paris or Lyons, Ghazan was likely
looked at as being one step above a migrant camel herder.

Sienna glowers at him through her hair.

That Pashtun boy picked the worst possible way to get his
self-respect back.

The younger guy fidgets. Ghazan can't decide between
standing or squatting down to be eye level with her. He leans
in awkwardly, studying her without enthusiasm. He probably
expected his life as a "freedom fighter" to be more enriching.

Ghazan's folks don't know where he is. Maybe he told
them he was going on leave from university to find spiritual

enlightenment in India. In reality, he has paid the Chechen to hook him up with the local Khorasani warlord, this Artuk guy. The one who told them to watch her but not beat her too badly. Ghazan expected to take part in a few easy, victorious battles and do his fair share of sport killing at terrorist summer camp.

But Khorasan is full of killers, all better at it than foreign newcomers. Holiday terrorists are valued for their cash contributions, little else. All Ghazan ended up doing was hauling water and guarding the few worthless prisoners in this reeking hell-hole of an underground jail. Before she dropped in, Ghazan was well on his way to realizing he was again a wretched outcast.

By the flickering light panel taped to the wall, she can see a glint in Ghazan's eyes. Sienna is struck by a realization. She, her body, her dignity, her stubborn existence, have become his pathway to imagined glory. And Ghazan is not about to tread lightly.

"You." His voice low, he inches closer. "You kidnapped the great leader. Then you fell. You have no uniform, no identification, making you a *spy*. We can do as we like to you."

Sienna stirs, her chains rattle. Ghazan shrinks back. He checks to make sure she is still bound firmly. For all his desire to seek redemption through inflicting pain and death, the slender man wants to be absolutely sure that no injury can come to him.

Trying his best to be intimidating, Ghazan snarls from a safe distance, "You will tell us where he is!"

Sienna tries to project cold flintiness from a face which is surely lopsided by swelling.

"Oh yeah, him…" she slurs. Sidewinder. The great leader. *What a joke … What a …*

The room tilts like a flight simulation she's just screwed up. Jumbled thoughts, images, sounds, sensations fight to cram to the front of her brain like passengers exiting a crowded bus. The helicopter, the little girl, something wrong with the RAPTEK on her back. She tried to get it off; her limbs were frozen. Then floating, weightless, even before falling out into the dark rushing wall of hurricane-force wind. Freefall.

She shakes her head, as if inside there's some kind of ball-bearing maze puzzle and flipping it at just the right angle could solve it. All she gets is blood pumping through eardrums, slamming home the irony: it was only a few hours ago—*it has to be hours*—that she and the Dogs were taking prisoners and she was asking the questions.

I must be underground. Not deep, though.

On the far side wall are fungus and condensation. The floor slopes. The structure is set into a rise or small hill. Very hard to detect. A platoon could walk right by and never know she's there. Next, she figures what tactic to use against her interrogators.

Ghazan, the college boy who switched his major to terrorism and kidnapping, gets tired of her stalling by drooling blood bubbles. "Well? Do you need another wake-up call from my friend?"

The Pashtun thinks he's some kind of intellectual, a Che Guevara of the desert steppes. If she can get him angry, he might make a mistake. The sloppiness of amateur rage, not much use to her while she is chained and unarmed. Later, who knows?

Sienna replies slowly, as though she's been settled into a beaten-down stupor. She emphasizes her North Carolina accent.

"Last time I saw your great leader, he was doing fine." Sienna does not look up. "He had a real powerful sense of self-preservation, if y'all git mah drift. He's probably havin' drinks on a beach somewhere, rattin' out everyone he ever knew. Including this place."

Notwithstanding swelling cheek and jaw—and hair recently given a conditioning rinse with sewage—she tries to project sullen confidence. "Y'all won't even hear the Stymph drones comin'."

If ever a place needed a peppering of cluster bombs.

Of course, they'd blow her and the other prisoners up as well. It would be nearly worth it. "Naw, you won't hear a thing. You'll just experience a whole lotta deadness. That's what you'll do."

But there will be no rescue. No drones are coming. There was no provision for large-scale search and rescue in the official Sidewinder mission plan. In her haste and arrogance she'd seen to that. The profile was strictly slash and dash. The price tag of her screw-up is being in here with these two guys and the bag of rotting goat guts they must have hidden.

"Pay attention, you ignorant woman! You will tell us who has him."

Sienna feels Ghazan's smaller hand grab her. He's imitating what he's seen his torture sensei Rasul do. This fellow has been watching too many old cop shows where roughing up the suspect actually works. Judging by his accent, they could even have been French ones, which can get pretty darn violent.

At least the Chechen doesn't make any pretense at having moral superiority or a greater mission. Hurting people simply brightens his day.

After each question, Ghazan's thin, bony hand slaps Sienna's head.

"Americans?" *Slap.*

"Zionists?" *Slap.*

"Russians?" *Slap.*

"Saudis?" *Slap.*

The amateur geographer tries his best to give her a world tour of pain. She snaps back to the singular flash of blue light into which her previous reality had vanished. Maybe the RAPTEK power shorted out. Whatever it was, she did it to herself. If they'd only kept course straight for the *Lee*, it wouldn't have happened at all.

Ghazan rocks backward on his heels and nurses his aching hand. "You think you are better than us? I went to the Sorbonne in France. I am educated. I left to follow higher laws. To become a fighter for ideals greater than your pathetic rights and freedoms."

He's just given Sienna more intel on himself than he's ever going to get out of her.

"Well, I didn't go to no Bon-bonne college," she says. "But I do know somethin'. And I knows it real strong. The one thing that gives me the edge."

"Ha!" Ghazan pokes Rasul. The Chechen seems to be dozing. "And what is that?"

From under her mass of filthy hair, she fixes him with a gaze that seems to heat up her own eye sockets. "You'll kill anyone," Sienna tells him. "I'm just gonna kill you."

Ghazan's pupils dilate even more in the dim light. Instinct tells him to be afraid. He's never been threatened quite like that, certainly not by a bound prisoner, a female one at that. Then, reason lulls him back into confidence.

You should have gone with your instincts, bud.

Ghazan looks at the bored Chechen. "Hey, I suppose that means you, too, Rasul." He laughs nervously. "Do you feel the danger? Do you feel maybe we should let her go? Save ourselves?"

Ghazan takes a swig of water and smacks his lips. "This is the sort of farce that happens when they send peasants to battle the blessed elite." He leans even closer. Oral hygiene is a sacrifice he is making for the cause.

"As soon as you are no longer useful, then we are going to make a movie." He reaches into his shirt pocket and pulls out a video recorder. "Maybe it does not win any prizes at Festival de Cannes. Heh. But my people will give it, how do you say? Five stars."

Sienna's prepared; she's made herself ready. But thoughts of sadistic execution videos go through her mind and nearly bring her to the edge of the pit of despair.

Sarge Bryan, Annalies...

"Now, how did you say you were going to kill us?"

24

Sienna does not respond. The gulf between her and them is too wide. They think they know about hate. For them it's something learned. They were each taught their particular brand. Its power helped them fill some void. The thuggish oaf Rasul. The out-of-place Ghazan. After they had enough of Khorasan they could leave. She is different. There is nothing between her and them. Nothing to say.

Her silence makes them laugh. The cinderblock rectangle echoes with mirth, as hollow as dried bones, emptied of marrow. Ghazan's bluffing. He won't do anything until he's told.

Tumblers clank. The door and the lock set are not rusty. Both are new. Brushed stainless steel. She'll need the key or have to ask someone real nicely to open it when she checks out.

The man who enters is different. He carries his weapon on lean shoulders, like it's part of his body. One of the local fighters. He prowls like a voracious sand lynx next to two domestic house cats with a poor attitude.

His face causes images to burst through Sienna's mind:

six gently sloping hills,

a burnished cane of ironwood with more than a few skull splinters in it,

and something vast that understands her completely. She can feel it stir... the earth.

McKnight! Snap to! You're still on the Army's clock. Hallucinate crazy shit on your own time. Sienna obeys. Her head creaks sideways on swollen neck joints.

The village fighter looks at her, at Ghazan, at Rasul, then back at her. He closes the door and locks it from the outside. Sienna gets a glimpse of her third guard. In the corridor is a guy with a really round, shaved head. He could be the dullard brother of the village fighter. They've put outsiders in with her and put a trusted man, Round Head, in place to watch all of them. Smart. Cautious. Dangerous. The real threat is not down here with her but up in the streets of this charming little hamlet.

Her hosts clam up. Sienna looks to the only source of daylight. Crossbars block ports along the top of the far wall. Sienna cannot consider them windows. There is no way she could ever crawl out through them, even if they starve her down to the size of a supermodel. Adding to the ambiance, dark plastic has been taped over these.

Sounds carry down from what must be the main drag. Several well-tuned vehicles arrive. Nobu might have been able to suss out the make and model. Her radio operator spends enough time immersed in games like *Road Rage Cataclysm V*. She can only tell they are SUVs. High-end civilian ones, not local military.

Tires kick up sufficient wind and dust to blow in the plastic sheets covering the grates. Ghazan takes a good blast of grit and starts coughing like he's been hit with mustard gas. The goof gags for a full thirty seconds. A blob of snot ends up on the skanky beard he's been trying hard to grow. Despite her pains and more pressing items on her to-do list, Sienna thinks it would be nice to have that little video recorder just then. *Khorasan's Funniest Terrorist Videos* would have a new star.

Sienna gains a narrow view of the street. By the angle of the sun, she gauges compass directions and time of day. The newcomers decide to park with their backs to what is likely the sturdiest building in town—her jail.

Rasul looks up suspiciously. He does not understand much local Persian. The Chechen does get that his position as a foreigner is tenuous. He brought Ghazan here for a fee and now has nowhere to go, if the villagers let him leave at all. Rasul's main fear is that the college dropout's money runs out and Ghazan is seen as more valuable locked inside a cell awaiting his own ransom. Rasul has no currency value. As soon as he appears useless to Artuk, a peckish sand lynx might be gnawing dinner off a thick Chechen skull.

A voice speaking clipped Dari comes through the grates. "Master Artuk." The guy sounds arrogant and is likely the leader of the visiting group. "I bring greetings and blessings from 'one who is known.'"

Sienna watches through the gutter-style openings. A second set of feet, in dusty leather shoes, walks up to the man in the new desert boots. A walking stick *poks* along. Below frayed pants legs, tanned skin covers sturdy ankles. Artuk.

Sienna can just make out the opposite roof. On it, a

local gunman adjusts position. He does not sight in on the newcomers. That's as cordial a greeting as anyone can expect in these parts. Below the gunman, the sign of the silversmith's shop rattles. Heavy, rolling shutters slam down. The most prudent businessman in town locks up, just in case. The back room of that shop has tools which could pry apart her chains.

The local chieftain stands a moment, sizing up the situation that has rolled into his town. Finally he says, "Khalid-ban, your presence honors us. Let us have tea in my son's house and discuss what brings you all this way."

Artuk does not sound honored at all. He uses the local diminutive "ban." That's appropriate when you're talking to a shopkeeper's assistant.

Ghazan understands most of what's being said. He is too distracted to think of sticking her head back in the bucket. Sienna drinks in every scrap of information. Anything can be useful.

"This will not take long, honored grandfather," says Khalid. "You have something that has *fallen* to your hands but belongs to one who is known. I have come to retrieve it, in this." Khalid drops an empty leather carry bag. "While our mudarris owns this item, he has decided to allow you some compensation for keeping it safe."

Another satchel falls to Khalid's feet. This one is not empty. Artuk prods it with his walking stick. A multicolored bank note flutters over the edge.

Sienna's grip on her chains tightens. Not just because a generous offer is being made for her by a motivated buyer. The new guy, Khalid, said "mudarris," an Arabic term meaning teacher. It is sometimes used as a cover name by despicable evildoers. One in particular. Must be a coincidence. Judging by her bruises and state of dehydration, she's only been here a few hours. There's no way *Scythe* could know where she is.

On the other hand, it looks like she has other fans. The empty bag sports a snowflake-shaped button next to the fancy label. It has a self-chilling cryo mechanism. They sell knock-off versions on late-night shopping channels. These bags are for housewives who want to look stylish. They keep meat and fish cold, even on a hot day. This one looks to be an authentic fashion item. It is just the right size for stashing and delivering a human head. Who would show up so soon with a small fortune and a designer decapitation tote bag?

In his arrogance, Khalid has made a huge mistake. He's shown the lean, hungry men of the village a bag of money. Artuk and his men surely count it as theirs no matter what happens. If some of them have to die to get it, so be it. The only question is, how much more does Khalid have for the local sand cats to take?

Sienna watches the two men's feet. Khalid's boots stand solid, cautiously tense, not jumpy. Artuk shifts his weight from left to right and back again, like he's uncomfortable with newcomers being so close to the cell holding his most valuable commodity.

If Artuk is the sneak she hopes, he'll try to move her to increase his negotiating position. Once Khalid finds himself outmanned five or six to one and the package he came for spirited away to some hole in the hills, then the real negotiations will begin. To move her, they'll have to unchain her. *Could be my chance!* Greed and violence to the rescue.

Artuk convinces Khalid to have some tea and discuss

their business off the common streets. The new guys look intimidating. They are better armed, with at least one crew-serviced heavy weapon. Judging by how the second SUV rides low on its shocks, this could be a .50 cal or a Dushka 1938. Even so, the newbies are at an overwhelming disadvantage.

"You must see the Russian samovar in my son's house," Artuk says with pride as he and Khalid walk away. "Its operation is quite complex. As a young man, I asked the general in whose camp I found it to explain its workings more than once before I cut his throat."

Sienna's throat feels seriously parched. There is a plastic water bottle next to the disassembled AK. But neither Rasul nor Ghazan have thought to torture her by pretending to offer her a drink not containing urine.

The most pointed of her pains, strangely, is the hard clamping on her wrists. The chains are new. The big shackles are old and encrusted with enough rust to come with a free tetanus shot. Her hands and arms are filthy. She feels worse than barnyard rank. Her befoulment is worthy of that crazy hillbilly Glantzer.

Her injuries are surprisingly minor. Shoulders and back have a good range of motion. After that fall and undoubtedly being handled like a sack of potatoes by her rescuers, she should have ended up in as bad a shape as Roger after Antarctica. Getting away without a major compound break or massive internal bleeding is a huge bonus. All things considered, she should really be ecstatic.

These shackles are her impotence. And that's what Sienna can stand least of all. She has to find a way out. She tests her bonds. They are tight. Slipping them would mean breaking or gnawing off her thumbs.

And they've been good thumbs; no sense getting rid of them now.

Rising heat and the closeness of the cell have worn down Ghazan's zeal. He must also be pondering the cryptic transaction between Artuk and the new arrivals. Dealings he is not part of. He sits on the bench set into the wall opposite Sienna, idly cleaning the rifle. He's so far out of his element, Sienna nearly feels sorry for him. Nearly, except for the whole execution video thing he has planned for her. The aspiring director must have been waiting for just the right subject.

Mr. DeMille, I'm not ready for my close up, thank you.

The Chechen, having no specific task to occupy his beefy hands, takes to thinking. This he can't do without rambling.

"You know how we fix up people in Chechnya?"

Sienna quietly takes measure of her captors.

"We shoot them."

Bribery? Rasul is greedy, but won't take risks. The other one? No way. He's probably rebelling against rich parents.

"We shoot them early."

Distraction? Can't start a fire.

"And many, many times."

Fake illness? They'd only laugh.

"Until they stay fixed up."

Wait, then. Wait for a mistake or a miracle. Wait and survive.

"Tell me, I forget," Rasul says with genuine curiosity. "Why is this one still alive?"

"Commander Artuk said keep her," Ghazan says. "Try to make her talk, but keep her."

"Maybe he gives me some fun time with her," Rasul says, looking at her with red-rimmed eyes. "This Colonel Bitch?"

Sienna's stomach heaves some more as he approaches her with a hideous curiosity.

"What is this stuff on her arms?"

He investigates the only way sensible to him, by digging into her bicep with a bayonet knife. Sienna gains a new sharp pain to go with all the others. Completely awake, she pretends to be groggy. Pretty quickly, the area he's jabbing at becomes a bloody mess. The would-be surgeon abandons his idea, sensing a more urgent calling. She, on the other hand, is intrigued. Furtively, Sienna looks at her arm closely for the first time since waking. A line of fiber-optic relays seems to be melted into her skin.

The guts of the RAPTEK.

*Last time I saw that, it was **ON** me. Now it's **IN** me? Maybe it melted like plastic in a fire.*

Unlike scalding from hot metal or blistering from burning body armor—both of which she's familiar with—these areas of her arms do not hurt at all.

She studies her fingers through swollen, grit-filled eyes. The dim light does not help. Scraps of her gloves hang down. And something else. Something pulses beneath her shackles, underneath the dirt and crusted blood.

That strange fire. The same thing must have happened on her hands as on her arms. More bits of the RAPTEK. Whatever the crud is, she can scrape it off later. Experimentally, she grips and flexes quietly. Bones and tendons are intact, working well enough to press a trigger. She looks greedily at the field-stripped vintage AK and the tantalizingly full magazine next to it. Well maintained, an AK is the workhorse of personal killing machines. Many of them have much longer lives than their successive owners, and they have been notching kills for generations in the hills and plateaus of this place.

The Chechen turns to the far wall. He prepares to urinate. And keeps preparing. He has trouble getting a good stream going. His hip gyrations and whispering to his privates are so morbidly comical Sienna nearly laughs out loud. She stifles a spasm of inappropriate hilarity. This pains her bruised ribs. The ironic jabbing in her midsection only makes her want to laugh more.

Talk about gallows humor, as the Brits say.

Rasul's persistence pays off. Pee dribbles into the floor gutter. Only a prodded squirt or two actually make it to the cinderblocks. To distract herself, Sienna goes through a more detailed inventory of available weapons, tools, and her injuries. It could come to a close-quarter fight—she should be so lucky. The mechanisms binding her wrists are no more complex than the spring ratchet of a standard handcuff. But she can barely put her hand to her face, much less touch the left shackle's lock with her right hand. Her mind works furiously. Her arm oozes blood. She remains motionless.

Finally, Rasul gets a good finishing stream going. Droplets, colored dark yellow and green by the lousy light, splash against his trousers.

Damn, these guys know how to show a girl a good time in a hurry and on a budget.

Rasul pees on the dead mouse and snickers.

Right.

She evaluates her head and neck. Her cheek could have

been hit by a baseball bat. Hematoma swelling has levelled off. It affects her vision as much as it's going to. There is another pain. A cracked jawbone? That could be bad. She's relieved when one of her back teeth comes loose. She spits. Out it comes with a stringy gob of bright red saliva. It plops into her right palm.

Over by the wall, the Chechen wraps up what seems to have been a thoroughly enjoyable bladder emptying. His boots slosh in muck.

Of the two men, she feels more kinship with the one fiddling with his zipper. His brutality and his aims are unrefined. He has no veneer of ideology besides his pride in his countrymen "fixing people up." Sienna can't help thinking this makes him more like her. So she hates Rasul the most. With contempt and a juicy sliver of hate, she flicks her tooth at him.

Here. You knocked it out. Have it.

She aims at the back of his head. At four yards she hardly expects it to hit—

splutch!

As though struck by a cattle-slaughtering bolt gun to the back of his bald scalp, Rasul's grin explodes in a geyser of gore. What looks like a vapor trail traces back to Sienna's manacled fist. The body, still standing, twitches for a nerveless moment then collapses into an unsightly heap. The thump Rasul makes greeting the floor is louder than the flight of the molar missile that killed him. Sienna's forearm, hand, and fingers tingle with energy.

That felt like... like the RAPTEK, but different. Stronger.

25

Ghazan's features twist into a rictus of horror decorated with pink spray. Aerosol of Chechen brains.

What now?

Any more thinking and she'll be as dead as messiest urinator ever. Rasul has most certainly shuffled off his smelly mortal coil with the help of her hyper-accelerated tooth.

That really, really happened.

Their three-person world has turned inside out and become a two-person world. Ghazan stumbles back to the corner of the cell. He wipes at his eyes, smearing gore in a thick stripe.

"You salope! You shot him—I kill you!"

His rage is terror-fueled and bloodlust-driven, and it is incoherent. He grabs the closest thing, the boltless AK. Holding it like a club, he lunges. The clumsy attempt to crush her skull snaps her back into reality.

She's been here. She's done this. A thousand times. In play, practice, and war. An enemy coming at her with lethal intent, well, that's just like the feeling of her bare feet hitting the cold barracks floor after 4 a.m. reveille at boot camp.

Sienna flips the switch. The stillness of a fight settles on her. She dodges the butt of the rifle coming wildly at her head with room to spare.

Way obvious, dick.

Her leg, the one she worked quietly and diligently to get feeling back into, kicks out. Its shin hits the attacker's extended knee. Something snaps. Ghazan falls and howls. Coolly, she watches him crawl back to the bench, one leg gratifyingly twisted.

Good. He won't be trying to stand up and bash my head in again anytime soon.

Ghazan's hair hangs in sweaty streaks. Dripping glasses hang half off his face. In seconds he has gone from looking forward to directing an execution video, to being alone, disabled, and wracked with pain.

He loses the last shreds of his wits. Ghazan forgets about his ideals. Vanished are the highfalutin arguments he had with professors in Paris. Gone are thoughts of how much he hates his parents.

All this descendant of Pashtuni tribesmen can think about is ripping into his enemy with nail and tooth if he has to. Most importantly, he forgets about Round Head.

Instead, Ghazan's lust for the kill causes him to tunnel-vision focus on one thing: re-inserting the bolt carrier of the AK.

His sole need is to perforate Sienna with as many 7.62mm holes as possible. Normally, reassembly would take about five seconds with steady hands. Ghazan's hands are not steady. They twitch and shake. At first, he turns the bolt the wrong way round. Then he lets the rifle slip off his lap.

Ghazan is in shock.

It is one thing to kill prisoners while they are chained and on their knees. Captives aren't supposed to shoot back with some kind of hidden weapon.

Sienna can read Ghazan's thoughts on his face as though he were shouting them.

We aren't supposed to get killed. He glances at the lump of former Chechen. This is so… *unfair!*

Sienna pulls at her shackles. The rifle is problematic. At this range, even this idiot will eventually hit her. She looks to her hands. *What just happened? What did I do?*

Her life depends on the right answer. Could it be some residue of charge from the broken RAPTEK? It is, was, only supposed to work on metal. Was there a filling in that tooth?

No time.

Only chance is to hope I can do it again. Just once more.

She looks for something—a rock, a nail, anything. Sienna's eyes search the small space in reach of her hands or feet. Nothing. Only dirt and filth. The bucket? No. Too big. Anything usable has to be about the size of a fléchette projectile.

As if there's any logic to this! She snarls. Her chains rattle and clank.

Sienna glances up. Ghazan presses his back against the wall farthest from her. Does he know he's wearing a facial of gray matter puree? The Pashtun has gathered enough sense to realize his worst nightmare is still chained up. And *he* has the gun. If only he can put the pieces in the right spots.

Drool quivers down from his lips. He locks the rifle bolt home in the correct position for firing. Fingers fumble with the magazine, trying to slot it. There's a unique backward and forward motion needed to load this model of AK. On the first try, Ghazan misses it. He barks an incoherent caveman grunt of frustration.

Alarm builds inside her. Not panic, *never panic.* But close enough as the magazine finds its spot. The well-oiled bolt racks backward with a distinctive *ca-check.*

The metallic sound echoes pitilessly between bare walls.

Sienna feels something scrape against her left shackle. Her class ring. Under the blasted remnants of her gloves. They haven't stolen it.

But how can my ring work? The RAPTEK had no effect on it. *That's why I didn't take it off.*

In a bizarre flash, she recalls picking the ring's design in her senior year at West Point. Bryan suggested the more ladylike casting. She wanted something substantial, just in case she had to punch someone. The men's style was also cheaper and even less expensive when Ennis gave her a chunky tourmaline stone to have set in it. It was a memento of all the good times they had since they met during the Battle of Beast March.

Sienna looks at it. The shiny band is crusted with blood and mud. Her captors had either not seen it or had each been waiting for a chance to steal it for themselves.

However she's kept it, the trick now is getting it off before Ghazan starts shooting.

Sienna can just barely put her hand to her mouth. She prizes the ring off with her teeth, the front ones which the late Chechen so thoughtfully left intact. With effort and loss of skin, it comes off. She spits it into her right palm just like the tooth.

The charging bolt of the AK slams forward.

A rifle bullet is in the chamber behind the slant-tongued muzzle. Eight millimeters wide, it is a suddenly huge pit aiming at her chest. She's not looking at the Pashtun or his weapon. Sienna concentrates on her hand and the object in it.

"USMA" is inscribed on the side… there's something else— her class motto. She helped translate it with a Latin dictionary. The side of the ring is too crusted with crud to read.

What is it? What a stupid thing to forget… to think of now.

Sienna stares at the ring. And then it isn't in her palm anymore. For a measureless instant, it floats up between her fingers.

Oh yeah.

Et factus est vera lucis tenebra

"In darkness…"

The heavy-cast West Point class ring makes a snapping sound as it bridges the distance between her hand and Ghazan. He's crouched over his weapon, bracing for the satisfying kick of the AK's recoil.

"In darkness become a true light."

Made invisible by sheer speed, the small band impacts the side of Ghazan's head.

Maybe he feels a kick, if so it's definitely not satisfying. Ghazan is killed instantly. More gore matter sloshes against the wall. The dead man's fingers convulse, mashing on the trigger. The rifle is set to automatic. It rattles off half a dozen rounds.

Luckily, the AK's muzzle no longer points at her. When the weapon goes off, it is stuck in Rasul's posterior. The sound gets muffled. Loud enough in the enclosed space. It might not have been heard up on the street, especially if everyone is crowded around Artuk and Khalid and that big bag of money.

Fat as the Chechen's body is, the metal-jacketed bullets rip through his guts and bounce off the floor and the walls. Sienna ducks. Shrapnel of metal, stone, and bone ricochet.

The deadly jackhammer stops.

She is unhurt. No shouting comes from the street. The buttock-suppressed noise didn't carry. She has another problem. The commotion must have been heard in the hallway. Round Head.

Outside the door, keys rattle.

26

Smoke from the cheap ammo just fired off has hardly risen to the ceiling when her third guard enters. He must be the slowest thinking of the three. Ghazan and Rasul were glad to keep him outside. It meant more loot for them, the two now very dead guys. Sienna does not get a good look; she pretends to be unconscious. Her hands, empty and bound, hang listlessly in full view of the newcomer.

She can almost hear Round Head's simple thoughts.

Both guards dead. They look shot. Uh oh.

Prisoner unconscious, maybe dead. Can't tell yet. She is still tied up, well and truly tied. And unarmed. Okay.

What could have happened? Will I be blamed? Maybe they shot each other arguing over loot. Why would Ghazan shoot that Chechen man in the ass? What a disgusting way to kill someone. I should have stayed. They were trying to cheat me! But, hold on a second, then I'd probably be shot, too. And I'm not. So in that case… in that case, all the loot can be mine. Good for me.

Sienna has new confidence. Once with a tooth was a fluke. A second time with her ring is a trend. Three times will get her free!

Got to find something. I should wear more jewelry, like Snakelips. That was my one and only ring. Slow as this guy is, I don't think I can con him into unlocking my chains.

A spent cartridge ejected by the wildly firing AK sits just out of reach. Sienna tries to attract it using the loading motion. The same one she used to pull Sidewinder's knife away from Anis's neck.

The brass shell does not move.

That would have been too convenient. Maybe this ghost remnant ability of the destroyed RAPTEK can only repel things. Whatever. It only has to work one more time.

Just please look away, you dumb little…

Round Head bends down over the Chechen's exploded, hairy butt crack to check the body for valuables before getting help. Hard times in North Khorasan. Soundlessly, Sienna's foot flicks out and kicks the empty shell into the air. Her left hand catches and palms warm brass with hardly a sound. Round Head looks in her direction.

He reaches for… not his pistol. His walkie. He's going to call for help.

Can't let that happen.

The slow-thinking man clicks on the grimy transceiver button to activate the microphone. He clears his throat. Someone answers. The reception is crappy: *"What—shhrk—is it? Who is this?"*

The guard can only reply with a gurgling sound, his neck having been punctured by a hyper-accelerated brass shell casing.

"Stop playing around," the radio squawks. *"If I find out who*

this is, you will be in for plenty of hurt! No signals. You know the rule!"

Sienna watches Round Head sink to the floor and bleed out. His uncomprehending eyes are open. They lock on hers as he dies.

Around his belt is a ring of keys. One of them must fit the locks on her wrists. Way out of reach. She considers shooting the shackles. Too much risk of blowing her hand off. She has no idea how finely she can aim or control this, whatever it is, or how many "shots" she has until the RAPTEK realizes it's scattered over the desert in a thousand pieces. Well, not all of it.

The railgun worked through the fiber cables. They're melted into my arms…

Maybe this energy is like static electricity. That can affect plastic, even make socks stick together in the dryer. She looks at the splattered room and the three dead bodies.

Some socks. Some dryer.

Her chains clink against poured concrete bases. The whole place is falling down, and the one thing they don't skimp on is prisoner accessories. She has an idea. Gathering a length of chain, she shields her face, then sends it crashing into the cement stay. The sudden pull nearly breaks her wrist, but the chain starts to warp.

Again. Again.

Whump. WHUMP!

The warping opens a break; the break releases the next link.

Free. One hand at least.

She still can't reach the keys. The other chain is easier. It's a rough tool, but powerful. Nearly silent, totally deadly. Just the thing for a jail-break.

She grabs keys off the far-staring guard's belt. Round Head was probably some local mook trying to earn enough to keep his family in goat's milk. Here, in this place, you are either with the local carnivores or you and your kin are fair game. She covers his face with a decrepit piece of tarp.

The two others, the world is well shed of. She searches for anything of use. In between, she drinks warm but clean water, sparing some to wash the class ring and irrigate her swollen eye. Though at this point, developing pink eye and enduring T-Rex's inappropriate comments are probably unavoidable. Welcome jibes from her people. Back home.

From a stairway at the end of the corridor past the other cells, a bolt gets thrown. She glances down the narrow row of steel doors. Fight here in this dead-end space or evade? She darts out, quietly opens the latch on the next cell, and ducks in.

And she freezes.

27

Two pairs of downcast eyes stare at her feet. They are eyes that blend into the gloom of an even darker chamber than the one she's just escaped. In them she sees the hurt of an abused animal resigned to once again receiving the lash. Sienna raises her finger to her lips in the internationally recognized sign to please stay very quiet. The haggard, half-seen faces could be made of wax. They remain as still.

This cell is about one-third the size of the luxury suite next door. Sienna posts herself against the door. On the other side, movement. Footsteps clomp down stairs at the end of the hall. They come closer. Artuk and Khalid must have made a deal. Or one is double crossing the other. Either way, those guys need to get ready for a surprise.

The two men in the hallway are not frantic. They do not fear imminent attack or know she's missing. They pad forward with intent, eager to do something. Only inches away from them, she controls her breathing and checks her surroundings.

The locks on all the jailhouse doors are flat circular mechanisms, similar to ones in hospitals and mental institutions. They might have been stolen from an NGO's charity construction site and ended up being used for a much different purpose than the donors intended. The good thing about them is, unless the men outside pull on each of the dozen doors, there is no way to see if a particular one is locked or not. Sienna grabs the inner handle and braces a still-throbbing foot on the wall just in case. It won't move a millimeter. She won't let it.

"Her cell is here," says an old raspy voice in the local dialect. Artuk. His tone reminds her of a wizened antiques dealer about to make the deal of a lifetime. "We have put her in the most secure part of our newest prison."

"It's usually better if you shoot them first," Khalid says. "But in the chest mind you, Master Artuk. The mudarris will want a clean trophy."

There's only one trophy outsiders could want here, and Sienna is bound and determined to keep it on her shoulders.

Artuk. The name, spoken aloud, reverberates in Sienna's mind along with images and stories hissed into the wind by the rasping tongues of sand wraiths. She shakes off the mild touch of creep. The last few hours have had more than their share of strangeness. She glances at the couple. They huddle at the back of the cell.

Out in the hall, the village elder takes umbrage. "Please, young man, give me some respect. I can read the note you gave me as well as anyone. Since before you were born I've been cutting off heads. If there is one thing we know how to do here, it's that!"

Footsteps pass right by. She could kill these two and take their weapons. But both men's factions will be waiting up above for them to come out. What happens next is way better than any distraction she could have improvised. Their idle debate over decapitation techniques stops when they see no guard outside the cell. The door of her former accommodation creaks open, unlocked. A wild scuffling comes from the hallway as they search. For what? A hole in the ceiling? Then, a satisfying wail of agony sounds down the corridor.

"AAARRRGGGHHH! She was right in there."

"Go! Get going, old one!" Khalid's voice betrays both anger and terror. "She must be trying to get out of the village. Find her, or the mudarris's disappointment will sting all of us. Everyone."

That'll set the enemy in all directions. She turns. They didn't make a sound. They could have betrayed her, maybe bargained for their own release. She could not have stopped them while keeping a grip on the door.

Daylight comes via a small aperture near the ceiling. The sun's rays filter in through trash blown against bars. She can see the two more clearly. It is a man and a woman. They look twenty years older than what Sienna guesses is their actual age. The man's arm is bent backward at an odd angle. His forearm points about thirty degrees in the wrong direction. If he's lucky, it's only snapped cleanly at the elbow. That's something she can help with and save the future use of his arm.

No one on the street heard the shooting. It's unlikely they'll be overheard talking quietly.

"You will soon be free," Sienna whispers encouragingly. "Let me set that arm and we'll find the best way to go out from here."

The woman swats Sienna's hand away. "Are you insane? Do not touch him."

Her hostility stops Sienna cold.

"How can you fix anything?" The woman explains like she's talking to a dull child. "They will come back. They'll just do it again, and to me as well!"

"I understand, uh, you must be in shock." Sienna assesses exfil options. She can't leave them here. Maybe they have friends in the hills. "We've got to move—"

"You speak with an accent that is perfect." Impatience joins irritation on the woman's weathered face. She studies Sienna's skin and features. "Are your ancestors from this land?"

Sienna pauses. Hamida. Khorasan. The land. It knows its own daughter. She shakes her head.

"No. My parents are American."

We don't have time. Sienna holds up her hand and listens at the door. If Artuk and Khalid find no sign of her outside, they might come back and make a more detailed search of the cells. This is no place for a fight. Not here. Not now. Behind hostile lines, escape, and evasion is SOP.

No time for payback. I'll help this couple, maybe they can help me get clear. They might know where I can find a good vehicle, or even a sat phone. Get to safety. Call the cavalry. Figure the rest out. Bryan, have I got a story for you that beats the battiest stuff T-Rex ever made up!

Sienna nudges the woman into the corner as she prepares to ease open the door. "We've got to get moving."

"No we don't, outlander." She pushes back. "Even if I don't see your smooth face, I would know you are a foreigner by the utter nonsense you talk, with our words in an accent which is perfect. If you really knew us, knew this place, you would know there is no 'out from here'. Not for us. Where do we go they don't find us? Are you going to take all of our family, our children, and their children? No?"

The woman quietly hacks the last word out as though it were a stubborn pomegranate seed stuck in her dry throat. She puts her hand on the man's shoulder and guides him back down to sit against a wall.

"No, I don't think so," she hisses with finality. "Here, we go through what we must. Maybe they let us go, maybe we disappear. But what is certain, what we Wise Tribes know, is when you outsiders come, you only make things worse."

Still speaking in hushed tones, the woman's indignation fades into rhetoric. She points to Sienna's torn clothing, which reveals her shoulder and presumably the yellow rose tattoo.

"You, you, foreigners." She rolls her eyes. "With your immodest dress and body-art tattoos—is that astrology? Sorcery? *Ach*! Save us from blasphemy!"

Now she's just ranting. Sienna hopes she won't have to gag her hostess. Fortunately, the opinionated prisoner pauses, considering something. After a moment of straight-up staring, she asks, "Why do you come here?"

"To serve. Protect the innocent. To make a difference."

"Phah!" It's a good thing the local woman is dehydrated, otherwise Sienna would have a coating of Khorasani saliva to go with the rest of the filth on her torn Army shirt. The woman shakes her head.

Sienna's saving them. And the old bat is giving her guff?

"Listen to my words, elderwoman," she hisses back in the harshest Khorasani accent she can manage, which is pretty darn stern. "Are you calling me a liar?"

The woman doesn't flinch. "Maybe it is *a* truth. But

we of the Six Hills are called the Wise Tribes. And it is not *your* truth. Not all." She studies Sienna. "You answer like my grandchildren when they have done something wrong. All practiced, reciting. Yes, even with my old eyes I can see you are still young and not shamefully plain. And not so dumb, either, to escape from these jackals. Why you not stay in America? You could have rich husband, easy life. But no. You risk everything. Why?"

I should move. These two—they've given up.

Instead Sienna gives voice to something in a way she's never expressed to anyone else. "To find... someone. Someone who took something from me." While this cell is small, her voice seems even more meager.

The woman nods, seemingly kinder now, in the harsh way of desert people. Revenge and payback, these things all Khorasanis understand in their souls.

"And if you find this person," the woman asks. "What he took from you, will you get it back?"

"I... I don't know."

Sienna took some local currency off Ghazan. She hands it to the woman. "Here, you might need this. Hide it."

"I know what to do." The woman snatches up the cash. "Finally you offer something useful."

She waves Sienna out. The weary, canny woman concludes the coast is clear at the same time Sienna's years of training tells her the same.

"Now you go."

The woman inclines her head slightly to the left. It is a subtle, polite gesture of acknowledgement one sees exchanged by women passing each other. An elegant and friendly motion if a woman is clad in ḥijāb or chadri. This woman is not. She and the man have been stripped nearly naked.

"You have been kind to us according to your own naïve, foreign ways," the local woman says. "For that I give you the blessing of our wisdom. We the Wise Tribe of the Six Hills say: Beware, for the wound that bleedeth inwardly is the most dangerous." In a motion that is half pat, half push out the doorway, her companion signals their time is done. "Lock the door after you."

Sienna eases the door open. Air hangs hot and still. She slips out. As the door eases shut, the matron's final admonishment follows.

"And we also say: Those who plant thorns must never expect to gather roses."

28

Sienna ducks into the hall. The small stream in the gutter runs more thickly with the mixed blood of three dead men added to its flow. It trickles by the door to the couple's cell, a metal tombstone. Quietly, Sienna steps over. Those two are going to gut it out. Here. In Artuk's world. Maybe they would go south, to the Fertile Spear. Maybe they already rejected the idea of putting themselves under the Serpens banner of Worldwide Help. She doesn't have time to wonder about other people's choices.

People dickering about the Buy It Now price for my head? I got other worries.

Still, the beat-down pair deserve one last solid. The local militia will soon be busier than a one-eyed cat watching nine mice. Their top priorities will be looking for her and avoiding the wrath of Artuk and this mudarris guy for losing her in the first place. She's seen enough horrors of prisoners forgotten in cells without food or water. She cannot obey the tough old matron's last request.

She twists the key off in the lock. Passing the other cells, she does the same to each one. Unlock, snap, on her way to the stairway. It's time to leave this no-horse town.

Past a plywood hatch onto the roof, Sienna feels direct sunlight on her body. The warmth makes her realize she's bruised and cramped down to her core. Sienna's aching face reacts to the pain. The pain of freedom regained. She feels her swollen cheeks crease with a wide Cheshire Cat grin. The hurts and indignities she has suffered are overtaken by the thrill of escaping that dank cell, which was supposed to be the last place she'd ever enter alive.

And underneath her cautious relief? Something else. Something she does not want to acknowledge. Not even here. Not even now. A longing, within her, deep and dark.

I won't listen. Not today. Got to get away, quickly, quietly.

Though… a reconnoiter can't hurt, just a quick one. Artuk and Khalid will expect her to make for the fastest way out. There's time. She makes it to the top of the jail roof and climbs to the next building over. There, Sienna crawls under a rusted water tank. She looks down. The view only makes her want to smile more. Despite the pain, despite the blood oozing from the socket that used to hold a molar. *Lucky tooth.*

In the dusty streets below, a pantomime of confusion and suspicion bordering on hysteria plays out. Artuk's village fighters wear farming and street clothes. The new guys, Khalid's men, wear crisp black desert gear. There are no official markings or hastily painted slogans on the SUVs to indicate who sent Khalid. This mudarris, he's a mystery.

The two groups of fighters are nearly at each other's throats. Artuk's men pad around, circling. Khalid's SUVs have taken up defensive positions in the square around their ace in the hole. The visiting team rolled into town with a ridiculously heavy piece of ordnance. It is a much showier piece of military bling than an ordinary heavy machine gun. The back of an open-ended truck is weighed down by a Soviet-era quad ZSU anti-aircraft gun. The Zeus, as it's affectionately known in terror circles, would look comical mounted like it is. It would, except for the weapons system's ability to level every house in the village in a few minutes. That kind of random destructive power isn't comical at all.

The villagers must be wondering if the interlopers have stolen her to avoid paying ransom. On Khalid's mind must be the possibility the village elder has killed his own men to fool them now that her head has an opening bid.

Unarmed villagers—shopkeepers, bicycle repairmen, farmers, herders, beggars—they all know a fight is coming. The dry air is electric.

She ducks down, rolls over, and contemplates the sky. Admittedly not standard procedure during a prison break. Sienna stares at the wide-open blueness certain people never meant her to see again. She withdraws into shadows, and watches. And waits.

Jittery men brandish pistols, grenade launchers, and long guns. Shutters slam down, children are whisked inside. In the dust of the alleyway below, a soccer ball rolls aimlessly. The locals will take shelter in basement sanctuaries, behind thick stone walls. Later, after the mayhem, they will carry on as the hard people of this hard land always do.

Sienna only half-lied to the old woman in the cell about her origins. Her mother was born in Khorasan, as was she. Maybe what she feels is her connection. No time to wonder. Only time to act. And survive.

To do that, she has to be realistic about her ability to run or fight if she's forced to. After all that trauma, maybe the surge of adrenaline is the only thing keeping her up. Maybe she's a hair's breadth away from being paraplegic like Ennis. A combat medical case she studied comes to mind. A French Legion convoy got hit by an IED. Three feet of rebar went through the gunner's torso. He used it to prop himself up in his turret. Claimed he didn't feel any pain until they got back to base.

She feels along her spine. Nothing much there. No jutting vertebrae. No gaping rent in her flesh or cauterized gouge where the power source had been. Just the standard-issue body of one Colonel McKnight, plus some smooth bits. These are firm and painless areas where the main bulk of the RAPTEK formerly sat on her shoulders and hugged the middle of her back. The part that held the power pack and other gizmos.

I gotta start reading user manuals all the way through.

Some stale water is caught in the pipe of a roof tank. She washes off mud and blood. Underneath the grime, a slick fiber-optic material is fused into her. It is warm and looks different than she first thought. When it was brought to her attention, she was kind of preoccupied.

The stuff is sunk in between the bones of her forearms, ulna, and radius. It is not a stripe. Not like Kinesio tape at all. The embeds trace latticework in three dimensions as wide as a quarter inch, fading to a wisp, then curving and expanding. Blue-green and translucent, the material has a slight luminescence. Or maybe it's just sunlight and shadows and her throbbing head playing tricks. Whether this is borrowed light being conducted by optic piping or some inherent radiance, she cannot tell. It's a little like filigree gilding. No. Not decoration. Not deformation, either. This is not her, yet it is. If she concentrates, the patterns are almost like… language?

The smell of recreational smoke wafting up ends her self-scrutiny. Two armed village guards stand in the alley. One puffs a hand-rolled cigarette containing what passes for local tobacco weed.

"I tell you, those bastards took her," the taller one says. "So they didn't have to pay for her head."

The pair have decent cover. If general shooting starts, they will not be the first ones hit. They feel at ease enough to enjoy a smoke and talk about local economic matters.

"It was a whole suitcase full of money," the second one says. "Probably more in the cars. Not that we'd see any of that coin in our hands. Artuk is too greedy, the old bastard."

The other one spits in agreement. "He must have eighteen sons by now, and I hear he's getting a new wife in the spring—URK!"

"What you say?" The shorter fellow leans back around the corner. "I told you smoking those things would—URK!"

29

The two militiamen were paying close attention to the scene of rising belligerence in the village square. Sienna crept up behind. One glanced back at the wrong moment, and it was over for them both. As her conscious mind raced through the best ways of taking out the watchmen, her new ability and older inner self cut to the chase. She found two jagged rocks in her hands. In a blink, they were no longer there but neatly severing the spinal columns of the combatants.

One slumps over his rifle like a limp marionette. The other slides down the brick wall, leaving a dappled smear as mouth and nose exhale a final lungful of tobacco smoke. Sienna stops questioning the source or nature of her abilities. Inside her throbbing skull, her fighting mind takes charge.

And it has company.

Sarge Bryan called it the racht. Where he got that term, she never learned. It is a part of her that urges her to do things. Terrible things. It was born the same time she was. Five red gashes inscribed its brief, eloquent creed on her body and her soul. Sienna knows this, though she's probably never been able to put the entirety of it into finite human language. The racht is in her, just dying to come out and play. She suppresses it with practical thoughts.

She picks up a flat stone a couple of inches in diameter. It floats in the palm of her hand. She's aware of a tingling sensation. The energy feels like when you're pressing the ends of two magnets together, positive to positive. The energy is seductively powerful. Her body is the source. She realizes instinctively that she can control the speed projectiles fly by changing how tightly she grips them before letting go.

The stones around her feet are smooth, as though honed into perfect shapes in the bed of some bygone river. They look just like the ones in her illustrated Sunday school books, where young David is shown putting five of them in his pouch before contending for the Valley of Elah championship belt. That bout happened three thousand years ago. Back then, the boy and future king was fighting way above his own weight class. His Philistine opponent's armor and weapons weighed twice as much as David. He only had a strip of leather.

Sienna has no sling. She does not need one. The men who want to kill her are no giants. But she'll need more than five stones.

In irregular actions, especially ones involving the tactic called running like hell for your life, being aware is essential. It can often mean the difference between popping a brew with the gang back home and ending up as a prize exhibit in some ghastly deviant's trophy room.

She does not pick up the weapons of the fallen sentries. They are not suppressed, and she has no idea what affect her ability might have on centerfire ammunition. Volatile primers can be set off by heat or static as easily as impact from a firing pin. She could blow her hand off. She scans each dwelling, looking for signs of advanced com equipment. She looks for anything she can use to help her get out of Dodge.

Best option seems to be a dash for the truck she saw behind a village shop. The owner must be hiding in the basement. It's laden with supplies and petrol. If she drives away slowly, avoiding lookouts, she will be just another villager departing the anticipated bloodshed. It could work. It might be hours before anyone figures it out. It's the right thing to do.

Like I said, time to blow this—

"Don't move, bitch," snarls a voice behind her. A door swings open and a gun is cocked close to her ear. "This is *my* place. *My* jail."

It is the same man she heard in the street above her cell, and later through the jail door. Old Artuk, in the flesh. Sienna stays still. Artuk has the drop on her and sounds pissed. She raises her hands, palms forward. Her right hand gently cups a stone washed smooth by an ancient river.

"You don't think I know every inch of it?" Artuk rattles on. "You think you can just sneak around here like… like…"

He sputters, struggling for just the right word to express his thoughts. He finds it.

"Like a *BITCH*?" The old man is apoplectic as he vents his outrage at her bitch-like behavior.

That curse word is getting old. Don't these guys know any other terms of endearment?

The lack of gunfire accompanying the curses means Artuk's pride and greed have, for now, overcome his impulse to just shoot her and flaunt his decapitation skills. He wants to find out more about what she's worth alive before committing to dismemberment. Canny Artuk. She prepares to turn around and show him bitch behavior like he's never seen.

"Don't you move! I have seen what you did with those two idiots." Artuk stays a few feet back. "No wonder you are so valuable to the mudarris. Asking for your head was just a trick."

Artuk crumples a piece of paper in his free hand. "They order me around. Pretend to offer me a dog's wages. Pah! They want you for themselves."

What is a human railgun going for on the black market these days? Sienna relaxes a little. This guy's definitely not going to shoot her now. Dismember her and auction her body parts, maybe. But he'll do nothing until he finds out more.

Sienna decides on the angle to take. She coos compliantly, "You are a wise one indeed, old master Artuk. I am worth a lot. In fact, I was trying to get away from my people and meet contacts from Russia when I had a small accident. For me, they will pay you gold and currency, whatever you want."

Then, thinking his concept of money might be as limited as his vocabulary, she adds, "And weapons. Great and terrible weapons, Master Artuk. Your power could stretch over the Six Hills and far beyond, very far. You can hold the *TYR Lens* and all who depend on it for water hostage to your will. Let us get away from this mudarris fellow, whoever he is, and I will tell you everything."

Sienna can almost feel the greed vibrating out from the old guy. The per capita income of this area is about the same as a Happy Meal back home. The more Artuk thinks she is worth, the less immediate danger she's in.

This could even work out better than—

From behind the village chief comes the unmistakable sound of a large submachine gun bolt being thrown.

—or not.

"I *knew* you were hiding her, you old goat."

"Ah, Mr. Khalid, there you are," Artuk says, switching to his own mild and compliant way of speaking. "I was just coming to find you. I have got her!"

"Drop your pistol."

"Now don't do anything hasty, my friend," Artuk stammers. "And don't let her turn around, she's dangerous—"

The elder's pistol has no sooner clattered to the ground than the squishy, raspy sound of metal being driven through cloth and flesh comes from behind Sienna. Blood sprays over her shoulder as Khalid pulls out the bayonet that has passed through the old man's body. Artuk is dead on his feet. He falls.

"Turn around, Colonel Sienna McKnight," Khalid says. "I want to tell the mudarris I looked into your eyes when I killed you."

Sienna turns around. Looming over her is a brutish, hulking man with dark, enraged eyes which have bored their way out of his wicked soul. These stare at her from above a bramble of beard. Whether from the urgency of the situation or the man's resemblance to someone else, something inside her surges. Something ancient connects with something brand-new. And a power she has never felt before, never knew existed, courses up her shoulder to her right hand.

She looks into his eyes. Then she kills him.

The flat river-washed stone in her palm disappears into a vapor trail with a crack of dry thunder. It is imbued with *such force*. Sienna squints as the heat of incinerated atmosphere splashes back on her cheek. The dark smoke tail smells like brimstone. She has launched a miniature meteor of wrath and given away her position with the sonic crack. At that moment, though, her reason is on leave. Her rough racht beast is delighted by the explosion of mud bricks behind Khalid, which she can see through Khalid, or at least the fist-sized tunnel that appears in the dead man's torso.

Someone must have heard that. Naw. Everyone must have heard that. She can still make for the truck. If she's lucky, the two groups, with their respective leaders dead, will fall into disarray. Confusion with homicidal overtones can only help her escape. She looks at the smashed mess of Khalid. His body is a broken rag doll, his rifle charred and shattered. The mess lies on top of rubble that used to be the foundation stones of a building.

How strong am I? Is this? Gotta watch blowback and collateral damage.

Footsteps sound, running in from the main street toward her and the two bodies. Sienna remembers something, something she wants to make certain of. The old guy had a note. She searches Artuk's pockets. There. She unfurls the paper and sees the two-bladed Scythe symbol.

**YOU HAVE A PRISONER.
KILL HER AT ONCE.
GIVE THE HEAD TO KHALID.**

Asrah. He IS the mudarris.

Him.

Him!

30

Her hand closes on the paper. Instead of crumpling, it burns. She swats away floating embers. Her world bleeds into two colors: red and black. She does not run from the approaching footsteps. She runs toward them, stooping to pick up stones.

No muzzle flash.

No sonic crack. Unless she wants one to echo between buildings to further confuse the enemy.

Unlimited ammo.

Nice.

Her fast assaults on both factions has them firing wildly at air and, better yet, each other. Khalid's men, in neatly tailored black pajamas, fall into disarray. Whatever their training, they are not ready for super-heated stone shrapnel coming at them from nowhere. From shadow.

The rocks Sienna has in her hands are one to two inches across. Some are brittle. At first she uses too much energy to propel them. They break apart in the air. By the third one loosed in rapid succession, she has the hang of it. The last of a trio of oncoming combatants receives a neat, skull-crushing dent between the eyes. No messy exit wound.

Sienna approaches the jumble of bodies, weapons, and spent casings. Others will come soon. Sienna looks for a communications device, a stolen sat phone, a civilian Lux/Net device. Nothing doing.

Spak, spak, spak!

Incoming rounds go way wide. Harmless. But there are more. Khalid's goons have come out of cars and covered trucks. Local fighters emerge from basements and take positions on rooftops. They are eager to impress Artuk, unaware he lies dead in the alley, his alley, stabbed in his back.

She dives into the doorway of a solid, oval structure, grabbing more ammo along the way. Held now in the sway of her rough inner beast, she muses that if there is one good thing about this country, it is the endless supply of well-formed stones. A good-sized stream must have flowed here, back in the day. Back when the Six Hills were ringed with green. Perhaps as it now is, eroded down to windblown clay and gravel trimmed with prickly brush, it is more its true self. This place has always been sustaining, never nurturing. How different, how alike, is its daughter?

Sienna has astonishing accuracy. No line-of-sight target is safe. She prefers to hold spares in her left and fire with the right. Coming up to a tricky corner, she stops short. There's a gap between buildings. An alleyway funnel. A chokepoint. Danger. On the ground in front of her, just above her own shadow, is someone else's. A guy on a rooftop is ready to ambush her when she steps out.

She doesn't step out; she leaps. Spinning around in mid-air, she lets fly with everything she's holding. The resulting devastation would make any 30mm cannon envious.

Stones are bulky. There have to be better types of projectiles, but this is not a great time to start experimenting. Sienna finds drop-leg belt pouches on a guy who has no more use for them. Deep inside a sheltering doorway, she pauses. The stone hovering over her palm becomes hot. It nearly burns her finger.

Ow!

She flips her hand open. It falls, giving off heat waves like a barbeque coal. If she holds something and grips, heat promptly builds up. That almost makes sense. As much as any of it does.

A figure pops up in her view, his rifle ready. Her left hand flings out instinctively, and the man goes down sprawling. With her personal artillery making no sound besides a whipping impact, her enemies have no idea where she's shooting from. They line up like ninepins.

One veteran village fighter sees others, men he must have fought beside for years, go down one by one. He senses the rain of death has to be coming from a window or a doorway, but his mind cannot process just *how* that's happening.

Suddenly, his last remaining companion's shoulder is struck and obliterated. The fighter is alone. He loses it and runs away screaming. In his terror, he lapses into his home dialect, a variation on Nuristani. It has florid, emotional terms for expressing shock and awe. Perhaps he has not used these words since he was a boy listening to scary stories about demons told by his grandfather around the dying embers of their communal hearth fires.

"FROM THE SHADOWS!" the man shrieks. He falls briefly to his knees, as though the ground has been pulled out from under him. Scrambling to his feet, he keeps shouting to his dead friends and no one in particular. "From the very *shadows*—bolts of death. It is the Iblis made of the smokeless fire! It is come to kill us all for our sins. NO ONE CAN SAVE US!"

Unfortunately for him, he does not drop his rifle. He could run away until he thinks he's safe, then turn and take pot-shots at her back. The village fighter, scared out of his wits as he is, is still a threat. She has a smaller rock ready. It's about one inch across and pointed like an arrowhead. The hysterical man scuttles around debris, dodges between burning wrecks of cars. Funny thing is, Sienna hasn't thought about aiming at all. Not from the time her first projectile, a surplus molar, left her hand and found its necessary target.

This guy here, he's two hundred meters out and more. Running wild. A single bullet to center mass using iron sights? Difficult. A rock to his right kneecap? Impossible!

Until it happens.

The projectile skims out, leaving a razor-cut vapor trail in the mid-morning air. It takes out the running man's knee in a gout of bloody gristle and torn pants leg. He drops, rolls. He is still screaming, just not words anymore. He is out of the fight, but alive.

She feels she could have shot a mosquito off his shoulder if she had wanted. Crazy. Absurd. *Mine.* Her life depends on it.

She replenishes her ammo. Something the man yelled echoes through her combat-clear mind. *Iblis.* The sassy jinn angel who refused to bow to Adam. Bolts from shadows.

Shadowbolt, not bad.

On the bullet-pitted wall of a cellar doorway cling pieces

of mirror. Fragments reflect fiber-optic material embedded in two arms. They glow with unearthly energy. *My arms.*

***

A few minutes later, things suck, bad. Bullets snap, close enough to feel. She keeps her head behind solid cover. The hostiles are delighted. They have her pinned down; they have the hated Iblis dead to rights. Her assertive tactical plan has gone south hella fast. Sienna is caught in the middle of the town square. She jams herself up against a jumble of bricks that used to be the town's main well.

It crosses her mind that maybe, when she had the chance, she should have rolled on out in that truck. But if she had done that, quite a few of these guys would have had the pleasure of gnashing crooked yellow while cussing her out for having crawled off, as expected, like a whipped bitch.

And it is my sworn Army duty to exceed people's expectations.

Suppressing fire keeps her pinned. It is all she can do to keep her hard point from being out-flanked. Having seen their fellow killers taken out individually, Khalid's people amass down the street, supported by clumps of Artuk's men. They are preparing an all-out assault. One of the black robes screams with joyous hate to the white-bearded driver of the Zeus.

"Nasir! We have her now. USE THE BIG GUNS!"

As his buddies keep Sienna from dashing to better cover, good old Nasir cranks the chassis that holds four cannon barrels. Through a brickwork crevice, Sienna watches the turret swing from its normal vertical position to an awkward horizontal angle. Down the main street. At the well. At her.

This ruin-spewing monster is the guts of a quad ZSU. An anti-aircraft gun capable of letting loose a hailstorm of high explosive shells that can knock a modern jet out of the sky a mile straight up.

And here they are aiming it at poor little Sienna. She does not know whether to be shocked by their savagery or flattered. If they let loose with that fusillade of shrapnel, she will be neither. The mud bricks she huddles behind will be no more effective protection than tissue paper.

She seethes under the chastising lash of her inner demon. If she gets killed, they, the two of them, won't be able to hurt the rest of their enemies. And that would be unforgiveable. More offended at her own mistake than afraid, Sienna scans her six. No one's angling for a better shot. They don't want to be in the sights of the Zeus when it opens up.

There's a rusty piece of metal. Something that shook loose from a cart or trailer. She reaches out quickly to retrieve it, wincing slightly as the thud of rifle and pistol bullets impact where her hand has just been.

Getting ready to shoot at me with a freaking anti-aircraft gun! They must really feel threatened.

The ZSU has a hell of a kick. It's normally mounted on a twenty-ton tank. This one is perched on a civilian flatbed. And not a big American one at that. The first shots will be way off. She's sure. They have to be.

Sienna's assailants are so focused on her, none of them notice what's parked farther down the main drag. What they are all lined up in front of: a fuel truck. The long tanker sits low on its suspension, but that could be due to poor maintenance.

Let's hope it hasn't made its delivery yet.

To hit the fuel tank well and true, she will have to angle over a yard. Or two. Into the open street. The piece of metal in her hand starts to glow orange. Then its center blossoms white. Just when she feels her hand start to blister, the ear-splitting *WHUMP WHUMP WHUMP* report of the AA gun starts.

The muzzles of the Zeus are so close she can feel the overpressure as the weapon warms up to its firing rate of four thousand rounds per minute. The first shells hit dirt. Nasir over-compensated for the anticipated kickback. He lets up the trigger to adjust his sights.

Dust as thick as a smokescreen conceals her desperate lurch. Sienna lets fly. She can't see crap. She does not hear her projectile hit the oblong metal of the fuel truck. Yet she's certain it does.

It's called situational awareness, you geniuses.

A jet engine roar accompanies concussive fists of air, which fling a sandstorm of dust and a year's worth of gutter trash and her back down the street.

She sees

   hard-packed ground

    a patch of blue sky

     a gout of oily black smoke

    hard-packed ground

   a patch of blue sky

as she rolls like a tossed rag doll. Still, she's doing better than the enemy. They were in the gullet of the blast. Everything in the V-shaped avenue in front of her that can burn is suddenly, gloriously, on fire. Smoke chokes her nose, mouth, and lungs.

Sienna struggles around flames. A baser need competes with her desire to breathe. She can feel it. The battle is done.

Her racht is not. Into the empty spaces underneath human words, it whispers. Its desire permeates the hollows between sentient thoughts:

That Monster—he still hunts us. Hunts us as surely as we hunt him. These are his people, his hands. Crush them. Show no mercy. Make them feel your pain!

In front of her, a black-robed combatant tries to prop himself up on a splintered arm. His other hand holds a rifle. Sienna's kick to his head sends his neck snapping back and his body reeling into a dusty heap. He moves no more.

The shockwave from the fuel tanker blast has flattened half the village. Still, that leaves the other half for her enemies to hide in.

After them!

31

Airborne filth from burning gasoline and tires churn through streets, darkening them at mid-morning on this cloudless day. And Sienna is not finished, not by a long shot.

Somehow, Zeus-gunner Nasir survives—most of him anyway. With blackened, bloody hands he clutches the burnt drumstick stump that used to be his leg. He sees her and, incredibly, remembers he has a sidearm. He reaches for it with hate in the one eye not broiled out of its socket.

Sienna speaks quietly.

"This here is my big gun."

She sends a flat stone to crush the ribs over his heart. Bones splinter. The grizzled, broken fighter slumps against a pile of debris.

After the explosion there is an interlude, a stunned lull. In other places, one might expect to see a gathering of the brave or compassionate or curious. In other towns, there might be some influx of first responders who would sort through the wounded and fight fires as best they could. But this is old Khorasan, the north, the unforgiven land that scorns redemption. And its half-breed, bastard daughter has returned to kick over the hornets' nest. She dares them to come out and sting.

All semblance of command and control ceases for both newcomers and locals. Khalid's remaining men are convinced they have been betrayed. After regrouping to a strong point, the black robes shoot wildly at anything that moves. A few of the village fighters leave. Most of them, greedy for the hoard of cash known to be in the visitors' trucks, wage a counter-offensive in the streets and alleyways they know well.

Goaded by this offering of frail human hostility, Sienna feels her racht cast off its final restraining chains. She can no longer control it. She does not want to.

With the reflexes of an Olympic athlete, a lifetime of physical and tactical training, and her new abilities, none of them stands a chance. Two of Khalid's group hunker down beside the Toyota across the square. Black-coiffed heads pop up looking for a target. They are decapitated. Another runs with a belt-fed weapon to higher ground. That one's pelvis explodes and his body folds limply backward, like a rag doll.

With each pulse of energy, with every hyper-accelerated bolt fired, Sienna feels not weaker but stronger. The eerie fiber she can see in her arms and feel in her shoulders and back innervate, giving her ever more confidence in her destructive capacity.

She has the accuracy of the best scoped rifle she's ever fired, the stopping power of an artillery shell, and unlimited ammunition. She hears scuffling behind the last standing wall of a wrecked produce store. Two rifle muzzles poke up. She does not even break her stride. Four stone projectiles peal into the cinder blocks, blasting them into a jumble of dust and vaporized body parts: gray, pink, and brown. A final bolt bounces the rubble and makes sure.

Pent-up feral energies tear through Sienna's mind and body. Older than human reason, more powerful than conscious will. She accepts their singular purpose: to LASH OUT and make them all know her *Wrath*.

Sienna has been wary of going into close quarters since the debacle with Artuk. Nothing like having a seventy-year-old duffer get the drop on you to make you think twice about entering the maze of narrow alleys. But that's where her quarry is hiding. She follows.

Her powers and her liberated aggression prove effective against AK, pistol, and bayonet. One man's body ends up draped over a second-story balcony, carried along by the enormous energy of a half-pound projectile traveling just under the speed of sound. His corpse makes a mess of a window box stuffed with flowers and radishes.

Concussion can kill as effectively as shrapnel. And it does. Sienna sends a two-handed bolt into the midst of four ambushers. Bones snap, organs rupture, ears and eye sockets run liquid scarlet.

I am your Beast, straining at my bonds, tied up, abused, taunted beyond enduring. Now unleashed. I am racht, I am all of you and more!

One of Khalid's black robes searches for the phantom enemy in the cellar of a house. He rips up a flimsy wooden trap door. A frightened teenage girl in a rust-colored scarf stares up. She's not the female he's looking for. A local. Useless.

Frustrated, he rifle-butts the village girl full on her cheek. She sprawls back into the hiding place, into a cluster of the young and the elderly. This black robe is one of the group paid to cut the head off a chained captive and return the trophy to their master. Him!

Sienna hears herself whisper, "Look."

Khalid's man spins around and sees her. Then he sees no more. Two small rocks go through his eyes.

Look! And find only my merciless gaze staring back.
No tears for you as you fall.

Another man comes out of a doorway, his machete raised. Sienna jams her elbow in Machete Man's throat. She takes the two-foot blade out of his hands and wings it, hardly looking. It sprouts out of the chest of another onrushing enemy.

No tears of sorrow.
None of exultation.

Machete Man comes up off the ground and grapples with her, eyes bulging, gasping through a bruised airway, still trying to strangle and gouge her. Sienna might have knocked out Machete Man. She is not that far gone, she can tell, still tell, the difference between combatants and bystanders. Or disarmed guys trying to give up. But the poor fellow is persistent. And clearly, he is a man who loves his knives.

He pulls another blade from his belt. Sienna punches him behind the ear and spins him around, facing him away from her. He jabs backward at her head as she wrestles his left hand into a hammer lock. Sienna does her best to choke him unconscious without killing him. He doesn't appreciate her gesture. He cuts his own shoulder in his bloodlust to carve Sienna's features off.

Sienna has no stone. But improvisation is always at hand, and so is the man's spine. As she slides left to avoid his wild backward stabbing, she presses her palm against the unruly guy's back. Her new sense of touch extends a few inches above her metacarpal bones. She can feel through squishy skin and fat to something round and solid: one of his lumbar vertebrae. Must be L1 or L2. In the heat of the moment, she can't be sure. It does not matter. It feels much like a rock. The man bites her forearm. It hurts. Before Machete Man can tear off a juicy chunk of her flesh and wriggle away, L1 (or L2) comes shooting out of his chest. It hits the wall opposite with a wet *thunk*.

No tears, only yearning.

Hunger.

For More!

The silversmith's storefront explodes out into the main square. Sienna ducks the blowback of brick splinters and shattered glass. In the village square, the crater made by the exploded gasoline tanker still burns. It forms a ring of fire, as if someone slit the navel of the Wandering Desert to let the intestines of Hell peek out. There are no more shots. All the gunmen are dead or incapacitated.

Recklessly, Sienna launches herself over tumbling rubble. She is thirsty, possibly severely dehydrated. She can't stop. She's getting good at stacking her shots up to three in each hand at once. Acrid smoke from pooled machine oil smells like air drifting across the clear, wide lake near her North Carolina home. Brimstone contrails of her bolts add gentle incense. Venturesome licks of fire find a home on shattered timbers. To either side of her, these flare and crackle. Nothing moves. Nothing living dares make noise as she walks, slowly now, down the smoldering avenue.

To her left, movement. More nourishment for the

insatiable? Her hands charge up with power, now as natural for her as drawing breath. Ready to rend flesh and deal death in an instant…

She stops.

In her sights is a trembling, filth-encrusted man. A desperate beggar. He sees her and stops searching a fallen body for some meager allowance that will allow him to survive one more day. He recognizes his peril. So does his companion, a bony mutt with a pitifully tattered coat hanging over jutting ribs. Only one of the man's legs will bend. He kneels on the one that works in supplication to Sienna. His dog adopts a similar posture, lowering its head to the ground.

Sienna meets the beggar's wide-open, bloodshot eyes. Her arms are streaked with soot, her hair trails ash. Embedded fiber optics glow. She must appear to be a spirit, an elemental goddess of destruction.

ENOUGH!

NEVER!

They've had enough.

No!

Sienna recalls herself and is suddenly, utterly exhausted. She looks at the beggar. He is a cripple wandering in a merciless land, forced to loot from the dead. But even he has a friend and loyal companion.

Enough.

Seeing it will receive no more sustenance, the coiled thing inside her retreats. Hissing and snapping its greedy jaws, it ebbs—for a time.

Sienna's racht passes.

She is alone.

Destroy is all she can do. As for mercy, the most merciful thing would have been never to come to this place. She surveys the devastated settlement. A full-on air raid could not have done more damage.

The locals. They're beaten. There's nothing left to destroy. What little they had, gone. The shop fronts of what used to be the main drag are burned out. Khalid's men, all dead. The village's fighting men have been killed or crippled, leaving it vulnerable to roving bandits or the designs of hostile clans. Seeing the smoke, displaced fighters from all over the Six Hills will be incoming soon. They will see an opportunity to take advantage of the power vacuum left by the sudden passing of Artuk.

Her knees fall onto the dirt of the street. Small puffs of dust rise. She does not have the strength to find shelter and collapse. Wreckage of buildings and vehicles flare spates of flame. These daytime torches illuminate the last three players on the stage of her Armageddon-themed morality play—the beggar, his pet, and her.

Improbably, inside an overturned Jeep, the radio has switched on. A woman's cheery voice chirps.

"...and now back to BBC International News, updates from around the globe with Jeremy Greffer."

"Thank you, Christy. News from the world of science tops our stories today. Correspondents in Europe are still sorting out the somewhat conflicting reports coming in from the Lichtstrom. Eye witnesses have reported some kind of glitch during the super collider testing of the artifact popularly known as the Ansible.

"And while we wait on those updates, we can happily report a major advance in unmanned space exploration. Have you ever *wanted to get away from it all? Well, today the probe launched by China's CNSA, which they've appropriately named* Adventurer, *landed billions of kilometers away from Earth on Eris. Named after the Greek goddess of Chaos, this lonely planetoid is as far as you can go out in space and still be in our solar system..."*

32

I am a trapdoor spider.
Sweat-stained folds of a kufeya headdress frame a window into a blasted wasteland.

You'll never see me till I want you to.

Every small movement sends dust motes swirling out into the steady rays of the sun. Every exhalation pulls precious moisture out of her body. For some reason—maybe successive blows to the head—she thinks of heat blasting from a pizza oven. A specific pizza oven. A place in Fayetteville where she worked one summer. From shin to shoulder, the cooks all had symmetrical burn scars from each of the six heavy doors. If she passed by while these were open she'd have to hold her breath. Heat. Unbreathable. The broiling inside would blister a hand in seconds. Now she's in the center of one hundreds of miles across.

An hour ago, her ride bled out. Cracked hoses impossible to patch, it was a goner. She got far enough to see the Six Hills from the other side. The low mounds float off the ground on a cushion of heat waves. Behind them, a small trail of smoke fades up into Khorasan's callous blue sky. This signal of distress did not go unnoticed.

After the battle, scores of bandits from the Six Hills descended on the crippled settlement. Like eager ants and flesh-hungry beetles, they came singly at first, then all at once. The community she tore apart lay like raw carrion left on the edge of the scouring maw of the Wandering Desert. Nothing would go to waste. As unsavory as Artuk's successors are, her fight is not with them. She found a working car and this time had the good sense to drive away. Lucky for the invaders.

Besides avoiding hostiles, her priority was to find a satellite phone. One that worked. One whose plastic housing was not melted into the fingers of a rudely severed hand. That didn't happen. And the best choice of working vehicles did not last long under the relentless assault of heat and dust of the open road. It's only use now is as bait.

She takes a small sip of water and thinks on ways to continue her sojourn away from Dodge. One method would be to let herself be captured and do the old "Surprise! I'm a railgun and you're dead" trick. But she hates repeating tactics. There is also the nagging problem that the story of her violent escape must have hit the terror chat channels by now. That would scare her pursuers. Scared people shoot first, then send dogs in to bite the corpses. Then they shoot again.

The battered egg-shell blue car slumps in a roadside depression. Only partially hidden, dirt randomly covers shiny parts, and the roof is topped with dry twigs. Sloppy and dumb. *Perfect*. It looks like someone incompetent tried to camouflage it.

Her real ambush dugout has a decent view of the winding road and even a good patch of sky to watch for friendly aircraft.

From the outside, the viewing gap is just another crack in a brittle landscape. She crouches, sips water, and does anything to distract herself from the one thing she dreads: looking at herself.

She rolls up the light cloth covering her arm. It's still there. *Was it just going to disappear?*

Maybe it will come off with a good scrubbing, using sandpaper if necessary. She runs her fingers over her arm, along the seamless join where her flesh meets the border of deeply set something. Cyan and magenta and iridescent silver, those are the colors the stuff reveals.

Something's been bugging her. The RAPTEK magnetics are only supposed to work on metal. She picks up a car key bauble. The garish lips-and-tongue trinket is a pretty racy accessory in this part of the world. The owner was risking a flogging for the sake of personal style. It's made of only plastic. Sienna thinks about closing her fingers. Only thinks about it. The bauble floats, starts to bubble and melt. It becomes a tiny, Daliesque icon. Before it can scald, she flings it.

Okay, then.

Next, she checks the improvised bandage covering the spot where the Chechen went all Dr. Zhivago on her arm with his bayonet. The area is scabbed but not infected. The gouge is closed and raised. Tender. Could it be healing? Equipment doesn't regenerate. It works until it breaks or gets junked.

At least the power plant didn't blow. One item stuck in her mind from her glance over the instruction manual. There was no maximum amperage or voltage. Perdix and his bunch hadn't analyzed all their Ansible-based invention could do. They were more concerned with keeping it all a big secret.

Boy, were they gonna get all grumpy when she showed them what was left. Was it such a big deal? They must have the blueprints somewhere. And they could always clone more power chips.

The weapons system… the power source… the Ansible.

My accident. Could they be connected?

What really happened in Europe at the Lichtstrom on March 19? First home, then answers.

Sienna waits.

The sun slides down the inverted bowl of the sky like a fiery eye, staring, greedy. Sand scuttles down the rim of her hide. Like an itch in the back of her brain, she's teased by the notion the sand grains are being kicked back by the spiny feet of a scorpion. A scorpion which has become so much a part of the landscape it is now invisible to self-aware observers.

No. No scorpion. But yes, movement.

Vibrations. Farther off. She feels them moments after the sand sensed them. And right after that, she hears. A motor. Coming closer. A truck. She remains motionless in her spider hole.

***

Twenty minutes later, Sienna is still an unfulfilled carjacker. The armed men on the road below her position are not cooperating. They just sit in their truck. And chat. They look at the badly hidden car. Look at each other. Look in their empty back seat. But they don't get out. They're supposed to get clear so there's no chance of her replacement ride getting damaged during the double helping of mayhem she wants to serve up.

They sit. In the heat.

The longer this goes on, the greater the chance they'll call reinforcements. For now, they're just talking and smoking. Exhaled fumes billow out the half-rolled-down windows. The truck is a fly ride. It looks in good shape, with plenty of water and gas. Well worth stealing, T-Rex would say. They must be trekking somewhere special, maybe a marketplace.

I can't let it get away.

Sometimes a bat-crap idea can result in a good plan. It better, because her next move probably involves a bullet hitting her.

She does not have any firearms. There were no serviceable bolt guns. Even loading up a semi-auto mag could lead to unwanted and explosive results. No matter. Using rocks and pieces of metal bare-handed, she had as good a range as she'd have with any gun.

Sienna wraps a stick in a cloth. Exhaling, she tightens the straps of her salvaged torso armor. It is wraparound articulated rhino-skin armor, rated for multiple hits. Hopefully, she will not have to test its limits. An empty water bag filled with hydraulic fluid completes her outfit. She prepared it with notions of spattering the windshield of a passing car or mixing it with the diesel to signal friendly aircraft with a multicolored smoke smear. The fluid is red. She can use it.

Bursting out of cover, she accelerates a small rock. The projectile makes a hypersonic crack and impacts just in front of the stopped truck. Two men wearing track suits jump out. To them, she's a figure on the ridge who has taken a badly aimed shot with a weapon bundled up against sand exposure.

This could work.

Incoming bullets kick up sand around her.

Or not.

Sienna pretends to be frightened by the overwhelming force her assailants bring to bear, and flees. She keeps her head down and runs straight away from the gunmen. Only the upper A-zone of her back presents a target. A near miss makes her grimace and duck her head lower.

Spak!

Wide. If she pretends to be hit, they won't believe it.

Elbows in. Head down... *Okay, where did these two learn to sh—*

Crack!

Right above her kidney, an impact like a horse's kick sends her sprawling. She eats sand.

Freaken AKs. Why can't they shoot each other with 5.56s like polite folks?

Sienna makes sure her fake gun is still bundled and flung well away. She squeezes the bag of hydraulic fluid; it dribbles out of the ragged hole over her back. Then she sprawls her hands out, clutching loose sand as if in a death grip. That should be unmistakable.

Sienna keeps her breathing shallow. Tense seconds tick by. One of the guys approaches. Only one climbs up the dune. Good. The other stays guarding the truck in case she's a distraction for a larger group.

She can't risk looking back. In front, all she can see is the shadow of a man. He stands, tense, ready to fire at any movement. She stays still. The moment passes. The shadow man looks back to check on his friend, then slings his rifle backward. He prepares to use both hands to search her for valuables.

He's closer, then closer still. When he's good and close, she turns over. And gets a blast of sunlight in her eyes. When she formulated her original bat-crap plan, the sun was higher in the sky! She can't see anything. There's a soft clatter as the startled attacker reaches around for his weapon. The stone she prepared flies out of her fingers too soon. With a snap and a whistle, it flies off. No time to fish for a new one, Sienna uses what she has. A handful of sand.

A stream of tiny particles jets in the direction of the silhouetted head of the gunman. His face gets sandblasted to the bone. He collapses back with a strangled cry from a lipless hole. Sienna blinks at black spots in her vision. She can see well enough to bring the stick down good and solid behind his ear stump.

Right then, the second belligerent decides to join. Sienna tries to drop him with the piece of wood. It only careens off the sand, totally missing its mark. Too big. Her opponent kneels and aims carefully. Body armor or not, this fellow will not stop shooting until she's full of holes and leaking real blood.

She dives forward as though she were on the grass field on some school ground, lurching for a touchdown. The first burst of incoming bullets misses, though not by much. He eases off the trigger to get her back in his sights.

There's no cover.

A mess of gravel-sized stones score and cut her palms. She clenches them in her fists and accelerates them the twenty-odd meters at the crouching enemy.

Tiny rocks whiz through the air like a hundred shotgun

pellets, peppering the antagonist's chest, arms, and torso. Some debris flying at supersonic speed must also have lodged down the barrel of his weapon. Sienna can tell, because when he fires at her again at point-blank range, the rifle's breech explodes. The shooter's headgear, scalp, and a good chunk of forehead bone burst up and out.

The echo of the AK breech rupture eddies between escarpments along the road. It fades into a malevolent silence. Sienna scrambles to the lip of the sand precipice and looks down. No movement on the road. There is no third guy.

She sits down. This hurts. So she lies down. That also hurts, as does breathing.

Close. Way close. The ceramic inserts over her back are cracked. One more good hit...

Forget about that. Like Carlos Hathcock said, a miss is as good as a mile. Of course, the famous jarhead rarely missed.

On your feet, McKnight. Gotta get away from here before more of them show.

Fake blood runs down her leg. It joins with her enemy's genuine gore and the mix is lapped up by omnivorous sand. She lets the harness holding her body armor fall. The lightening of a few pounds throws her off, makes her dizzy. She has to brace on one knee. Maybe she's more dehydrated than she thought. Or else this thing, the thing she does, takes *her* energy as well. Either way, she has a working truck. Side-stepping down the dune, a fresh bruise welling on her back gives a sharp pinch with every step.

Latched to the flatbed of her new ride is not as much gasoline as she hoped, but certainly enough water for days. And in a milspec metal box, something else. Could it be the mythical satellite phone? She pulls it out and dusts it off. Cyrillic letters on the outside. It's a Russian GPS unit. She hits the power switch, and a cracked, dirty LED screen lights up.

ГЛОНАСС/GPS

RA.645876

IN.578531

That's where she is, down to the meter, as designated in New GLONASS grid codes.

"Fat lot of good that's going to do me."

For some reason, the numbers stick in her mind. It's not even a NATO grid, just some proprietary system the Russians have been trying to sell to private industry. Could be useful to know her coordinates; maybe there's a Luxphone in the cab. She flings open the passenger door. And then the only sounds are the rush of desert heat and the beating of two hearts.

33

A boy. Local, from the looks of him. He scrunches back in the bench-style seat behind the driver's chair. Sienna checks his hands. Empty. *Empty is good*. He looks… familiar? She pushes the impossible flash of recognition out of her mind. There's something else that jabs at her, something about the way he's sitting. The big jacket he's got on. It's zipped up. In this heat?

"Hey there, little man," she says in Dari. "I'm not going to hurt you."

Most likely he's a forced recruit or a hostage from a rival village. "Why don't you come up and sit in the front?" Sienna gently reaches back to bring him to the front. As he shifts away from her, from under the hem of his oversized jacket poke two loops of twisted electrical wires.

The only part of Sienna that moves are her pupils; they dilate and then relax. She'd been this close to live ordnance before. But a bomb vest appearing just like that, strapped to some kid, one who those two planned to use to attack some school or hospital while they drove safely away… this atrocity brings so many emotions rushing toward the already fragile dam holding her mind together.

It holds.

After trauma and torture. After killing and nearly being killed so many times in the past two days. By some grace, Sienna keeps it together, if only by a thread. And that strand has to be strong enough for just one more marvel. Just one more. It has to hold.

For one more.

That's what goes through her head as it vibrates with the rushing thumping noise of her own pulse. What she says out loud, as though she's just noticed an untied shoelace on the sneakers of the boy cowering in the back of the truck is, "Please, be very still. Let's see what you've got there. Let's see what they did to you."

Sienna slowly reaches forward. The kid is breathing fast. A sheen of sweat gathers above his upper lip and eyebrows. Slanted rays of the sun bore through side windows. They shine off the fine dark stubble on his close-shaved head. Gently, she examines, then eases down, the jacket zipper, revealing the device. It's a webbing-vest apparatus. Way too big for him. The bomb maker probably sewed it for a man. A man who lost his nerve. And then they grabbed this child from somewhere.

Somewhere not far?

The village of Six Hills? In the confusion of the destruction she caused, who would notice a kidnapping? If this isn't the same boy Denbow intended to kill, he could be his twin. She saved him then. She's got to do it again. She is going to. Just once more.

The explosive apparatus is padlocked, but only through the wire loops of the ammo carrier they rigged with explosives.

The boy can be cut free, but that would mean reaching around his back. No way.

From experience and everything the bomb jockeys have told her, each of these devices are unique. Not built to last. Volatile. The builder would have told them, the now-dead guys, not to lean forward, or to the left. She doesn't know, she can't know. She has to disarm it here in the truck.

Most of the triggering mechanism is hidden. On the practice models at the Base, there's normally a push trigger or dead man's switch. It's nearly always close to the arming trigger that sets the whole device hot. There is often a remote, in case the bomber gets incapacitated or chickens out.

Or happens to be a kidnapped boy who doesn't know he is supposed to die.

Sienna takes a deep breath and tries to let it out smoothly. Like she's glad. So glad just to be hanging out with her new chum in the middle of Khorasan's spacious Wandering Desert.

She forces a smile. The kid responds, a little. The trick will be cutting the enablers without closing any trigger circuits. The vest in front of her has too many wires sticking out. Probably just extra junk the bomb maker looped around and didn't bother to trim off. She has to check each one.

"What's your name? If we're going to hang out here for a while, I can't keep calling you 'little guy.' No, you're too old for that, almost a man."

The boy does not answer her. More troubling still, he does not look at her.

"We'll have you out of this in no time. Just sit still."

Slowly she pulls out her multi-tool. Sienna opens the smallest, least scary penknife she thinks will do the job. Then, covering it with her hand so as not to frighten him, she brings it forward.

"Hold still, just like that. You're doing really, really well. You know, my mom used to tell me a story. Whenever I was getting my hair cut or she was measuring me for clothes. It was about a beautiful butterfly that was sitting right on top of my head…"

The sun's slanted rays are a boot heel crushing their small metal box into the brick oven of the unpaved road. Every part of Sienna perspires.

On the boy's closely shorn scalp, moisture drips. Liquid materializes seemingly from nowhere and streams down over his quivering eyebrows, down his face, drip dropping off his chin. It lands, pools, and makes blotches on the dusty, olive drab jacket that looks ridiculous in this heat.

Outside, across the desert landscape in the windows, the land has become impossibly still and hushed, as though it is watching. As though it is feeding on their life force. Hers and that of the boy.

With skilled hands, ones that seem to move on their own, Sienna ferrets out the looped dead ends. Three in total. And the single trigger set. This device is a quick and dirty job. No wireless connection. Just a timer and push detonator. The timer is off.

No use thinking about whether her changed body might set off the bomb. Her hands are the only tool she's got that can save the boy. The wires are exposed, no extra conduit housing. Easy to trace their circuit. Good. Just one wire to cut. Just one.

"…and if I moved, the butterfly would be scared and fly away. But if I held still it would tell me of the wonderful, far-off lands it had been to…"

Just one…

She brings the multi-tool blade up to the dirty, twisted wire. The crucial circuit.

Just…

She clips the twitchy, death-summoning copper ligament cleanly in two, twisting one end down and away.

… one.

It's done. Safe.

Now to find some bolt cutters or keys for the—

Suddenly the boy flings open the side door and bursts out. Sienna grabs his coat.

"NO!"

He struggles out of it easily. The bomb vest remains padlocked to his narrow torso, secured over a drenched undershirt.

He runs off. One, two, three, four, five paces over the sand. She lets go of the dusty jacket and reaches out—

He explodes.

Something she missed. The cut wires touching somehow. A lousy crimp job on the primer, anything could have been the cause. Or nothing at all.

The result is instantly fatal to the boy.

Shrapnel had been loaded in with the charge pouches—nails, bent screws, scraps from a metal workshop floor. The maker, to save resources, only loaded the front pockets with explosives.

The concussive blast slams the truck door shut, then rocks the whole vehicle so fiercely Sienna's dazed body flies out the passenger side.

The whole ruin threatens to tip over. The truck teeters above her momentarily insensible body like the jaw of some huge spring trap. It totters on the whisper blade edge of chomping down.

Then the smoking bulk slams back down onto torn shock absorbers and burning tires.

Sienna's face is bloody; she can see it in the side mirror dangling in front of her. Pieces of glass string along her forehead like the front of a tiara. As soon as she can draw breath back into her lungs, she releases a hoarse cry.

Just one, just one more, why couldn't, why couldn't you...?

She runs out of words, out of coherent thoughts.

Fingers tighten around palms full of sand. Hate for the men who did this. Guilt over another failure. Frustration at *another innocent life lost!*

Her hands convulse. Sand superheats and turns into globs of molten glass. Like her anger, she cannot hold it any longer.

With an anguished yell, she lets fly. Fat glass beads strike the hood of the wrecked Jeep like brittle-skinned pieces of a useless falling star. Pinprick needles burst upwards into a thousand prisms, they scatter through the air, gouging out a million colors from the pale, fading rays of the unflinching sun.

The thunder clap of her rage. Its heat and the heat. Then one heart beats against the sand.

34

She speaks to an oddly shaped stick. Her words are thin. They pass through her ears and awareness without trace.

"   "

_{Hey bub, get outta my way! I got places to be.}

She's on all fours. No. She wants to be on all fours. First, though, she'll do one elbow. Then figure a way around this stick in her path, and then, when she's good and ready, she'll get back to crawling.

The day's throat has been slashed neatly across at the horizon, and darker blue oozes up out of the wound. It is almost done, and she with it. Her forehead stopped leaking blood. The ringing just behind her jawbone has quieted. Concussive mementos left by the child-bomb.

That seemed like it could have been the last. The one she wouldn't get up from. Worse than any of the assaults during the village battle, more wounding than any bodily insult courtesy of the Chechen. The dead one, whose name escapes her just now.

Even down there in that cellar, down there she felt freer than she did moving away from the destroyed truck. Crawling, then walking, now crawling again, away from the kid-sized crater on the other side of the road. That jail held more liberty than the empty horizon and the jeering sky. Back then, down there in that dank, foul chamber, there was something which had burned away in this crucible: a chance the good guys could win.

Out in the open, she wants to escape. Alone in the Wandering Desert facing a stupid stick, jutting out of nowhere, she feels hemmed in. She's got to get away from this crowd.

Harrr.

Irony buzzes in her skull like a fly in bottle. She's dying of dehydration. She needs a deluge of water to come up and over her. Not to waste on drinking, she needs it to engulf her, to wash her clean. Her skin, so crackling hot and dry, the water touching it would cause each drop to hiss and bubble and burst into steam. Steam she could disappear into.

This last wish, the mirage grants.

***

A rushing noise. It grows closer. She can almost make sense of it. She knows what it is. A cool stream feeding a lake, deep and clear to many fathoms. Just out of sight. She can hear and smell that water. She arrives at a place that invades her mind, and there is no need to drink, she can just breathe in… the cooling…

Sand and sun melt into rolling green hills. Fog shrouds sixteen-year-old Sienna as she stares at her father's grave.

A stoically carved headstone stands alone. The weather-pitted gray cairn is surrounded by highland moors so floridly green they hypnotize the eyes of outlanders.

Kelley O. Langton
Beloved Son and Brother and Friend
Aged 21

No mention of his being a parent on the headstone. But after a long search and a hack into Britain's National Health Services database, Sienna had no doubts. The DNA on file proved Kelley Langton, son of middle-class Scots, became a father at seventeen and died four years later in a riding accident.

No hint he ever knew what happened to Hamida after she was deported. Had Kelley Langton heard of her death? Her murder? How would he ever have learned the true facts of that final hour?

It had taken Sienna the better part of a decade to reach this place. First had come the revelation from Annalies that she had not been orphaned by a car accident. Bit by bit, teenage Sienna reconstructed her personal history. Public records from Cambridge University provided glimpses. Hamida had come from what is now Khorasan to study English and sciences.

Archived news stories and videos yielded jumbled facts. A few column inches on back pages reported a short-lived public protest led by a women's shelter group. A thirty-second news clip showed them petitioning energetically against Hamida's deportation. They spoke and wrote in vain. She was a pregnant minor in the UK. Hamida's nearest male relative demanded her return. Forcible repatriation was inevitable. For her, there was no sanctuary.

In all of the documents, the names of participant minors were cut out. The deeper Sienna dug, the more shocking the possibilities. For some horrific days and nights, Sienna thought her biological father was the student who attacked Hamida in her rented Cambridge apartment soon after she arrived.

She needed a reliable source. Then Sienna's darkest fear was dispelled by the oddest of characters. A year before visiting Langton's final resting place in the highlands, she had a long Lux/Net talk with an English woman. A woman who had answers.

Seventeen years earlier, this woman ran a small storefront women's shelter in Chelmsford. London's *Citizen Juggernaut* quoted her in interviews advocating Hamida's case for asylum. When Sienna tracked her down, her organization had grown into a charitable network all over the UK and beyond. She was Fiona Fitzgibbons, registered nurse, retired. She talked a lot.

"Oh, yes, yes, dearie, I remember. 'Orrid thing. 'Orrid. Sixteen years ago, t'was, but still like yesterday for me."

The stout, gray-haired woman shook her head morosely in Sienna's monitor.

"Now she, your mum, wot a brave girl she was, through and through, brave 'n steadfast."

The year before Sienna was born, university records showed Hamida stopped attending lectures. The same week, local Cambridge papers reported a disturbance and an attack on an unnamed female student.

"That was 'er, for certain. We talked fer hours. 'Er English was very proper. Poor lass. And the one who done it, she was still deathly afeared o' 'im."

There was one thing, one thing above all Sienna had to know. Was the attacker... Could he somehow be her father?

"Oh, no! Ne'er that! Work it out, girl. You was born in

September. Hamida run away from Cambridge not later'n October year previous. The villain weren't no more yer father than Jack the Ripper."

Mrs. Fitzgibbon's face pinched with memories of old upset and simmering resentment.

"I always suspected Whitehall political tinkerin' with the case for her asylum. I did, and I do! T'wasn't right, sendin' her back like that. For all it's worth, I think she'd be proud o' you. All you've done getting into your nice military college. West Point. I do like the sound o' that. Keep you out o' mischief, West Point will."

Sienna's next question was obvious. Her genetic father was referred to only as Joe Bloggs, the UK equivalent of John Doe.

"I seen 'im once, I did. Tall fer 'is age, but just a lad. Only seen 'im once, mind. Only once. 'is parents whisked 'im away back ta the highlands. Had to leave 'is place o' work. They had a scandal when they come back from vacation and found a girl livin' in the barn with a bun in the oven. Sorry missy, tha' bun woulda been you."

Fiona Fitzgibbons had smiled so meekly Sienna could forgive her immediately for referring to her as a bun, and missy.

"Now, the one in charge o' the case, chief inspector at tha', Coriander-Phelps. 'e'd have all the records. 'e's since died. Sorry ta say, 'e'll be no help findin' yer poor pa."

On that score, Mrs. Fitzgibbons was wrong. The late Chief Inspector Coriander-Phelps kept meticulous notes. Getting them cost Uncle Bryan a favor with someone at the Military Intelligence Corps. An official request to Interpol got them her father's name and the medical files from the inquest into the accident that killed him. These included a sample of Kelley Langton's DNA. A mail-in paternity testing company confirmed the final link. There could be no doubt.

Langton's parents never learned anything about their granddaughter. Sienna never contacted them. Perhaps she couldn't face the possibility they might look on her with prejudice. She was a half-breed. Or, as Bryan used to term it, they were both "made to order". Perhaps the Langtons would be suspicious she was after money. A bastard child turning up out of the blue was not something Sienna could be. And for what? To reconnect with distant family? To ask for answers they didn't have? No.

By then Sienna knew who her real family was. She was a McKnight. The trip to West Lothian, Scotland, was booked with Sarge Bryan's travel miles and made with Annalies's blessing. After a hike to the cemetery in the hills, she rested in front of the small grave mound.

The weight of Hamida's murder, the reality of a dead father she had never known and who would never know her, all came crashing down upon her there above the sodden, loamy earth. There, alone on the moorland, her tears merged with the dew dappled on her cheeks by fog until she could no longer tell which was which. Kelley Langton's marker stone also gathered and sheathed off tiny water droplets borne by imperceptibly moving air. The stone, hard and weathered, also wept.

35

Something snaps her back. Back to where scalding day is stalked by tendrils of freezing night.

Some primal trigger deep within her nervous system causes one final surge of adrenaline from nearly exhausted glands sitting on battered, withering kidneys. Swollen eyelids scrape over tear ducts long since dry. The deflation of the lush green mirage leaves her in a backwash of lucidity and sand.

She recognizes the insolent twig in her way, the one topped by curious bumps. A foot in front of her, it nods at her. Not wood, rather a scaly, brown-speckled snake adorned with devilish horns.

El-ṭorîsha. Also known as the horned desert viper… *poisonous.*

They look at each other. Both on their bellies. Eye to eye. Nose to darting tongue. They share a moment. It passes. The viper bids her a frosty good night and slithers home.

In front of her, pads of moisture, blood and sweat, even some thickened saliva press onto the sandpaperish topsoil. Her skin betrays her. *Benedict Arnold skin!* The natural pores in it, the newly added collection of cuts, even the openings of her sinuses, all let liquid escape. The patterns they make are a Rorschach tease. Before Sienna can make them out, they evaporate.

She's up. *Don't remember doing that.*

She's walking. *Where to again? Oh yes.*

Away from the horned viper. South, to the Fertile Spear; it's her only chance. Irrigation pipelines run all over. All along them are remote first-aid stations. Once activated, Worldwide Help will come. They are among the select group of people not likely to kill her on sight.

A sound. Loud enough to penetrate the dry fog rattling around her head.

So unnatural. It must be real.

Awareness of it causes her body to move. Her groggy conscious mind is a step behind her lifetime of training and hunter's reflexes. When it catches up, Sienna finds herself crouched behind a big rock, listening.

Noises get sifted in the space between her eardrums and her thinking. She recognizes them. Muffled ATV engines and the odd brief command coming from men's mouths. She cannot make out the language or the words. Whoever it is, they are coming closer. Quickly.

Her dehydration-addled mind still works, just slower.

Doesn't make sense.

Those dune machines are only short range. There are no towns around except the one she has destroyed. Perhaps those two monsters, the suicide-bomb kidnappers, had radioed in her position. Except they had been driving dark, off the grid, with a switched-off GPS unit.

USA friendlies then? The promise is nearly tempting

enough to believe in. Sarge Bryan's liquid-gold cybernetic eyes finding her in the distance before anyone else saw her. His smiling face. And, as long as she's fantasizing, she has to add Nobu with a cryo twelve-pack of brew borrowed from Captain Bobblehead's private stash.

Not likely.

The *Lee* and Bryan could have picked up on her position by stealth drone. But SOP would be to get her attention, then drop a survival kit with an encrypted handset. She'd have a few hours to sip milspec electrolyte replenisher before enjoying a chopper exfil after dark.

The ship's XO, Bianchi, would definitely not send a bunch of cowboy Marines on four-wheeled motorcycles.

"This way!" one of her cowboy pursuers shouts, his accent indistinct.

Whoever they are, they've got her tracks.

Gotta hide and find some ammo.

Minutes later, Sienna slumps at the mouth of a gorge. Dark soon. They will have night-vision. She will have a great chance of breaking her ankle. Her persistent trackers spread out through the jumbled rocks of a canyon. One wanders too far.

In real life, creeping up behind people hardly ever works. Waiting for them to come round the corner of an outcrop and slamming them on the head with a log, that has a higher success rate.

Her arms are nearly as wooden feeling as her club. She has to put her whole body into it. Thankfully, she connects with a discreet *whunk*, one his companions didn't hear. Sienna drags her insensible pursuer into the shadows. He looks Caucasian.

Long hair. Unshaven. Cute when asleep. She searches him for water.

Nothing. Not even a crappy energy bar. It must all be on those ATVs. Odd insignia. Not the WWHI Serpens. She checks his other gear. The desert kit he has on is no standard outfitting of any armed forces she knows.

Dreaming Boy has a lot of custom stuff, like special-ops rigging, but traveling much lighter. There's a sidearm, but most interesting is his shoulder weapon. An EEL launcher. Dubbed the "sea cucumber round" by T-Rex because of the—to him—hilarious shape and texture of the projectile it fires. Electroshock enveloping ligatures are purposed to incapacitate, not kill.

Maybe friends of old Artuk, bent on taking me alive for my salvage value?

Sienna turns her captive over, crosses his hands and slaps an EEL stun-cuff round onto his wrists. The smart non-lethal emits a small electric jolt. Then, sensing no struggle, stops. Epoxy goo hardens, securely binding the commando's wrists. She stashes the remaining EEL rounds in her new webbing. She leaves the launcher. At about three pounds, in her state, it looks a might heavy. Good thing she's got her own launchers, as long as the batteries last.

She rises to her feet. Too quickly. Sienna catches herself before collapsing. The small nook of dusk shade fills with stars of her own making. She sits down again until her vision clears. Shaking her head does not help much. She realizes the fix she's in.

Too many.

They're not amateurs either. They'll have their

transportation guarded.

Got to make… make it out of this damned canyon.

The canyon has other ideas. Annoying geology formed it with only one entrance and a sheer back wall. No use trying to climb it. Even if she had the energy, a fly would be visible trying to make the ascent.

The hard way, then.

"Crikey, she's a fast one!"

"Up there, I sawr her!"

Australians and South Africans? What the heck is going on?

"Careful. Don't shoot off any EELs unless you hafta. Someone get eyes on, now!"

Whoever you are, *get eyes on this!*

Sienna dips out of her hiding place and sends out a chunk of sandstone. A puff of dust explodes off a soldier's flak vest. Deciding to return the non-lethal favor until they force the issue, she uses less than full acceleration. Not that she has much choice. Each discharge of energy leaves her battered and worn body weaker.

Too weak. And that's no good for anyone. Sienna feels *it* rising. She barely restrained her smoky wraith at the Six Hills village. Hours have passed like a blur. Hours filled with dehydration. Filled with getting shot. With watching a kid get blown up by the cruelest of monsters. She feels its seductive strength. Her vǫrthr, whose plaything is indiscriminate death, rises.

No!

Sienna looks to her hands. She can barely focus. Her breath comes in short rasps. The next piece of stone won't even float in her palm.

Out of juice. Guess… we'll have to give… 'em the old fastball then…

You are weak. So weak.

If her hand were not on the rock outcrop, she's sure she would keel over. Preparing to hurl her projectile, she dips out again—

Let

And slams cheek and shoulder into one of them. The great big, bearded fellow takes a half-step back. Tactical sunglasses the color of a rainbow at sunset study her. He reaches into a chest pouch.

me

As he rips open a Velcro flap, Sienna finds an EEL round. It takes both her hands to hold the few ounces of metal and plastic without dropping it. That is all the strength she, the weakling girl, the spent soldier, the failed warrior has.

Out!

Before she can even try to plant the EEL onto Bristleface's forearms, her pursuer shows her something that makes her drop her guard and think she's dreaming.

The last rays of the day shine through a gash in the surrounding crags and splash vivid color off the last thing she expects to see.

His dusty gloved hand holds out a yellow rose.

"Sienna McKnight, I presume?" her assailant says with a white-toothed grin. "We're here ta rescue yah."

Sienna cannot cling to consciousness, cannot fend off the malevolent darkness that will surely kill the man in front of her and all his companions. She does not know the bearded man, but she knows what is rising inside her all too well. In the instant before her vǫrthr takes over, she decides.

She slaps the EEL round on her own arm.

Above her, as the world of consciousness falls away, Bristleface's grin turns to shock. And then he skids out of sight as her eyes roll back in her head. Fifty-thousand volts jolt her. Sienna pitches forward, losing consciousness. The mercenary drifts yards away, down an elongated tunnel. "Missy!

What've

you

done?"

That pisses her off.

The EEL's electro-tendrils sap the last of her strength and confuse the other.

She thinks she hears someone who sounds like her mumble back: "Who you callin' miss—?"

36

FAR FROM THE WANDERING DESERT

"…your arms right now."

My arms?

At the sound of a woman's cheerful Saturday morning cartoon show voice, Sienna tries to raise them. At first they feel heavy, or numb, like after she's rolled and slept on them. She looks. Padded leather restraints latch her forearms snugly to gleaming stainless-steel bed railings.

"Hgggh wasssthisssmm?" Sienna's tongue is as dry as a chalkboard eraser. She pulls on her bindings. Rising up as far as she can, she pretends to check them out more closely, while also checking out the room. Before asking the obvious, she needs to arm herself with enough information to ferret out lies. She scans for any clue as to where she is, and anything she can use as a weapon.

No windows. Most of the equipment is ultra-modern. It looks like what they had in Roger's room back in Washington, only the markings are in a bunch of different languages. The vaulted ceiling is not covered by drywall drop panels. Carved and fitted stones arch above. These have been painted over many times and give the impression of being very old. The place has a distinct subterranean vibe.

Captivity. This is getting old. Her soft shackles clink.

"Sorry about those. It was that thing that you were doing. We had to put those little wrist warmers on ya."

A phone on the wall chimes a lively tune. Not a Lux/Net handset. It is an actual telephone with a receiver and curly, tangled wires. She hasn't seen one like that since visiting a Cold War bunker during a history field trip. Full, heavily glossed lips purse at the interruption. A long, manicured finger raises politely in Sienna's direction. As if her being patient is a choice.

"Let me take care of… Hello? Oh, hi."

Her attendant is about her age or a few years older. She's thin and tall, very tall. She pirouettes away from the bed. She's balancing on heels at least six inches high. And that accent. It is pure mid-Atlantic, a hybrid made up in Hollywood when talking pictures were invented. As natural as the color of her huge hair. From the back she looks like a human dandelion. She twirls back to face Sienna, phone cord wrapping around slim waist and prominent bosom. Sea anemone false eyelashes flutter.

"Yes, our little patient is up."

The strange woman is a multitasking contortionist. While balancing the plastic receiver on her shoulder, she pokes at Sienna's bed monitor, and at the same time undoes the leather restrains. Colorful ink on one of her arms depicts a serpent coiled around a bright red apple.

"Yes, yes, she is. After the grogginess of the anesthetic wore off. Uh huh. Really well, considering. She's pretty alert."

A flashlight contained in the base of what looks like a

lipstick tube flits over Sienna's face and deftly checks her eyes.

"Pupillary response… really good. And so adorable hazelly too!" Her caregiver's voice chirps with delight. "Her pictures totally don't do her justice. Yes… no. Scans show no concussion or cranial pulmonary events. Aside from the obvious, she's in good shape. See you soo-oon." The receiver clacks back onto its hook. Sienna's arms are free of restraints. "There. That must feel better."

Two fingers press delicately on her wrist. The woman's nail extensions are also ten miniature display screens. They play a video of animated kittens which somersault, hide, and do kitten things. The medical exam is accompanied by giggles.

"I know you've got a pulse. I was in a healing ashram last year and the doctor guru guy proved sparshana touch could diagnose early-stage conditions better than a clunky old MRI. Wild, right?"

Sienna welcomes the freedom of her arms. Still, she's been given no reason not to be wary. Who was on the phone? Is she a prisoner? If so, of whom, some transatlantic glee club? There's a small chance this is some off-the-grid DARPA black site. Maybe they are humoring her while they figure out how to extract what's left of the unique RAPTEK from one standard-issue soldier's body.

"I… don't," Sienna finally manages to croak out. "Don't think Army medical is going to cover that sparshana stuff."

"Don't worry about… Oh, you're joking." The woman's mass of curler-bound hair shakes merrily. "Joking is good. I'm Melanie, by the way. How is your pain level, on a one through ten scale?"

"Hi, Melanie. I'm at about a hard three, I guess." This is

accurate. Her body throbs all over. It's a challenge keeping her balance sitting up in the bed. Full-on getting up and walking will take some prep time. Her head feels like it has been mushed by a huge nutcracker. Wide swaths of skin have been peeled off, as though by sandpaper.

It was sand all right. Minus the paper.

On the upside, the amateur Chechen-style surgery wound on her upper arm is covered by a transparent dressing. It's closed up and stitched properly. Elegantly, really.

"Yeah, a three." *But with ambitions.*

Sienna cranes her neck to look around from a different angle. Shooting pains greet her movements. "I've been in a few military medical centers. Don't recognize this one."

"That's because it's super-secret. Which is quite a lucky coincidence because you're a secret agent or something. General Bryan will tell you everything."

The mention of the name is at once comforting and baffling. "Wait, general?" Sienna asks, still fuzzy. "Either I've been out longer than I thought, or you mean Sergeant Bryan, right?"

Blonde curls shake above her like fronds of a huge fern. "Military ranks, who can keep track? Admirals, field marshals, prelates, magi—the list just goes on."

"You know Sarge?"

"Sure do. He said you prefer your lattes foamy and you like an extra snuggly blanket when you've got sniffles or are recovering from shrapnel wounds."

Finally something familiar.

"Let me talk to him."

"Not a good idea just yet," Melanie says. "Remember the

secret agent part? He's supposed to call us when he can."

Sienna tilts up on an elbow. Under clean white sheets, her whole body is a glowing ember of hurt. She knows this feeling. The results of accelerated healing, sonic orthopedic casts, hyperbaric treatments. While she's been out, her body has been given the platinum card health care treatment.

"So, Melanie. Where are the doctors?"

Sienna lurches her legs over the side. The strange woman involuntarily backs away from the bed. Not scared, but definitely mindful. Melanie recovers from her start. Her eyes twinkle; she giggles.

"Oh, I should have asked you before. Now that you're back to your senses, can we set some ground rules? Number one being: no more throwing neurosurgeons through walls."

"Huh?"

Melanie gestures to the wall across from her bed. There's a distinct man-sized indentation in the drywall plaster.

"Or me. Just so we're peachy clear, okay?"

"I did that? To who?"

"You were kind of out of it. And the nice man forgives you, though he is charging us double his normal hourly for the time he was knocked out. We had to take all the sharp objects out of the room so you didn't hurt yourself. At first I thought only ferrous metals, then you made that little hole in the ceiling with a glass thermometer." She points a kitteny finger up. "Then I thought, alrighty, let's try dampening the electro-conductive valence." Melanie pauses her torrent. "Maybe we leave that for later. You must still be tired. And as for doctors, I'm afraid I'm it for now. Ta-dah!"

"You're my doctor?"

"Well, I started full-time at Eurolincx right after I left med school. I mean, hee, I did all the work, but I stopped handing things in when they got so cross with me for disagreeing with the textbooks. And just between us"— Melanie drops her voice to a whisper and looks over both shoulders for no apparent reason—"I'm not exactly certified in England. But I won't tell if you don't."

She winks. And unless Sienna's seeing things, the ends of her long lashes sparkle pinpricks of light.

England?

Her attending cheerleader/physician continues Melaniesplaining. "Great thing is, we had all your medical files. Right from when Theodora McKnight delivered you. She kept detailed records, even how your poor little heart stopped for a spell. Which reminds me! The same thing happened to Audrey Hepburn when she was small due to a really bad case of whooping cough, her mother revived her and knew right then and there Audrey was destined for great things. Just-like-*you!*"

The bizarre deluge of information delivered with such unflagging pep starts to make Sienna wish she was back in a coma.

"Wait… why would you have my medical records? And Melanie, I think I have to ask you…" Things were getting weirder, not clearer. Time to change that. No point delaying the cliché. "Where am I?"

"Oh!" The flighty physician stops in her thought tracks. "I thought you were going to ask me something hard. That's easy. My boss always insists we keep up to date with everything, just in case. Though falling out of a helicopter and the other, uh, things that happened, definitely low-probability bimodals. You're in the super-secret hospital wing of your father's house."

Suddenly, it was not just a concussion making her head spin.

Uncle Bryan, you got some explaining to do.

Thank you for reading
New Praetorians 1: Sienna McKnight.

The next volume is:

NEW PRAETORIANS 2:
SHETANI ZERU BRYAN

Available soon on Amazon.com

Sarge Bryan watched helplessly as Sienna McKnight fell from a speeding helicopter. He was certain the brilliant, accomplished, and brave woman he had known since she was a girl was dead. Almost certain. He has to know for sure. He has to get back to the hostile sands of Khorasan's Wandering Desert.

Twenty-three years ago, Sergeant Shetani Zeru Bryan was on the military plane that brought Sienna and her adoptive parents home to North Carolina. A steadfast friend to the McKnights, he has supported and mentored Sienna throughout her life. The shocking secrets he has harbored for years might save her, or could turn out to be the most dangerous revelations yet.

To get advance alerts on book release dates and free items, send an email with "list" in the subject line to:

syrus.rk@gmail.com

THE NEW PRAETORIANS NEED YOU!

Your honest reviews help this indie project on:

Amazon.com
Goodreads.com

Posted on your blog or social media? Send us a link.

Visit:

https://www.facebook.com/NewPraetorians/
https://twitter.com/rksyrus
https://www.instagram.com/NewPraetoriansFanArt/
https://newpraetorianssite.wordpress.com/contact/
WeChat 微信 hui960697

NEW PRAETORIANS WIKI

1st Special Forces Operational Detachment-Delta: 1st SFOD-D, a unit of the US Army garrisoned at the Base, along with a small auxiliary squad.

*

2016: The first year the Refugee Olympic Team joined the Games. The athletes competed under the Olympic flag.

*

Adaptive Execution Office (AEO): A segment of DARPA (the Defense Advanced Research Projects Agency of the US Department of Defense). AEO was created to accelerate the transition of DARPA technologies from concept to active use for the military and private-sector partners. Rumored to be headquartered at the Cheyenne Mountain Complex bunker in Colorado Springs, Colorado.

*

Ansible: Popular name for an artifact recovered by the exploration team of Everett and Akan. Its dimensions, known properties, and exact location are classified. There are no known photographs of the object, only artists' renderings.

Ursula K. Le Guin coined the word "ansible" in 1966 to refer to a system of faster-than-light communication. How this term came to be applied to the object in question is not clear. However, the term began to be used shortly after its retrieval from the Bentley Subglacial Trench in Marie Byrd Land, Antarctica.

According to FREENET conspiracy blogger &OrwellLives!, the object defies photographic recording, both digital and analog. Everyone claims to see a different glowing shape inside a so-far-impenetrable shell. &OrwellLives! also claimed governments are developing weapons systems and mind-control devices using Ansible-based technologies, as well as employing it as a beacon to offer wealthy interstellar species visas to come live on Earth.

Other names include **Antarctic meteorite Everett-Akan MBL/BST 00001**, **The Aleph**, **The Spirit of Rajan**, and **Elemental Squark ñt**.

*

The Base: The Special Forces section of the large US Army installation outside Fayetteville, North Carolina.

*

Bellingshausen Station: A Russian Antarctic station at Collins Harbor, on King George Island; rumored to be home base to the next generation of nuclear subs and specialized Arctic cyborg units of battalion strength.

*

EEL round and launcher: Electrostatic Enveloping Ligature.

A less-lethal round used almost exclusively by Special Forces military due to its cost and specialized training requirements. The projectile employs a combination of electrostatic epoxy resin, nano-charges, and a small internal mechBrain to disable enemy fighters at up to one hundred meters. The concept is a combination of the Mossberg X12 and the M320 40mm grenade launching platform. EEL rounds are also known as Sea Cucumbers or Goober rounds, due to their gelatin-like appearance. US Army designation: M588.

*

Formula 0 Racing: Originally an amateur university student-run event, zero fossil-fuel emissions racing has been taken over by large corporate sponsors. The annual races overseen by the governing body still include the original track along the Eyre Highway a 1,660-kilometer (1,030 miles) paved road linking Western Australia and South Australia via the Nullarbor Plain. Claims of cheating and corruption on the part of race safety officials are constant during the active season.

*

Hinge: Slang for a US Navy lieutenant commander (LCDR), Officer O-4.

Refers to the cranial procedure that is supposedly mandated as soon as a naval officer is promoted to this rank. Half of his/her brain is removed and a hinge is inserted that allows for reattachment of the removed gray matter if required. The hinge limits the LCDR's head movement, O-4s are constantly nodding in the affirmative and saying, "Yessir, yessir" when in the presence of the CO.

*

Hovercopter: A generic term for the V-560 and variants

manufactured by Bell Helicopter, Lockheed Martin, and Lichtwerks. Persistently called "helos" by Navy personnel.

This fifth-generation tiltrotor aircraft employs captive induction as primary thrust instead of rotors. Maximum speed and range are classified but estimated to be 300 knots and 1,000 nautical miles, respectively. Advances over the Valor and previous FVL craft include significant increase in visual and sonic stealth due to incorporation of guanine nanocrystal mechanisms on exterior and the unique design of the nacelles.

*

IceCube Neutrino Observatory: A neutrino telescope near the Amundsen–Scott South Pole Station in Antarctica. Its thousands of dark-matter energy sensors are distributed over a cubic kilometer of volume under the ice.

*

Khorasan: A newly sanctioned nation in Central Asia; its constitution requires it to have open borders and accept all refugees regardless of origin, race, or religion.

Geographically, Khorasan incorporates the former Afghanistan and a section of previously uninhabitable wasteland connecting to the coastline. Administered by Worldwide Help International (WWHI), the south of the country has been transformed into an area often referred to as the Fertile Spear. This is the last sanctuary for many desperate refugees from all over the globe. The north retains its traditions and stubbornly resists change.

Other historical map redrawing initiatives in the region by superpowers have included:

The Durand Line (1893) which established Afghanistan as a buffer zone between British and Russian interests in the region.

The Wakhan Corridor (1873)

Russian Turkestan (1867-1918)

The post-WWI dismantling of the Ottoman Empire and the creation of artificial states the boundaries of which overlapped tribal, ethnic, and linguist identities.

Pax Syriana (Lat., "Syrian Peace") a concept invented by superpower think tanks during the late 20th century to describe a hypothetical reshaping of the Middle East. Some models proposed erasing post-Ottoman borders and re-establishing the Persian Empire to improve stability and benefit commerce.

*

Licht/Net: A photon- and neutrino-based communication network. In most countries it has replaced the Internet. Many people surveyed were not aware they were using the system because mobile devices and computers connect automatically, without charge. It is a single network but known by different names in different countries, notably **Lux/Net** in English-speaking countries, **Réseau/Lumineux** in France, and 光ネットワーク (**Hikari/Nettowāku**) in Japan.

An early demonstration of the principle that every light bulb in the world could be a communications node was documented in a 2011 TED talk in which modulation of the light from a single LED transmitted far more data than a cellular tower. Licht/Net is now ubiquitous due to cost factors and the network being entirely wireless. Handheld and other devices connect via light emitted by Licht/Net-enabled bulbs or panels. Inside the light sources, photons interact with a neutrino stream generated by Lichtstrom particle colliders. Data is transferred to the central switching hub (the supercolliders formerly known as CERN), then the process is reversed, completing the network.

The most distant member of the network is the Chinese space probe "Adventurer" 冒險家 in its mission to Eris (planetoid 136199, discovered 2005). On the date of landing, Eris will be approximately ten billion kilometers distant from the Earth.

Internet protocol suite (TCP/IP) still exists, but due to Licht/Net's services being free and unlimited globally, fiber-optic and other networks carry much reduced traffic. Primary legacy users are gamers, pornographers, and fraudsters. Fake money transfer schemes are often carried out through .trans domains registered in the Balkan republic of Transnistria (Републикэ Молдовеняскэ Нистрянэ).

Licht/Net site addresses are designated by /* top level domain names with /licht being the equivalent of .com. The network supports the exchange of **LichtCredits,** the virtual national currency of the Lichtstrom and an open transaction conversion system which provides most of the benefits of a single currency with fewer disadvantages. Known internationally as **LuxBucks**, **Argent d'alion**, and 電気マネ ー **(Denki mane).**

*

Lichtstrom: A corporate nation between Switzerland and France.

Based on top of the physical structures of the privatized

CERN supercolliders, it serves as the world's leading information hub. Lichtwerks Corporation is primarily involved in communications systems, but is expanding into aeronautics and materials science. Dr. Wolfgang Licht's most high-profile project is a space elevator system, currently under construction.

While often translated into English as "light storm," Lichtstrom translated from German means "luminous flux." In photometry, this is the measure of the power of light perceived by the human eye.

Other corporate nations in history include Rhodesia and the East India Company.

*

MARSOC: United States Marine Corps Forces Special Operations Command, the Marine Corps' contribution to Special Operations Command.

*

mechBrain: A portmanteau slang term for any mechanical device or system which demonstrates interactive behavior. Often used disparagingly when the mechBrain is perceived to frustrate human intentions.

*

Metcalf-Chang device: A neural PET scanner. Manufactured by a division of Eurolincx Corp.

Its sales literature claims it can interpret brain activity to a high degree of pragmatic competence. Essentially a brainwave to text/image machine. It's currently restricted to governmental use. Detractors claim it is merely a different version of the fMRI brain scans used decades previously as documented by Gallant et al. Initial test subjects scanned by device prototypes have filed lawsuits claiming dementia and other side effects.

The name refers to West Point Professor Dorothy Metcalf, MD, nPsychD, and Noonian Chang, a reclusive researcher at Ao Kazan Corporation in Japan. The device is based on their work, but its construction did not involve them.

*

microSwarm: A coordinated unit cluster of small aerial drones.

Used for civilian and military purposes, they can carry chemical or biological payloads and deliver them with high precision. Worldwide Help International is one of the few non-governmental organizations (NGOs) known to employ microSwarms, often using them to immunize or cull remote herds of animals. Agricultural microSwarms are used to pollinate essential crops in areas where insect pollinator numbers are not adequate to ensure a stable food supply. Terran models use visual, olfactory, and DNA sensors to achieve highly accurate targeting. Once initialized, command and control is decentralized. A number of drones may be incapacitated without disabling the swarm. Communication between drones is normally frequency-hopping ultrasonic. Marine models typically are nested inside larger conveyances such as Ao Kazan cetacean robots until they are close to their final deployment zone.

Offensive military uses of microSwarms are prohibited

under the protocols of the "Convention on Prohibitions or Restrictions on the Use of Certain Conventional Weapons Which May Be Deemed to Be Excessively Injurious or to Have Indiscriminate Effects" (Geneva Conventions of 1949 and Additional Protocols, and their Commentaries).

*

Miggle: Slang for the revolver-style six shot Milkor Multiple Grenade Launcher. The USA designated variant M32A1 has been adopted the Marine Corps and by USSOCOM.

*

Neutrinos: Elementary particles with very small mass which move at near light speed.

Neutrinos interact only via the weak subatomic force and gravity. Many pass through the Earth without any known interaction. "A neutrino of moderate energy could easily penetrate a thousand light-years of lead." - David Griffiths. Neutrinos can be created in nuclear reactions such as those that take place in stars, supernovae or Earth-based reactors. Neutrinos are the primary carrier wave of Licht/Net. Neither the "flavor" of neutrino Dr. Licht uses, nor how these particles are modulated into wireless signals, which can be interpreted by mechBrains in phones and other hardware, is known.

*

RAPTEK: [**unsubstantiated FREENET rumor**] Railgun: Ansible Powered Test Kit. A DARPA-developed, single-soldier weapons system based on Ansible-derived energy generators in contravention to international treaties.

The US Navy tried for years to create a working railgun system for its Zumwalt-class destroyers. DARPA is said to jealously guard this technology and the only alleged prototypes are being tested by the US Army at an undisclosed facility.

*

Red Mist (Rubri a'ris polyaminopyridine): An extremely useful local and general anesthetic commonly found in military and civilian hospitals. It is also used recreationally. Its popularity has surged due to low toxicity, general availability, affordable street price, and the drug's uncanny ability to mimic other narcotics the user has previously enjoyed.

The compound was developed through genetic manipulation of the venom-producing cells of scorpions. Its characteristic red color and typical aerosol delivery mechanism have resulted in its popular name. A catalyzed compound, the drug only becomes active when in contact with certain types of metals. In medical use, these are pins or staples inserted into anatomical regions to limit the desired anesthetic effect. Clinical anesthesia is achievable even in cases of extreme blood loss. Among recreational Red Mist users, studs and piercings employed as catalyzers are ubiquitous. Vinegar renders Red Mist inert and not identifiable as a controlled substance.

Trade names include **Glazitraphane** and **Xanitanyl**.

*

scRamjet: Supersonic Combustion Ramjet (aka "flying stovepipe"), a form of supersonic air-breathing engine and the aircraft employing them. Military versions operate up to speeds through Mach 6 (4,600 mph; 7,403 km/h).

*

scrolls: Flexible, expandable filament screens which have replaced most tablets and portable monitors. Often housed in cylinders about the size of a fountain pen; larger, more expensive versions can expand to 38x68 inches. Opaque and rigid when locked open, they are compatible with all existing software and touchscreen drivers.

*

Stymphalian drones: Successor to the X-47B and the latest graduate of DARPA's J-UCAS program.

A semi-autonomous stealth unmanned combat air vehicle. Designed to continue operation even when cut off from ground control. Stymphalians independently coordinate with other mechBrain-enabled weapons platforms. Payload is classified but estimated to be at least 2.5 tons. A flex-munitions module allows the aircraft to decide what sort of payload to deploy at the last minute. Choices range from thousands of antipersonnel cluster bomblets to UAV expendable mode (colloquially known as "kamikaze mode"), transforming the entire drone into a single multistage bunker-buster. The fleet was temporarily grounded after a friendly-fire incident over the Ess Alüm peninsula.

*

TYR Lens: A large desalination and electricity-generating station floating in the Gulf of Oman.

Along with the **Great Wall of China**, the **Giza Pyramids**, the **ELON Transatlantic Hyperloop**, and the wind-powered undertaking to thicken the Arctic ice cap, **Project HODUR**, the Lens is one of the largest engineering projects in human history. It is the first large-scale use of metal-organic frameworks (MOFs). Most of its sixty-square-kilometer (average visible above surface) area is composed of calcium carbonate and was manufactured by the MOFs in the same fashion as mollusks produce seashells.

The *Lens* is a large energy plant. A combination of direct and stored solar energy as well as algae-biomass-generated free electrons (through exploitation of the TYR quark effect) power an extensive electrical grid. Total generating capacity is classified, but has been estimated to be in the terawatt range. This energy is also used to desalinate seawater from the Gulf of Oman. Drinking and irrigation water is pumped through aqueduct-style pipelines throughout the Central Asian region. The target of numerous terrorist attacks, it has never suffered significant damage.

*

US-SOCOM: United States Special Operations Command. Oversees various Special Operations Component Commands of the Army, Marine Corps, Navy, and Air Force.

*

Wandering Desert: (Persian: بیابان سرگردان) an extremely arid plateau region in Khorasan. Its topography is shaped by persistent winds and a nearly endless supply of sand.

It is moving westward, encroaching on agricultural areas. Worldwide Help International reports "hundreds of villages have been submerged by windblown dust and sand. Dunes nearly 15 meters (50 feet) high block roads, forcing residents to establish new routes." The region is sparsely populated by Baluchi and Pashtun nomads. It is also known as the Registan Desert ‫ریگستان‬. (Reference: "Advancing Deserts and Rising Seas Squeezing Civilization" By Lester R. Brown)

*

Worldwide Help International: A very large private humanitarian institution.

Under various names, antecedents of the modern organization date back to temples dedicated to the healer-god Asclepius, the scorpion goddess cult of Ta-Bitjet, healing hollows of !Xu the sky god of the Saan people, and others. Its banner designs most often incorporate depictions of the Serpens constellation, repeated five times.

Sources and amounts of its annual budgets vary. Public records reveal a close relationship between WWHI and Ao Kazan Corporation of Japan, especially during the building of the *TYR Lens* and the establishment of the refugee safe zones (RSZs) in Southern Khorasan. Because of the scope of WWHI global operations and its noted ability to discourage hostile actions against its aid workers, it operates in areas deemed prohibitively dangerous by other NGOs.

THE NEW PRAETORIANS SERIES CONTINUITY

TEN CHARACTER-DRIVEN NOVELLAS, ONE GLOBAL STORY:	Start date (Khorasan time)
New Praetorians 1: **Sienna McKnight**	March 19
New Praetorians 2: **Shetani Zeru Bryan**	March 20
New Praetorians 3: **Yama & Yami**	March 20
New Praetorians 4: **Anis**	continuous
New Praetorians 5: **Crush**	March 20
New Praetorians 6: **Ran Oliphant**	continuous
New Praetorians 7: **Khamseen**	continuous
New Praetorians 8: **Dr. Golem & Mr. Genji**	March 20
New Praetorians 9: **Heaven's Scythe**	continuous
New Praetorians 10: **Shadowbolt**	continuous
My Summer Vacation by Sienna McKnight (New Praetorians 0.5)	A prequel short.

FN   B   A   #   E

S LH   11/3

C J PARK 11/9

M G SAKE 11/4

R L H

Made in the USA
San Bernardino, CA
11 September 2017